GIULIA CARL<

AD MARTEM
12

Instagram: @Astro_Giulia and @AdMartem12
Twitter: @Astro_Giulia
Facebook page: Astro Giulia

Cover picture: © 2018 Eashan Misra
Instagram: @Mr.Kalopsia

ISBN: 9781791533977

This book is also available in e-book format.

Preface

Human Mars missions are a favorite theme of science fiction, but one of the most difficult ones. And the more we approach the time in which astronauts will actually set foot on the Red Planet, the more difficult it becomes to describe a fictional mission to Mars.

The difficulties grow exponentially if the author tries to speak of the mission in a realistic way.

To describe a realistic mission means to get rid of most of the factors which are at base of an attractive adventure novel: whoever will organize such a difficult, dangerous and costly mission, being immaterial whether the organizer is a space agency, a private organization or a consortium of agencies and industries, will do his best to avoid coups-de-theatre and unpredicted (or unpredictable) events to ensure that astronauts follow the predicted mission planning, without risking their lives, or, at least, reducing such risks to a minimum.

If we look to the past, the Apollo missions worked in an unbelievable routinely way (except for the Apollo 13 mission, in which the unpredictable stepped in and caused almost a disaster). In a cynical way, we could say that all the Apollo missions would have made for quite boring novels, except for the Apollo 13, which could have been a screenplay written by a master writer: there was the danger, the adventure, some coups-de – theatre and an almost unbelievable happy end. No wonder that it was possible to obtain a blockbuster out of the Apollo 13 mission without the need of introducing significant deviations from the actual story.

Most of the ingredients which authors introduced to add zest to fictional human Mars missions are quite unlikely and would just be the effect of serious errors (technical, organizational, etc.) made by the designers of the mission.

Giulia Bassani, on the contrary, succeeds in writing a book which is at the same time realistic and entertaining: adventure and unpredictable events are not linked with some unlikely errors made by mission planners, or even more unlikely things like the discovery of aliens or intelligent bacteria on Mars, but are the logical (and perhaps unavoidable) consequence of a very reasonable decision. After a number of successful human Mars missions – which are not described in the novel since they would be as little exciting as true successful space missions can be – the planners decide to proceed with the next step, a step which is strictly required to pass from exploration to colonization: to give birth to a few children on the Red Planet. In the beginning, this can follow the stated plans, and in spite of radiation and isolation, the three children are healthy and 'normal'. But, exactly because they are 'normal' human beings, they go through the difficulties and conflicts of adolescence. And, as all youth, they become allergic to rules – but a dangerous place like Mars is the worst place to disobey rules.

From these premises, the plot can develop into an actual page turner and the reader goes through the adventures of these nice and clever young guys to discover, at the end, that the idea of giving birth to Martians was, after all, not so bad.

Giancarlo Genta
Politecnico di Torino
International Academy of Astronautics
December 2018

When you are in your mother's womb, you have no certainties. You don't know who your parents are, you don't know where they are, you don't know how you will be born or where you will live. At first you don't even know if you are male or female. You know nothing about yourself and the world around you. You are sure of one only thing: when you are born, wherever and whoever you are with, you will call that place home, you will call those people mum and dad. You don't care where you are, be it a city, an igloo, the jungle, a ship or even another *planet*.

For you it will be perfectly normal.

Author's note

The passage of time on Mars will be measured with the Darian calendar (created by aerospace engineer and political scientist Thomas Gangale in 1985).

This is how it works: a year on Mars lasts 668 sols. *Sol* is the name of a Martian day and it lasts 24 hours and 39 minutes. There are 24 months composed of 28 sols each (even if every six months one sol is omitted). Each month has 4 weeks composed of 7 sols.

The days of the week are: *sol solis, sol lunae, sol martius, sol mercurii, sol jovis, sol veneris, sol saturni.*

Accordingly, the protagonists of the story will be eight Martian years old, which is equal to about fifteen terrestrial years.

The Martian months are:
Sagittarius, Dhanus, Capricornus, Makara, Aquarius, Kumbha, Pisces, Mina, Aries, Mesha, Taurus, Rishabha, Gemini, Mithuna, Cancer, Karka, Leo, Simha, Virgo, Kanya, Libra, Tula, Scorpius, Vrishika.

Moreover, the people living on Mars are used to say "*tosol*" instead of "today" and "*yestersol*" instead of "yesterday".

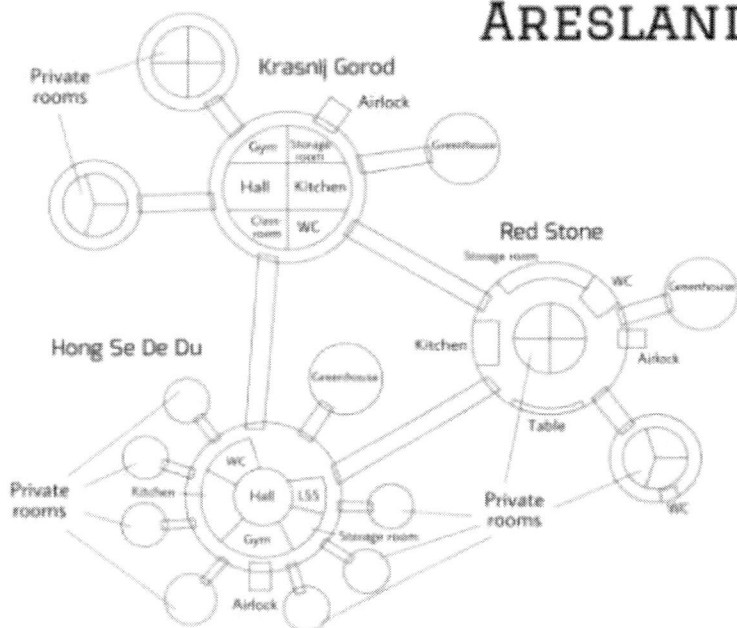

ARESLAND

Private rooms

Krasnij Gorod

Airlock

Gym | Storage (SSKE)

Hall | Kitchen

Class rooms | WC

Greenhouse

Hong Se De Du

Red Stone

Storage room

WC

Greenhouse

Kitchen

Airlock

Table

Private rooms

Kitchen

WC

Hall | LSS

Gym

Greenhouse

Storage room

Private rooms

WC

Airlock

PROLOGUE

It was 6:00 pm in Florida and the blazing sun was by now descending, hiding behind the colossal building of Kennedy Space Centre. It was May 22nd in 2042 and that day, at NASA, one of the most important decisions was about to be taken, not only for space exploration but also and most importantly for humanity.

The last, definitive meeting was about to begin in the briefing room. NASA's director, Robert Walmore, was observing attentively all the people taking a place around the table. When everyone had arrived and also the director of the future mission at issue had taken a place in front of him, then he spoke.

«Ladies and gentlemen, please be seated» he invited, sitting as well.

Everyone imitated him. Walmore was already over fifty but he wore his age well. His dark grey hair was perfectly still, his green eyes peered carefully at every detail, every person, while his fingers rubbed his chin absently.

The tension was tangible in the room. Walmore, his deputy Terry Coleman and the associate administrator Claire Dennis, sitting at his side, could perceive how hard the engineers and scientists in front of them had worked on this project and how determined they were to reach the goal.

«So,» Walmore began intertwining his fingers on the table «We are gathered here today to revise definitely every point of the twelfth mission of the Ad Martem program. Mr Torres, as director of Ad Martem 12, I turn it over to you.»

«Thank you, Walmore», an impressively slim man spoke up.

His small, dark eyes blinked behind two thick lenses. He stroked his long grey beard, preparing for a long speech.

«Before we think about the future, ladies and gentlemen, I would like to turn our thoughts to the past and revisit the history of our project. The missions of the Ad Martem program began in 2034, when we sent to Mars the first 3D printers, the robots and rovers which started to build a permanent space station. Throughout the following years, with missions numbers 2, 3-4 and 5, we dealt with setting communication and surface-monitoring satellites into orbit around the planet. In 2038, with Ad Martem 6, thanks to our alliance with the European, Russian and Chinese space agencies, we made history as the first three astronauts stepped foot on the surface of the Red Planet: George Jenner, Oleg Sokov and Cheng Li. Ad Martem 7 and 8 each brought three more astronauts. These nine, of which two Americans, one European, three Russians and three Chinese, gave life to the Martian station of Aresland, composed of the Red Stone, Krasnij Gorod and Hong Se De Du bases, located in Hellas Planitia. With the missions 9 and 10 we've sent to Mars supplies for the astronauts and scientific experiments. Now, Ad Martem 12 is scheduled to lift off in 2044, after Ad Martem 11, a set-up mission. In two years, six in total will be the astronauts heading to Mars. The goal of the mission is to give birth to a human being and keep him or her alive on a planet that is different from Earth. Six professional astronauts will take part in the mission, three women and three men who will do their best to complete their task: giving birth to a child and bring him or her up in the best of ways.»

A moment of silence followed during which Torres observed the effect his words caused on the audience.

«Now, James, show the project, please» he addressed a young man who had meanwhile linked his laptop to a projector that illuminated a wall, all those present turned to watch.

«With pleasure, John» James Walker replied, moving next to the projection on the wall.

The image portrayed the map of one of the most popular space bases of the moment. Two circumferences, one of which was smaller, were linked through a rectangle. Within the bigger circumference there was another, split into four slices, and all around it, alongside the perimeter of the major one, there were several rectangles and squares which followed the curve of the circle and represented more rooms.

«I take it you've already realized that this is the American and European base Red Stone, where three of our astronauts are currently living. Well, I guess we can start from here...» he addressed a laser pointer to the small circle divided in four parts «... These are the four private chambers for every astronaut and, at the moment, only three of them are occupied. With Ad

Martem 12, the base will have to be able to welcome two more astronauts, plus a future third, that is the new born. As such, a third geodesic dome will be built during Ad Martem 11...» Walker pressed a button on his laptop and a third circumference appeared in the map, it was linked to the main one through a rectangle and was divided into three parts «... similar in size to the greenhouse...» his laser pointed at the small circle that was already present «... and will provide three more private chambers. The bigger one goes to the child, while the other two will be for the parents. This dome will be entirely dedicated to the child and his or her needs, it'll contain all the necessary and will have a separate Life Support System.»

«This situation,» Walker resumed after a brief pause «will be repeated similarly in the Russian base Krasnij Gorod and in the Chinese base Hong Se De Du. This solution was studied with the teams of the national directors present here today, Natalia Romanovna Kurkina for Roscosmos and Kim Yao for CNSA.»

As he called the first name, a slender woman stood up, her brunette hair was gathered in a tight pony tail, her stony eyes were focused. Soon after an Asiatic man did the same, as serious as the woman next to him.

«Who accepted to support and collaborate at our project, in order to bring humanity to make a new giant leap.»

The two bowed their heads respectfully before sitting down again.

«I'll now briefly show you the situation in these two bases» Walker announced while pressing some buttons on his laptop.

The image changed, it now showed two maps at once, very different, but still composed of circles. The Krasnij Gorod was composed of two bases linked to the main, central one, while the Hong Se De Du was a large geodesic dome surrounded by six much smaller circles.

«These are the Russian and Chinese bases in the current situation. With the update for Ad Martem 12, we'll add a new dome to both of them, just like we saw for the Red Stone» Walker touched the keyboard once again and two more domes appeared in the maps «Where we'll set up the private chamber for the child and the parents.»

«And all of this will be ready within 2044?» Coleman asked.

«Not all of this, but the external and internal structures of the domes will. As from then, the astronauts on the planet will take care of furnishing, shall we say, fix all the necessary and activate the Life Support Systems. The children's birth is expected to take place in 2045 and everything will be perfectly ready.»

«But now let's talk about when those children will grow up» Walmore finally spoke up, after being silent until that moment «They need an education, they'll be curious and ask question. What will they be taught?»

«They'll be brought up speaking the native language of the base where they're born, but they'll learn the other two as well» Amanda Lynch began, she was a spaceflight psychologist, her fierce red hair contrasted against her pale skin. Her voice was smooth and unwavering.

«At age five they'll learn to read and write, at six they'll begin to study mathematics. At eight they'll start on a study path of science and geography, in detail of Mars and generally of Earth.»

«Of course, doctor Lynch» Walmore interrupted her «But my concern is: what will they be taught about Earth, about human beings and our history?»

The woman took a deep breath before answering.

«For what concerns our history, they'll be given a general education, they'll study our origins and the origin of the Universe most of all. The rest of their studies will be focused on Mars.»

Walmore leaned forward from his chair while his eyes peered into those of the woman.

«You are telling me that those kids will barely know what Earth is? They'll know nothing of the humans who live here, of the terrestrial lifestyle and cultures?» he emphasized his last word.

«That's not what I mean. I'm saying that it's not fundamental for them to know it as, despite life on Mars will be obviously different from that on Earth, they'll learn all the necessary by simply staying with other human beings. They'll be aware that there are other people on Earth, that's it.»

«That's it?» he repeated before moving his eyes away and sighing. «Doctor Lynch, I've told you many times already. Those kids have the right to know who they are!»

«The time will come for them to know everything.»

«That is, when?»

«When their body will be completely developed and therefore they'll be able to face a long-duration space trip with less probabilities to suffer serious damages.»

Walmore didn't reply, he continued to observe the woman, thoughtfully.

«They will be very intelligent and skilled kids, Walmore» doctor Lynch resumed with persuasive manners

«They will be the first human beings ever to be born on a planet that's different from ours. They will know they're born on Mars and Mars will be their home and their natural normality and the astronauts living in the bases with them will be their family. And until they are mature enough, we can't overturn their existence by telling them that actually the real cradle of the entire humanity is another planet and that they were supposed to be born there, together with all the other human beings. They will be just kids, first of all, before being experiments...»

The room fell into silence as those last words lingered in the air above the table. Walmore kept looking at the psychologist, who was determined enough to hold his gaze. He broke the silence with caution.

«And when they'll be twenty years old, instead, and it will be the moment for them to know, don't you think it would be equally upsetting to learn the truth?»

The hint of a smile curved the corner of her mouth, but she returned serious right away.

«They'll see astronauts come and go and between the bases and Earth there's a constant communication. It's very possible that after all those years they will have figured it out by themselves. Let everything be natural, nothing must be forced. Besides, this probable necessity to know and curiosity toward our origins and the past will be eventually lost generation after generation and everything will become more natural and normal.»

Silence returned, Walmore was thoughtful. Everyone observed him expectantly.

«Fine» he then said «The meeting's concluded, you can leave the room.»

His words were followed by a scraping of chairs and bags as everyone stood up to gather their things and leave. Walmore stood up as well to shake hands before they exited silently. When the last person had left the room, he closed the door and approached a window to look outside. Terry Coleman and Claire Dennis remained. The sun was by now set and the sky, adorned with soft rosy clouds, was spectacular. Walmore perceived the steps of young Dennis, his associate administrator, as she approached him.

«I hate that woman» he claimed keeping his gaze on the sunset.

He heard an amused chuckle coming from Coleman who stood by the door.

«Listen, Robert» Claire Dennis began and Walmore listened «You might also hate Amanda Lynch but she's right and you know it. It's clear that sooner or later they'll understand, but it's important that everything happens quietly and naturally and not rushed.»

Walmore sighed and decided to change topic.

«Tomorrow I'm going to meet the directors of ESA, Roscosmos and CNSA to take the final decision.»

«What's your decision?» Coleman asked.

Robert Walmore turned, finally, and looked at the woman and at the man in the eyes.

«Our engineers have convinced me. I don't like Amanda Lynch, But I trust Claire. Hereby...

I approve Ad Martem 12.»

ONE

~ *15 Virgo 239* ~

Finally Jordan Miles felt really useful.

No more bad-smelling feed, feathers flying all around and organic waste to be cleaned. No more of that junk, no. For a long, very long time (or at least, he hoped so), he wasn't going to see the henhouse and those messy hens anymore. Finally he felt free! Turned eight years and fourteen months old, event that he had been waiting for a very long time, he was assigned a new role: learning to drive rovers, taking care of them and checking their functioning, which had to be perfect.

This would mean roaming the grounds around the Aresland in complete freedom, on board incredible vehicles that Jordan had been dreaming to drive since he was a child. Of course it was still a great responsibility. Now the safety of trips and excursions depended on him.

And he was proud of it.

That morning he woke up sooner than necessary, but he just couldn't resist one more minute in his bed. Yet he would still have to wait a good hour before he could go to the Main Base for breakfast. He silently left his room through an automatic sliding door, wearing pajamas and grey silky socks. That curved corridor was empty and quite dark, the only lighting came from a pair of mild LED lights on the ceiling of the dome.

He slipped into the bathroom, a small structure that resembled a parallelepiped which was almost in front of his room. It only contained a toilet, a sink and small mirror. It was a little bit cramped, not much of a comfy place, but however that bathroom served for night or morning uses only. The sanitary facility with a shower and the medical compartment was in the Main Base.

Jordan washed his face and then passed a hand through his brunette hair, completely and constantly messy. When he decided he had achieved a sufficiently neat status, he headed back to his room.

He let himself fall back heavily on his bed and absently glanced over to a small digital clock on his nightstand. It was 6:23 am. He had forty minutes left before breakfast. He knew that he wasn't going to resist all that time doing nothing. Therefore he decided to make time fly by tidying his room that after all those years had become a real disaster. He got up from the bed and went to stand in the centre of the room to look around himself, it was difficult to decide where to start. After all he had owned that room since he was born, so it contained anything and everything. On the floor, next to the bed, there were some horrendous robots, built with some pieces of cork, plastic and some rudimentary gear that Jordan had tried to test many times, unsuccessfully.

Books of every genre were piled up on the shelves above his bed, from children's tales to entire scientific encyclopedias, everything hidden under a thin layer of garnet dust that covered some models of rovers and spaceships as well, leaning in balance next to the books. Jordan had never had many books, actually no one had. Until, with Dounja Douglas' arrival, they got a machine that printed works in hard copy. Before that printer, Jordan used to have only one small book entitled "Your first book about the Universe", that his mother had given to him. It was one of the few colored books in the Aresland because the new printer could produce only black and white volumes.

And then, ancient toys and plushes of every kind were holed up under the desk, under the bed and in every corner of the room. He had no courage to throw them away. His nightstand had three drawers containing his underwear and on it, there was a framed picture next to a small lamp and the clock. It portrayed a woman with long, dark hair and a kind face, who carried in her arms an unleashed one-year-old kid who just didn't want to stay still. She was his mother, Laurie Williams, with her baby Jordan.

It had been already six years since he last saw her and he almost wouldn't remember her appearance if it wasn't for that picture. She had fallen ill quite badly when he still was a child and therefore she had to leave for Earth where some experts would heal and keep her safe: this was what Jordan had been told. He was fine with it, he had accepted the fact that he wasn't going to see her ever again, even though he missed her. Jordan was serene: he had his father Alexander with him and all the others who lived in the base. He had always been the centre of attention for everyone, surrounded by smiling and kind people. He was fine with it, he was happy.

When Jordan heard a bell ringing and was taken out of his thoughts, he realized that all he had done was sit on his bed with the picture of his mother in his hands, without tidying anything. He figured that he would never manage to reorder a thing and that mess would reign forever. Alright, he thought. In any case that sol he was going to start driving rovers! The bell that woke up all those present in the bases stopped ringing and Jordan took off the clothes he wore to sleep and put on a dark green t-shirt and a pair of cozy cargo shorts. After he slipped on his sneakers, he turned off the light and left.

His room was part of a dome divided in three spaces: the other two belonged respectively to Alexander Miles, his father, and to Dounja Douglas, a young-looking woman that took his mother's place inside the Red Stone four years before. Jordan walked down the perimeter of the dome, that was again contained in a bigger geodesic dome, until he turned left and continued in a corridor. He walked at a deliberate pace until he came out in the Main Base. Right next to the entrance there was a long table which followed the curvature of that immense hemisphere, where two men were already sitting, having their breakfast: George Jenner and Frank Larsen were used to get up much earlier than anyone else.

«Already up?» Frank asked as he noticed him approaching.

He was a middle-aged man with a very pale skin, fading blonde hair, light blue eyes and flushed cheeks.

George, who wasn't watching, turned to look at Jordan as he took a seat next to them. He was the eldest inside the base, but despite the grey hair, his physical shape was more than fit, even if a little bit more achy. He had the role of leader inside the Red Stone.

«Eh eh, I know why he's already up, don't I, Jordan?» George gave him a wink and the boy grinned.

«Good morning to you too» Jordan said.

George chuckled. Everything that was available for breakfast was placed on the table and Jordan was very hungry. He filled his plate with scrambled eggs, grabbed a piece of wholemeal bread and framed it all with some dried fruit. He poured a glass of water and began to ravenously eat that yellow mush.

«Tell me, did I miss something?» Frank asked glancing between George and Jordan with a questioning look.

«Since tosol on I'll take care of the rovers» Jordan explained.

«Oh, you were promoted then. But anyway someone should deal with the henhouse.»

Jordan waved his fork dismissively.

«Not my problem anymore, Frank. I don't want to see those birds ever again.»

Frank turned to him completely and pointed a finger at his plate in a scolding manner while George chuckled, sincerely amused.

«You know, that stuff you're devouring so passionately is only thanks to those birds, Jordan. No hens, no breakfast.»

Jordan rolled his eyes without looking at him.

«Don't torment him, Larsen» a new voice spoke up. Alexander had entered the Main Base, followed by a sleepy Dounja. «Jordan did an excellent job with the henhouse all this time. It is fair that he receives a promotion, he deserves it. Am I wrong, Jenner?»

«Thanks, da'» Jordan murmured.

«I was just giving some life lessons» Frank argued with a low tone, shrugging.

«Very correct, Miles» George agreed «But, as Larsen rightly said, we need someone who'll take care of our hens periodically.»

In the meantime, the last woman who completed the crew came out of one of the four private rooms of the Main Base and joined her mates at the table. She was Klara Nowak.

«Good morning, Nowak» George greeted when he noticed her «Right on time! We're about to decide who's going to be the next to take care of the henhouse. Anyone volunteers?»

«Don't wait for someone to volunteer, George» Jordan suddenly said, after swallowing the last bite of breakfast «You need an extreme courage to endorse such a task» he brought the glass of water to his mouth, ignoring the amused looks everyone shared.

«Until yestersol I was the one who took care of the rovers, commander» Klara said, moving her short dark hair behind her ear. «I can deal with the henhouse, it isn't a problem and it doesn't take time from my main task. I've already done it in the past.»

«Excellent, I suppose we all agree.»

George's gaze scanned all those present, noticing a particular spark of relief in everyone's eyes.

«Nowak, we are in debt to you. You saved our life» Alexander said ironically shortly after.

Klara smiled and Jordan stretched.

A new sol had begun.

Jordan finished his meal together with all the others and then left to go to class, which would start at eight. The big cylinder in the middle of the Main Base hosted four personal rooms, three of which were occupied by George, Frank and Klara. Jordan walked alongside the perimeter, passed in front of the corridor which led to the Hong Se De Du base and, after passing the kitchen, he took the corridor which led to the Krasnij Gorod base, where classes were held every sol. Soon he found himself in a new large dome that contained a smaller one in the center. He turned left and began to walk down the perimeter again, passing next to the machines of the Life Support System: the oxygen generator, the carbon dioxide absorber and the water recycling system.

Just as he was about to get past the bathroom door, it opened and a girl of his same age came out in the corridor, stroking her long wavy red hair with her fingers, trying to untangle some rebellious knots. Jordan reached her.

«Oh, *Dobroe utro*, Jordan!» the girl exclaimed seeing him.

«*Utro tebe[1]*» he greeted back, smiling.

"Dobroe utro" meant "good morning". At the Krasnij Gorod they were all used to speak Russian, just like English was principal in the Red Stone and Chinese was protagonist at the Hong Se De Du.

Those three languages were the three main means of communication at Aresland. Jordan had learned them all as a child, even though English was spoken more often due to its simplicity and it was destined to become the only official language.

---

[1] Utro tebe: from Russian, "'morning to you too"

They were about to start down towards the classroom when they heard some quick steps approaching and they turned back again, already well aware of who was coming. A tall boy with dark hair and almond-shaped eyes had come out of the corridor that arrived from the Hong Se De Du.

«*Da jia hao!*[2]» he greeted cheerfully, reaching their side.

«Hi, Nunki» Jordan said, high-fiving with him.

«*Privyet*[3]» the girl said, finally giving up on her hair and throwing it backwards.

The real name of the boy was actually Yan Heng, but everyone called him Nunki because it was the first word that he said as a baby. On the other hand, the girl's name was Anna Yesfir Taykeeva. Jordan had a second name too, even though no one ever used it: Arcturus, it was the name of a very bright star that was visible at night. The three of them were the same age, they were born there, not too far from one another. They had grown up and lived together until then, Jordan had always considered them as a sister and a brother.

«Do you remember which sol is tosol?» Anna asked looking at her friends expectantly.

«Tosol is sol solis» Yan replied thoughtfully. «So what?»

The girl rolled her eyes at him, shaking her head in a defeated manner.

«How can you forget these things, Nunki?!»

Anna's question puzzled Jordan, who tried to think as much as he could to give her a better answer.

Suddenly a memory was lit in his mind like a spark.

---

[2] Da jia hao: from Chinese, "hello, guys", literally "hello everyone"
[3] Privyet: from Russian, "hello"

«It's Virgo 15th, 239!» he spoke suddenly. «The arrival of three new persons is scheduled for tosol!»

«That's it» Anna upheld.

Yan turned to him with wide eyes.

«Man, since when no one new arrives?» he asked frowning.

«As I recall, four years ago a new woman joined the Red Stone, so I suppose someone arrived at yours too. Honestly I don't remember much.»

«Precisely. No one has arrived for four years» Anna confirmed sighing. «Anyway, guys, we'd better go to class, Nastya must be waiting.»

The two nodded and together they started down towards the room that was adjacent to the bathroom.

«I almost forgot, I managed to develop a new super complicated videogame, it's a bomb!» Yan announced with enthusiasm as they reached the room's entrance.

«Impressive» Anna commented flatly.

«What's that tone? You don't appreciate my hard work?»

The girl snorted and pressed a button next to the door, ignoring his question.

«I think that's great, Nunki. Can't wait to try it» Jordan intervened standing up for Yan.

«See, Anna? That's a friend» Yan pointed out, passing an arm on Jordan's shoulders theatrically.

The door slid open and the girl entered first glancing at the sky and whispering "Men!"

Yan went in after her with narrow eyes and Jordan followed them laughing.

The room wasn't very big. Three desks with a laptop each were placed one next to the other in front of a multimedia whiteboard. At the end there was a small closet which contained some papers, notebooks, volumes and all the office supplies. Images of cosmic objects were hanging on every wall: several moons of Jupiter and Saturn, the Andromeda galaxy, various nebulae, and star clusters and then many, many images of planet Earth, with its blue surface, its whirling white clouds and the night lights of the inhabited settlements. Next to the multimedia whiteboard, a woman was sitting at a bigger desk, her hair gathered in a pony tail. As soon as she heard the door opening, she raised her eyes from the book she was reading.

«*Zdravstvuy*[4], Nastya» the three greeted in unison.

The two boys took their seats at the desks while Anna headed to the closet.

«*Zdravstvuytye, rebyata*[5]. How are you?»

Nastya stood up from the desk and went to switch the multimedia whiteboard on, while Anna handed a paper and a pen to both Jordan and Yan, just in case they had to solve some written exercises.

«*Ochen' koroshò, spasibo*[6]» the girl replied first with a resolute tone as she took her seat.

«Not bad» Jordan's voice followed.

«Everything's nominal» Yan concluded.

The lesson began, held in Russian. With Nastya Ivanova they studied chemistry. That sol they analyzed and mastered the reaction that happened between carbon dioxide and hydrogen and that gave methane and water as products. That chemical reaction was extremely important and fundamental in the Aresland, as it was

---

[4] Zdravstvuy: formal Russian greeting, translatable as "hello"
[5] Rebyata: from Russian, "guys"
[6] Ochen' koroshò, spasibo: from Russian, "very well, thanks"

used every sol by the Life Support Systems in order to provide potable water and propellant for the rovers.

Three hours later the three found themselves together in Yan's room, inside the Hong Se De Du. The boy was sitting cross-legged on an armchair as beige as the sky, in front of a screen, the joystick in his hands. Jordan was crouched on the arm of the same chair and observed the game moves of his friend with attention and interest while he explained everything, step by step. Anna, on the contrary, was laying on Yan's bed, her serious gaze was focused on a thick volume that she held in her hands, entitled "Earth and life".

«Okay, now we are in the foreign mother spaceship. We must refuel and leave immediately» Yan explained, completely absorbed in the game.

«What's that countdown?» Jordan asked pointing at the top left corner of the screen.

«It says how much time of invisibility you've got left. As soon as you return visible everyone will try to kill you.»

«How very reassuring. However, Nunki, you've got ten seconds.»

«O, huoji![7]»

«How long for refuelling?»

«Five seconds!»

«Well, you have… five left now! Geez, run!» Jordan was raising his tone of voice and slowly Yan too.

«It should be somewhere here!» Yan shook the joystick frantically. «Zai zheli![8]» he yelled.

---

[7] O huoji: from Chinese, "Oh man!"
[8] Zai zheli: from Chinese "Here it is"

«Go, go, go! Oh no, minus 3, 2, 1!» Jordan had even stood up.

«They might not find us right away. Come on, 4 seconds, 3...»

Shortly after, the text "Refuelling completed successfully" appeared on the screen.

«YEAH!» the two boys screamed in chorus.

«OH, COME ON! CAN YOU KEEP THE NOISE DOWN?!» a voice that they hadn't heard in a while thundered in the room.

«Why don't you play with us too? Always stuck on those books...» Yan commented without turning.

Anna got up to sit, closed the book and placed it on the bed next to her, glaring at Yan's back as he was turned towards the computer screen.

«And you always stuck on those videogames, where's the difference?» Anna hissed back.

«The difference is that books are boring and games are fun. Okay, let's fly away from here. Now we go into the fray.»

«Or the contrary» the girl retorted even if Yan wasn't listening anymore, again focused on the game.

She stood up and walked around the armchair. She grabbed the joystick out of Yan's hands with a snap, taking him by surprise.

«-the heck you doing?! The enemy army's coming!» he shrieked.

«*Otlichno. Vstavay*[9]» her tone didn't admit replies.

The boy didn't hesitate any longer, knowing the girl, and left the place to her.

«*Davay!*[10]» he added, moving to the other side of the armchair.

---

[9] Otlichno. Vstavay: from Russian, "Excellent. Stand up."

The two boys stood to watch. With her small spaceship, the girl defeated the entire enemy army in a record time that not even Yan had achieved before, despite he himself was the one who had programmed the game. Sharp blows, clear and precise, and all the enemies fell one by one. The girl stood up even before the text "You won" appeared on the screen and she headed to the exit. She turned back as the door slid open only to see Jordan and Yan staring at her, dumbfounded.

«Well?» she raised her eyebrows «What're you waiting for? Food's ready.»

Right at that moment the lunch bell resounded in the Aresland and the girl disappeared.

Yan shook his head and switched the computer off.

«She's excruciating» he let out in a heavy breath.

A weak smile was plastered on Jordan's lips.

«Yeah» he murmured.

His eyes still lingering where the girl stood few moments before.

---

[10] Davay: from Russian "You go!"

TWO
~ *196 sols before* ~

The sol proceeded peacefully. After lunch, during which the three guys returned to their respective bases, Jordan dedicated an hour to studying the chemistry lesson of that morning, in his private room. He finally abandoned the desk at 3:00 pm, leaving it completely submerged in flying papers, notebooks, volumes and periodic tables. All he did was switch his laptop off, change his clothes into something more sporty and leave his room, heading to the gym.

As he walked down the corridor, usually governed by silence, he heard several voices speaking animatedly, coming from the Main Base and somehow he perceived a weird ferrous smell in the air. He felt an invisible powder tickling his nose until a spasm crossed his body and he sneezed. He had stopped in the middle of the corridor to evaluate the circumstances. All of that could mean one thing only, Jordan thought, someone had arrived from the outside, involuntarily taking inside some dust. But no extravehicular activity was planned for that sol.

His heart began to race as he realized what was happening. He resumed to walk, more quickly, until he came out on the other side.

There were his father, George Jenner and Klara Nowak surrounding someone whom Jordan couldn't identify. He got closer to have a better look. It was a young man who seemed unable to stop smiling and had an exhausted look as if, instead of driving a rover, he had carried it on his shoulders for miles and miles. Jordan observed him with curiosity, as if he had never seen anything like that before.

He resembled Frank Larsen very much, only he was younger and his skin was a little bit more colorful. He wore a huge white suit that looked like those they used to exit the base, only it was much bigger and bulkier, an old-fashioned one. His father and George were helping him to get rid of it.

After several minutes, when the man had come out of the spacesuit, the three noticed his presence.

«Ah, here you are!» his father exclaimed before addressing the new one «Shäfer, this is my son.»

«Jordan Miles, it's really you! It's a pleasure to make your acquaintance» the man said with a strange accent, reaching out.

Jordan shook his hand, wondering how he knew his name.

«My pleasure» he replied, trying to hide the uneasiness and to look like someone who met new people every sol.

«I'm Hans Shäfer of the European Space Agency, I take it you've already heard of it» he introduced himself.

«Uhm, yeah… Yeah, I know it. So you truly come from Earth…» it was too late when Jordan realized he had thought out loud.

He noticed Hans sending meaningful looks at Alexander and George and he lowered his gaze, embarrassed.

«Sorry, I was just-» he muttered, but Hans interrupted him with a friendly pat on his arm.

«Hey, sorry for what? Yes, I come from Earth, of course» he replied and Jordan raised his gaze to see he was smiling at him.

«How long are you staying?» he asked, quickly returning to his senses.

«For a long time» Hans said vaguely.

Jordan wasn't satisfied with his answer, having no idea of what he meant. He observed him carefully for one more moment, then he decided to let it go.

«Well, I got to go now. Have a good stay.»

The boy turned and left as Hans thanked him. But when the adults resumed to talk among themselves, he couldn't help but stop next to a wall where they couldn't see him, in order to overhear some of their conversation, unable to repress his curiosity.

«Just as you described him, maybe a little bit taller than I imagined» Hans' voice said cheerfully.

Alexander laughed.

«All his father, isn't he?»

«Oh, he'll surpass you» George commented, «All because of the lower gravity and he hasn't finished his growth yet.»

«Can't believe I've just met a real Martian and I can't wait to get to know the other two» Hans continued with a dreaming tone.

«They're just kids really» George said, then Hans spoke again.

«Alexander, I almost forgot. Laurie gave me something for you.»

Hearing his mother's name, Jordan's heart threatened to jump out of his chest. He moved a step to get closer to the three.

«Finally, what is it? Some real coffee I hope.»

«Jordan, are you alright?» a voice spoke suddenly behind his back and he gasped, not expecting it.

He turned to meet Klara Nowak's gaze observing him with an amused expression and her arms crossed.

He straightened up.

«Yes, I was er… going to the gym» he concluded, swallowing.

Klara nodded once, before walking past him.

«Behave» she said at last.

Jordan took a breath of relief. He wished he could keep listening to that conversation, but in the end he just turned and continued on his path.

An aluminum ladder descended from the summit of the cylindrical structure. Jordan climbed up to the top, where there was another geodesic dome. He entered and found himself in a room full of computers whose screens showed images from the satellites orbiting both Mars and Earth, while others showed series of alphanumeric codes that probably only Yan's programming mind would understand. He walked past them and entered the adjacent section of the dome: the gym. There was a cyclette, a tapis roulant and other workout equipment for arms and abdomen. He wasn't alone, a woman wearing a sporty top and a pair of tight grey trousers was running on the tapis roulant.

«Hello, Dounja» Jordan greeted he as he went to sit on the cyclette next to her.

«Hey, how's it going?» she replied quickly, too busy trying to breathe.

Jordan began to pedal.

«He arrived, you know that?»

His gaze was fixed on the small screen that showed his speed. He tried to keep on twenty kilometers per hour.

«Really? When?»

«Right now. There are dad and George with him.»

Dounja slowed her run down until she definitely stopped.

«How's he? Everything went well? The name's Shäfer, is it?»

«I think so, but he seemed very tired. And yes, his name's Hans, Hans Shäfer».

«Later I'll go say hi» the woman said almost to herself as she headed to a sink at the bottom of the room to drink.

Jordan kept pedaling in silence, while some over-whelming thoughts continued to roam in his mind. He didn't know whether he had to admit them or keep them private. He didn't even understand them completely. In the end he sighed.

«You arrived four years ago, Dounja. I can't remember… I don't remember if I felt the same way» he tried.

At his words the woman returned to him and gave him a curious look. She leaned against the machine of the tapis roulant and crossed her arms, giving him her full attention.

«How did you feel?»

Her words lingered in the silence for some time, nothing but the muffled squeak of the cyclette was hearable.

Jordan decided to stop pedaling and passed a hand through his hair, thoughtfully.

«I don't know how to explain this. You know… Sometimes I wonder if I was born on the right planet» for the first time he raised his gaze to meet the woman's eyes.

Silence returned, Dounja seemed hesitant at first, but then she briefly shook her head.

«Oh, Jordan. What are you saying? Of course yes, this is your home. *Our* home.»

She placed a hand on Jordan's shoulder in a tender gesture and he simply nodded.

Those thoughts had whirred in his head for a while now. Maybe he simply had to ignore them.

«Do you need help?»

Jordan and his father were in the storage room of the Main Base. It was a long, narrow place which followed the arc of the dome and was located between the bathroom and the corridor which led to the Krasnij Gorod. It contained literally everything.

Among various working tools, replacement parts, lyophilized food supplies and mountains of boxes, some of which still packed, Jordan was putting on his EVA biosuit for the extravehicular activities. His father helped him seal it safely, he placed the life support backpack on his shoulders and connected it to the system. The boy grabbed his helmet and closed the cabinet from where they had taken everything. He felt invincible when wearing his EVA biosuit. It was completely adherent to his body, an intertwining of red and grey lines spread across his torso, arms and legs on a white base.

«Let's go» the boy said before heading to the door, carrying the helmet under his arm.

The two came out from the storage room and reached the airlock which allowed them to go out without blowing up the base because of the difference in pressure between the inside and the outside. Alexander wore his helmet after sealing his own biosuit in a couple of moves, then he helped Jordan, who was a little bit more troubled.

«Don't worry, you'll get used to it» he said, making sure his helmet was well sealed.

«I guess I will, given that since tosol on I'm going out every sol.»

After double-checking every system and ensuring that there was no pressure loss, the airlock opened and they entered in that small cubic empty room. The hatch closed right away behind them.

«You ready?» his father's voice resounded in his helmet. The boy nodded, but he soon realized that probably Alexander couldn't see him.

«Yeah, can't wait. It's been a while» he said aloud, trying to calm down his enthusiasm and nervousness.

Alexander pulled a handle on the wall and shortly after Jordan could hear three series of bip-bip. A green light switched on above the hatch in front of them and finally it opened.

«You deserved it.»

Jordan moved some steps forward until he found himself stepping on rusty, scarlet brown sand. He smiled, it always reminded him of when he was a child, of the first time he had exited. He crouched down and let some sand stream between his fingers and although he was wearing thick gloves, he thought he could feel every grain. But probably it was just an impression.

«Come on, Jordan. Don't waste time, we've got two hours and a half of air» his father's voice bounced in his helmet, bringing him back to reality.

«Yeah, I'm coming.»

The boy stood up and took one more second to look around himself: an endless lowland of sand and rocks spread in every direction.

It was the Hellas Planitia, the second largest impact crater existing on Mars and it was the deepest one with its seven kilometers below the ground level. It extended for two thousand and three hundred kilometers in the southern hemisphere of the planet.

Jordan spent an entire hour with his father inside the Red Stone garage, a structure which kept the rovers safe during sandstorms. They focused on a two-seater unpressurized rover that basically consisted of four wheels and two seats. During that hour, Jordan memorized the onboard instrumentation and its functioning and, later on, Alexander drove the rover around the Aresland, letting Jordan observe his moves and explaining every parameter he had to keep an eye on.

It was by now 6:30 pm and Jordan's working sol could be declared concluded. He was tired both physically and mentally and he stank incredibly. He went to pick up some clean underwear and clothes from his room and he rushed to the bathroom of the Main Base which was fortunately free, to take a shower. He soaped and washed himself quickly in order to use as little water as possible. He took some more time to dry: he loved being wrapped in his towel, enjoying the hot, scented steam until it was completely withdrawn by special fans. Once dried and dressed, he cleaned the shower and tossed his old clothes and underwear in the laundry, he would return to collect them later.

As he left the bathroom he met George Jenner who was exiting from his private room.

«Hello, George. Do you know how long till dinner?»

«It should be almost ready, tosol Dounja cooks. You hungry?»

«Yes, very much.»

«Let's go then, I'm heading there too.»

Jordan and George began to walk, following the circle of the dome.

«So, tell me, how did it go with the rovers?» George asked, sounding sincerely interested and moving his hands behind his back.

«All theory, dad drove. But I found out what a radioisotope thermoelectric generator is and how it works, therefore I feel sufficiently satisfied.»

George chuckled. They had already reached the table where they usually had meals and reunions.

«Alexander says you learn quickly, I'm glad.»
Jordan shrugged.

«It's about necessity and survival, George. Suppose one sol I lose my mind and run away with a rover. Suppose it breaks, I will have to come out alive somehow, despite my mistake, won't I?»

George sighed and Jordan observed him expectantly.

«My dear boy… Mars does not forgive.»

At his words, Jordan rolled his eyes, already knowing where all of that was going. George continued nevertheless.

«You might also be the most expert among the experts but if you commit a great mistake, you won't be forgiven. It's the Red Planet's Law, Jordan. Never forget that.»

«Yeah, the Red Planet's Law, I know. But don't worry, George, I'm not someone who loses his mind. I've got a perfect control over myself» he declared proudly.

«That's good. Come on, dinner's ready, let's go help Dounja.»

George walked up to the young woman who was coming out of the kitchen and took the trays with the steaming plates from her hands, while the dinner bell rang in every dome. Jordan recognized the smell of rice and asparagus and his stomach growled. He helped Dounja distribute the cutlery while the other inhabitants of the Red Stone were reaching them.

After dinner Jordan met Anna in her room and shortly after Yan joined them. They were all very tired, sol solis was one of the hardest sols of the week. They spent an hour chitchatting about the new entries in the Aresland and Jordan realized that his friends had felt his same new sensations. They didn't talk about that too much though, they preferred to laugh at how Yan perfectly mimicked the new man who had arrived at the Hong Se De Du.

They went to sleep early in order to recover some energy for the following sol that, certainly, was going to be no less tiring.

THREE
~ *195 sols before* ~

"Sol lunae, Virgo 16, 239.
HISTORY OF MARS."

That was what Jordan wrote on his laptop that morning. It was 8:00 am and the Martian history class had just begun with Frank Larsen inside the Krasnij Gorod. The three guys were ready to take notes, an animated image of the Solar System was projected on the multimedia whiteboard.

«So, guys, who of you is able to briefly repeat what we've seen during last week's class?» Frank asked leaning against his desk,

Anna's hand shot upwards first.

«You go, Anna.»

«In the last lesson we've talked about the hypothesis regarding the formation of Mars. It's possible that Mars was formed by an aggregation or accretion of small objects in the primordial Solar System. However, differently from what happened to Earth or Venus, Mars completed its formation in about four point two million years, without ever going beyond the embryonic planetary phase.»

«Very good, Anna, you got it. And you two, can you tell what happened later?»

Yan interjected right away, after briefly glaring at Anna, who looked way too proud of herself.

«Probably the decay of aluminium twenty-six transformed the planet into an ocean of magma. And after the cooling there was a long period of meteor bombardments.»

Finally Jordan added his contribution.

«The hot mantle pushed and raised portions of the crust, then there was another intense period of volcanic activity and lava flows. Finally the planet cooled down, the atmosphere became rarefied, mostly due to the solar winds and the absence of a magnetosphere.»

Frank nodded his approval.

«Good job, guys. So, tosol we'll start a trip back in time, towards something that concerns us more closely. And that is, the history of Mars observations» Frank turned and went to take something from a drawer under the desk.

He took out three big headbands with a device each, which had to be worn like a pair of glasses.

«Therefore I ask you to wear these visors for virtual reality, you already know how they work.»

The three didn't hesitate to take one visor each. They had already been thrown into virtual reality. It was the learning method that Yan preferred as it really felt like being absorbed in a huge videogame. In fact a big smile played on his lips, revealing his excitement. Jordan wore his visor and after few moments of darkness, a light grew wider until he found himself on Mars' surface, outside the Aresland. Yan and Anna stood at his side, the sky was dark and starry and the reddish desert spread all around them. Suddenly they left the surface at full speed and shortly after they found themselves looking at a blue and greenish planet from above.

«Mars observations began with many ancient terrestrial cultures» Frank explained and at his words they reached the surface, landing in a white desert.

Huge temples stood behind them while some people wearing simple tunics wandered in the sand. It was night, some of them occasionally stopped to gaze at the sky. They raised their gaze as well.

«They had noticed, in the sky, a bright dot, slightly reddish, that moved differently from the stars. The first ones to name that dot were the Greeks, who called it Ares, like their divinity representing war.»

«Like Aresland» Yan said.

«Precisely. Then, the Romans changed the name to Mars, that has the same meaning of Ares.»

«Who was the first one to spot Mars?» Anna asked.

«We can't say for sure, but probably the first ones were the Egyptians. The first real scientific studies, instead, began on Earth around 1600, when Galileo Galilei built the first telescope to observe the planets...»

The scene changed suddenly and they found themselves standing inside a small wooden room. An old man with long hair and a full grey beard was bent on a paper. He was tracking the path of stars and planets in the sky. There was a long tube standing next to him, pointing outside a window and with two lenses at the extremities. It had to be the first telescope ever.

Jordan observed carefully everything that happened around him. He wasn't so keen on studying what happened in the past, he was more attracted by the present technologies and innovation, but anyway those travels in virtual reality enthused him a lot as he really felt like he was thrown into the past or into the future or into a tiny cell or into the greatness of a galaxy. However those three hours passed quickly and the three guys could enjoy their free time.

Jordan and Anna were sitting at the table in the Red Stone hall. Yan had been called back in his base, he had been given the task to show the Hong Se De Du greenhouse to the new person, something that Jordan and Anna were going to do soon too in their respective bases.

«What're you doing tosol?» Jordan asked her, casually stretching.

«After lunch I'm having another class of a couple of hours, I'm studying the propulsion systems of rockets, how launches work, with or without a crew...»

«Wow, really? Is it complicated?» Jordan cut her off.

The girl shrugged, observing her hands.

«Well, it's not simple, but it's very interesting. After that I have half an hour of break, then I study and finally I have gym before dinner. And what about you?» she raised her gaze to look at him.

«I study after lunch, then gym and finally I work with rovers, I'm learning to drive them.»

A smile opened on Anna's mouth.

«Ah, what you've been longing to do for ages!»

It was rare to see a sincere smile appear on that always-serious face. And when it happened, Jordan wasn't able to move his eyes away from her or to think about anything else. He didn't understand why, or rather, he didn't even wonder.

His lips curved in a smile too.

«Yeah... I've finally left those damn chickens to the past.»

«I know how you feel, I guess» the girl admitted «Neither did I like to work in the greenhouse so much. For a long time I've had to deal with the mushrooms cultivation we have at the Krasnij Gorod. You have no idea, always having to check on the soil and humidity and temperature and all. Honestly I prefer learning how to launch rockets.»

«I imagine. Don't make me talk about the henhouse, please, for I don't want to bring back old nightmares.»

They both laughed, Anna shaking her head.

«Why don't you stay here for lunch?» Jordan invited out of the blue.

Anna gave him a questioning look, not understanding.

«Tosol my father cooks pasta, it might happen once a month if everything goes right!» he continued.

The girl sighed.

«Although your proposal is tempting, I can't stay, they wait for me in the other base.»

Jordan rolled his eyes, already expecting that answer.

«Are you really giving up a plate of pasta?»

«Jordan, you know the Aresland's rules. Every meal everyone in their own base. And then your father has to cook for you seven already, I'd be intruding.»

«What will you have at Krasnij Gorod tosol?»

«I think I heard... uhm... Burmese tea-leaves salad with... beans, cabbage and dried shrimps.»

Jordan raised his eyebrows and opened his arms.

«I mean, you serious?»

A chuckle threatened to escape Anna's lips.

«You don't even fight a little bit in front of a proposal of some pasta with tomato-sauce prepared with our greenhouse's tomatoes?» he continued.

The girl pretended to glare at him.

«Hey, I do like the Burmese tea-leaves salad...»

«Stop it now!» he cut her off.

The girl closed her mouth, keeping a laugh down.

«Shall we ask permission, for once, or not?» Jordan continued, articulating his words.

The girl sighed.

«Alright.»

In the end Anna joined the members of the Red Stone to try the legendary tomato pasta of Alexander Miles, which turned out to be truly one of the best meals of her life.

When Jordan and Anna had gone to her father, Viktor Taykeev, who was also the commander of the Krasnij Gorod, to ask that permission, he had accepted easily and, in exchange, he had invited Jordan to have dinner with them, that evening.

It was 3:00 pm and Jordan had just finished studying. Like the previous sol, he prepared to go to the gym and left his room. In the corridor for the Main Base he bumped into Dounja and Hans who greeted him with a wave of their hands. Dounja was showing the Life Support Systems to the new man.

At the end of the corridor, he walked around the central cylinder until he found the aluminium ladder and he climbed up. He entered the office that preceded the gym and as always he absently glanced at the screens of the computers. Usual codes, satellite images of Mars' surface, then an image that he had never seen before and finally a satellite view of the Aresland.

He was about to open the gym door when he suddenly stopped. He slowly withdrew his hand from the button that would activate the sliding doors. *An image that he had never seen before?* That sentence had a very strange sound in his mind. He frowned, turned and walked back towards a monitor in particular. At first he had thought he was wrong, but effectively that image of the Martian surface had something wrong. A dark dot in the centre of the screen couldn't be anything natural, but rather artificial. But how could it be possible? It couldn't be the Aresland. Jordan turned to look at the monitor that portrayed the three bases of the Aresland station, all connected through three small corridors. Then he moved his gaze back in front of himself, furrowing his eyebrows.

Jordan was certain that there was no other settlement on Mars, at that moment. He was sure one hundred percent. And so what was that? He quickly glanced around himself, but there was nobody else apart from him. He sat in front of the monitor and began to zoom in as much as he could. Despite the picture was very grainy, it was crystal clear that that was a base or something similar. Before he could decide to investigate further in that computer, the gym's door suddenly slid open and the boy jumped on his feet, startled, zooming out the picture with a snap of his hand. Now nothing could be seen but the red Martian surface.

«Jordan!» a severe voice thundered in the dome «What are you doing?»

The boy pulled away from the chair and met Frank Larsen's furious gaze. He swallowed.

«Nothing, I did nothing» he replied quickly.

«You don't fool me, boy. What were you doing there? What were you watching?» the man seemed almost nervous, Jordan had never seen him like that before.

«Nothing, just... curiosity.»

«Curiosity» Frank repeated «You haven't changed a bit, Jordan. As a child you did nothing but snoop around, even where you shouldn't.»

The boy stood silent, having no idea of what to say. He just wanted to get out of that situation and for a second he regretted his decision to find out more.

«Why are you here, in any case?» Frank asked in a calmer tone.

«I have to go to the gym.»

«Go, then.»

The man moved aside and kept his eyes fixed on Jordan until the sliding doors sealed behind his back.

Jordan couldn't remove that image for his mind. Even while he was doing lifts, laying on the gym equipment, that grainy image of an unknown base lingered in front of his eyes. He couldn't accept the fact that he knew nothing about it, that no one informed him about anything. And Frank's reaction? Unprecedented. As if... as if he was doing something wrong, but there was nothing wrong! He was simply checking the monitors linked to the satellite, as a member of the Red Stone and inhabitant of the Aresland. It was one of his rights.

In that moment he felt like doing one thing only: talking to Anna and Yan of what he had seen. Maybe they knew something more. But he wasn't going to see them until after dinner.

Once he finished his gym session, he passed in front of the monitors once again and his gaze fell inevitably on the computer that first showed the image. But now the screen was black and a text in the centre read "Access blocked. Enter password to continue". Jordan shook his head and walked past.

He went back to his room to change clothes and prepare for the exit with his father and the rovers. He was so distracted that he even crashed against Klara while walking to the storage room, he hadn't seen her.

«Jordan, are you quite alright?» the woman asked, giving him a worried look.

«I'm sorry, yes I'm alright, I'm fine.»

He resumed to walk and reached his father in the storage room, he was already suiting up.

«Hi» Jordan greeted.

«Hello, Jordan. Here» his father handed him his biosuit.

Once ready and certain that everything was in place, they left the base through the airlock and reached the garage again.

«Tosol you drive, you ready for it?» his father asked.

Jordan didn't answer right away. The truth was that he couldn't quite focus on what he had to do.

«You may drive again for once, then I try» he replied.

For the whole round, Jordan found himself busier looking around himself, towards the horizon, in order to see if he could notice anything strange, rather than following his father's moves on the console.

His turn came, the two switched their seats. Jordan observed the commands attentively and finally managed to push the rover forward. He began to drive around the Aresland. For a moment he forgot about everything: he was driving a rover and he found that it was an amazing feeling. He was controlling a huge vehicle all on his own and enthusiasm was mounting inside him.

«That's good, Jordan. Keep an eye on velocity and turn around major rocks» his father advised.

He continued to drive when slowly his thoughts began to converge once again towards that image. He wondered if he could reach that mysterious place onboard a rover and discover what was it all about...

«Jordan!» his father called, alarmed.

The rover stopped suddenly as a wheel got stuck against a rock, making the two jump dangerously, but they managed to hold onto their seats and Jordan returned to reality.

«Jordan, what was that? Are you alright?» his father's scolding voice resounded in his helmet.

«I'm fine, I just got distracted a moment» the boy replied hesitantly.

«Distracted? If that rock were bigger this rover would be gone! And we too, probably! This is not a game, you have a huge responsibility and you can't allow yourself to distractions, it could cost your life, are you aware of this?»

Jordan swallowed, his eyes still fixed on the horizon.

«I'm sorry» he muttered.

Several seconds of silence passed, he could literally feel the weight of his father's gaze on him through the helmet's visor.

«Something's wrong?» Alexander asked, now with caution. «It's not like you to be distracted while working. What happens?»

Jordan didn't answer right away, his eyes were glued to the horizon. He couldn't help it. He needed to know if he had found something he didn't have to find, a secret that so had to remain.

«Is there anything you have to tell me, by any chance?» he asked slowly, «Something that I don't know, that no one ever told me?»

Not receiving an answer, Jordan turned to look at his father in the eyes through the glass of the visor.

«What do you mean, Jordan?»

«You got my question.»

«No, there's nothing. You do know that you're aware of everything that happens, just like everybody else.»

Jordan moved his eyes away and stared into nothing for a moment, processing his words.

«I know» he finally said.

But what Jordan actually knew now was something else: his father had lied to him and something was kept hidden from him.

«We better reenter. It isn't safe if you're distracted.»

The boy nodded. The two switched seats again and Alexander drove the rover to the garage.

«You sure you alright?»

«Yes, I'm fine.»

Jordan took a shower, slightly longer than the usual. Then at about 7:30 pm he reached Anna inside the Krasnij Gorod for dinner. They ate chickpeas and beans tofu with mashed potatoes. He hadn't said anything to Anna yet, but he didn't know how long he was going to be able to resist. He didn't spill out a word for almost the entire dinner, shifting nervously on his seat and continuously glancing at Anna, struggling to keep his mouth shut.

At a certain moment, Anna turned to him with a questioning look and leaned towards him.

«You're acting weird, what's gotten into you?» she whispered so that he only could hear her.

Jordan shook his head sharply and the girl sighed rolling her eyes and returning to her meal.

«*Ya dolzhen skazat tebe koe-chto*[11]» Jordan whispered, observing his plate.

The girl had just filled her mouth with a forkful of tofu.

«*Chto?*[12]» she asked turning again and hiding her mouth behind a hand.

«*Ya nye mogù, seychas*[13]» Jordan nodded his head once towards the other diners.

«*Davay*!» she urged.

«*Nyet! Mnye takzhe nuzhno Yan*[14].»

«*Koroshò.*»

Their conversation closed and they didn't speak until dinner was over and they could go look for Yan.

«Will you tell me what's this all about?» Anna asked while they hurried down a corridor towards the Hong Se De Du.

«First we find Yan.»

They reached the Hong Se De Du hall, where everyone was still sitting around a long table. The two guys stopped at the entrance, waiting for Yan to notice them, thing that happened almost immediately.

«*Ni neng lai ma?*[15]» Jordan asked addressing the boy.

---

11 Ya dolzhen… chto-to: from Russian, "I must tell you something"
12 Chto?: from Russian, "What?"
13 Ya… seychas: from Russian, "Not now"
14 Nyet… Yan: from Russian, "No, I need Yan as well."

Yan turned to the adults sitting at the table and told them something in a low voice. Finally he stood up and reached his friends.

«What happens?»

«Jordan's having a premenstrual-syndrome crisis» Anna replied ironically.

Yan narrowed his eyes.

«A what?»

Jordan glared at her before speaking.

«It's important, I've got to talk to the both of you» he said in a low voice «Nunki, can we stay in your room?»

«Wow, the situation sounds serious. 'Course we can.»

«The situation *is* serious» Jordan retorted as they started down towards Yan's room.

«Uh-huh» he muttered before whispering to Anna «However, is this syndrome transmissible?»

She face-palmed.

Anna and Yan were on the bed, while Jordan was sitting cross-legged on an armchair in front of them.

«I'll ask you a very simple question» Jordan began, «How many bases are there on Mars at the moment?»

Anna raised an eyebrow and gave him a weird look, Yan frowned.

«There's the Aresland» the girl replied, looking at Yan for support and the boy nodded his agreement.

«And then?» Jordan insisted.

«And then what?» Yan repeated «There's nothing else, is it even a question?»

Jordan sighed.

---

15 Ni... ma: from Chinese, "Can you come?"

«You mean that there are other bases apart from the Aresland on Mars?» Anna asked, not believing to a word that she pronounced.

«There's another one.»

«Bullshit.»

«I saw it with my own eyes, Anna! In the Red Stone office, on one of the monitors there was a satellite image that showed something I'm sure was artificial, a structure.»

«This isn't possible, Jordan. If it were, we would know it.»

«Indeed, Anna's right. We're always told everything that happens, we're aware of everything» Yan intervened.

«That's what I've always thought. But this time they're hiding something.»

«But Jordan, are you really sure you didn't get confused?» she tried.

«Yes, Anna, yes, I'm absolutely certain. When I was looking at that image, a member of the Red Stone caught me and when I left he blocked the access to that computer. It's evident that they're hiding something from us.»

The girl sighed observing the floor, Yan was staring into space.

«If what you claim is true, however absurd it may be, then I believe it's necessary to investigate» the boy with almond-shaped eyes said. «Let's be careful of every detail from tomorrow on.»

«I'm still not sure whether to believe or not» Anna admitted, «But I trust Jordan and I don't think he's suddenly gone crazy, so... Let's discover what's going on.»

Jordan smiled and nodded solemnly, grateful for his friends' support. Yan clapped his hands once loudly.

«Great. And now who wants to play a match of my super crazy videogame?!» he exclaimed jumping on his feet and grabbing the joystick from the nightstand.

«Yeah, let's do this!» Jordan jumped on his feet as well.

Anna, instead, brought her hands to her hair and let herself fall back on the bed.

«Oh, no!»

FOUR
~ *191 sols before* ~

Several sols had passed after that decisive talk in Yan's room. The three guys had tried to be more careful of certain discussions among the adults or on the screens of the computers in their own bases, but nothing seemed different from usual. After he got rid of that weight with his friends, Jordan had returned to his senses. He had perfectly learned to work with unpressurised two-seater rovers and his father had promised him that as from the following week on they would start to work on a new, bigger model. Those last sols had been so intense that the three guys found very little time to stay together.

Despite everything, that sol veneris 20, at 6:00 pm, they found themselves sitting together at the table of the Krasnij Gorod main hall. Jordan had finished working with rovers earlier than usual and had just taken a shower; Yan had arrived from his computer science class and Anna had just finished studying.

«So, still nothing?» Jordan asked, after making sure that no one was present except the three of them.

«No, Jordan» Anna said, sounding not too sure.

«Everything's nominal as always» Yan spoke up right away.

«But...» Anna passed a hand on her forehead, her eyes lost on the white table.

«But what?» Jordan pressed.

She raised her gaze.

«Well, haven't you noticed that lately we've had very few chances to see each other, to talk?»

«Geez, yes! Never had so much to do!» Yan exclaimed throwing his hands in the air.

«Like if...» Anna paused, shaking her head, deep in thought.

«Like if they're trying to avoid to let us stay together long enough to...» Jordan continued Anna's reasoning.

«Long enough to plan something» she completed, finally raising her gaze to look at the two boys in the eyes.

«Something they want to prevent from happening» Yan added, joining the stream of thoughts.

Anna nodded.

«However it's just a hypothesis. Nothing is sure. Maybe it's just an illusion of ours.»

At those words Jordan glared daggers at her.

«What I saw is not an illusion! It's a photograph of this damn planet!» the boy raised his voice, enraged.

He suddenly found a hand pressed against his mouth as Anna almost fell from her chair to shut him up.

«Sssht! They'll hear you!» she screamed in a whisper.

«Guys, I don't know about you, but I don't feel good. I'm not good if I think they're hiding something from me. I mean... they've always told us everything! And now what?» Yan admitted.

«Me too, Nunki» Jordan convened with bitterness.

«Yeah, same» Anna agreed.

«We have to do something, but something concrete» Jordan began with a tone of importance, «So, if hypothetically it's all about a second base on Mars, it means that it is monitored by your satellites too, that are linked to your bases computers, right?» he looked at Yan.

«Right» he confirmed with a nod.

«Then I believe it necessary to check» Jordan concluded.

Anna sighed, visibly upset.

«I've never done anything like that, I've never used those computers, I've never had to...»

«Listen» Jordan cut her off and she passed a hand through her hair «Now you have to, Anna. It's fundamental that you manage to access them for a moment. One moment is enough to see if there's something wrong» he spoke with caution.

The clear green eyes of the boy mixed with the blue, serious ones of the girl.

«It's not against the rules» he added softly and hopefully, after few seconds of silence and their eyes were still glued.

«Technically not» Yan interjected and Jordan almost winced as he was brought back to reality and looked away «But that would certainly be suspicious, we three should have no real reason to have a look at the computers that are linked to the satellites» he pointed out.

Jordan rolled his eyes and hid his face in his hands.

«I was trying to convince her, you dunderhead!» Jordan let out in a frustrated tone.

«Oh» Yan glanced at Anna «Well, yeah, it's not against the rules.»

«I'll do it» Anna spoke suddenly and Jordan lowered his hand to look at her, unbelieving.

She nodded at him and he struggled to keep his enthusiasm down.

He turned to Yan.

«I take it you already agree.»

«'Course I do, commander. I'll act immediately» Yan announced solemnly.

Jordan huffed and smiled.

«Don't call me that, don't even joke. I'm not a commander.»

«Ah, I think you'd cover this role excellently. Look how you give us orders!»

«But they're not orders!»

«Am I right, Anna?»

The girl let out a brief laugh and observed Jordan smiling.

«Oh, yes. Absolutely right.»

He smiled at the girl as he felt overwhelmed by a weird sensation of weakness that lately took him often and off guard.

«Jordan Miles!» a sudden, new voice called.

They gasped and turned to the door. A six-foot-tall man with large shoulders and eyes as black as pitch had come in. They felt their faces going pale for the same worrying thought that crossed their minds: they could have been heard. He approached the table with a deliberate, imposing pace. Jordan stood up and faced the man. He was Artëm Levitsky, he secretly aspired to command the Krasnij Gorod since when he had arrived, but that role had always laid with Viktor, Anna's father.

«Idi v Red Ston. Alexander zhdyot tebya. U tebya yest zdaniye[16]» Artëm said with his bone-chilling, deep voice.

---

16 Idi... zdaniye: from Russian, "Go to the Red Stone, Alexander is waiting for you. You have a job to do"

«*No kak? Seychas u menya yest svobodnoe vremya!*[17]»

«*Nyet voprosov. Idi*[18]»

The boy sighed loudly, annoyed.

He turned to look at his friends in the eyes. That look was enough to know that they had understood each other. Something was wrong. And that was a new opportunity to separate them.

«See you later» he muttered to his friends.

Then he turned and left the room.

«Hans, this is the greenhouse. Greenhouse, this is Hans» Jordan announced at the entrance of the third dome of the Red Stone.

The man chuckled.

«It's a pleasure, really.»

His father had given him the task to show their greenhouse to the new man. He knew that sooner or later it was going to happen.

«Follow me, I'll show you our cultivations.»

The boy started down among the six big shelves that filled the ground floor, followed by Hans, who looked around himself scanning every corner. All the small plants on the shelves were illuminated by an intense red-purplish light that made their leaves appear unexpectedly dark, almost black.

«Every shelf is dedicated to a species» Jordan began to explain, then he stopped next to one of them and approached it to get a closer look. «These are radishes» he said, then he looked around himself «While over there we have spinach. On that shelf there's chives» Jordan pointed at every shelf one after the other.

---

17 No… vremya: from Russian, "Why? Now's my free time"

18 Nyet… Idi: "No questions, go"

He approached another one to look attentively.

«These are peas. And then over there we have lettuce and there potatoes. As you can see they're all illuminated by LEDs, because they're cold lights, so they don't damage the plants, they don't risk to burn and they grow peacefully.»

«You save a lot of energy this way.»

«Yes, indeed. And then LEDs last a very long time so we won't need to worry to change them for a good while. Shall we go upstairs?» he then asked, waiting for Hans as he finished to observe the shelves.

«Let's go.»

Jordan headed to the centre of the dome, where an aluminium ladder stood almost vertically. It was like the one in the Main Base, but this time it led to the first floor through a square gap. The boy climbed up the ladder until he came out on the first floor. He was right away overwhelmed by a familiar smell that brought him back with his memories, to the times when he worked with the famous henhouse. He felt a chill running down his spine, but he tried to focus on what he had to do. As soon as Hans had reached him, Jordan headed to the opposite side of the henhouse, towards other, taller shelves.

«And here we have asparagus, tomatoes, quinoa and every sort of legume.»

«Who's taking care of all of this at the moment?» Hans asked, stroking with his fingertips a small tomato that leaned out of a shelf.

«Frank Larsen» the boy replied «Usually we take turns, we change every month.»

Jordan proceeded towards a couple of long tables which stood one next to the other and the man reached him right away.

They were approaching the henhouse.

«Here we are, let's say, experimenting hydroponic cultivation. As you can see the plants are not in the soil, but in an inert substrate. They are irrigated with a special solution containing all the inorganic compounds that are necessary to provide the plants with a correct mineral nutrition. We have some corn, fennels, cabbage, carrots, basically a bit of everything and for now it seems it's working. Ah, and here we have strawberries, blueberries, raspberries and blackberries.»

«Man, if we go on like this I won't make it to dinner» Hans joked.

«Don't tell me, I'm starving and I hope it'll be ready soon. However let's move on, there's not much left.»

Jordan turned reluctantly towards the henhouse. He found some courage and together they approached a rectangular fence that on one side was delimited by a cubic structure that contained some beds of straw. A couple of hens scratched the thin layer of soil that was created specially for them. This time Jordan didn't say a word, so Hans spoke.

«I heard you've worked with them for a good while.»

«Unfortunately you heard well» he stammered.

«How many are there?»

«Four. Four nightmares. However there's not much to be explained here. They produce about one egg per sol and who takes care of them has to collect the eggs every sol and bring them to the kitchen and the other bases. And then everything has to be cleaned periodically, their excrements have to be kept to be afterwards recycled into energy and then, well, feed is not a problem, these creatures devour anything.»

«Why do you talk so badly of them? They look peaceful to me» Hans said, crouching down next to the fence to have a closer look at one hen.

«Once, one of the first times that I worked here, while I was replacing the straw inside their shelter, one of the hens ran away from the fence» Jordan began to tell, «You have no idea of what chasing a hen and trying to catch it means. Please don't make me remember, don't ask me any more.»

Instead of laughing or smiling, as Jordan expected, the man continued to observe the hens and a spark of hidden nostalgia seemed to shine in his eyes. The boy got curious and he furrowed his eyebrows.

«Did I say something wrong?»
The man seemed to return to reality all of a sudden

«Oh, no no. It's just... They remind me of Earth» he shook his head slightly and a small smile appeared on his lips, «You know, when I was a child I loved going to the countryside, to my grandmother's. She always had some hens and I had fun like crazy chasing them. Well, of course when it was them who chased me, it was another story. But I have some beautiful memories.»

Jordan was hesitant, he narrowed his eyes while studying the terrestrial in front of him.

«Countryside, you said? What is it?»

Jordan could say that for a moment Hans studied him with his same curious spark in his eyes.

«Countryside is... well, uhm, it's an open-air place, far from cities, where... there are immense meadows and houses are simple, people are simple. There's clean air, there's peace...»

While Hans was speaking, Jordan tried to imagine everything, even though it turned out most complicated. The man noticed his lost look and seemed to suddenly remember something.

«Wait! I have a picture» he tucked a hand into his right pocket and took out a small piece of paper folded in a half. «I always take it with me, wherever I go.»

He unfolded it and handed it to the boy. It showed a small wooden house, clung to the side of a green hill. As green as the leaves of the lettuce he had had for lunch that sol. Behind it, several trees stood tall and in the background, some mountains covered in woods spread to the horizon. The sky was blue, so intense that it seemed almost unreal, occasionally interrupted by some swabs of white cloud.

«This is my grandmother's countryside house, in Germany.»

«It's beautiful» Jordan whispered, his eyes lost in the depths of that image.

«I happen to see such pictures very rarely» he admitted, handing the paper back to the man «Thank you.»

He smiled, folded the picture again and put it back in his pocket.

«Hans» Jordan called after a moment of silence.

«Yes?»

«Do you think I'll be able to see the countryside with my own eyes... one *day*?»

Hans suddenly raised his gaze on the boy. His eyes were as blue as that far sky. He seemed hesitant.

«I don't know this, Jordan» he said, almost to himself «I really don't know.»

In that moment the dinner bell rang, interrupting Jordan's thoughts.

«Oh, finally!» Hans exclaimed, «Is there anything else or can we go?»

«This is it, we can go» Jordan replied, turning and heading back to the ladder. «The tour is over.»

Jordan was really exhausted and he desired nothing but going to his room, into his bed, to sleep and recover energy. But in spite of all of this, as soon as he finished eating, he got up from the table and turned to leave in the opposite direction to that which led to his room.

«Hey, Jordan. Where are you going?» Alexander asked right away, noticing his intention. «You look tired, don't you think it's best if you go to rest?»

The majority of those present had turned to look at him, he stood still. He swallowed and tried to quickly make up an excuse in order to move in that direction.

«I need the bathroom» he said, «And I'll take something for the headache.»

«You feel bad? You want me to come with you?»

«Oh, no no, thanks, really. I don't think that's necessary, thank you» he hurried to say, backing off, before turning and leaving definitely.

Once he was sure that the cylindrical structure and the kitchen inside the Main Base hid him from the eyes of his father and the other members, he turned sharply to his left, taking the corridor which led to the Krasnij Gorod. He didn't meet anyone, fortunately, thus he could reach Anna's room without being noticed. He wasn't surprised to find the girl laying on her bed with a book in her hands.

As soon as Anna saw Jordan, she whirled to sit and put the book down

«Jordan! What are you doing here?» she scolded in a whisper, standing up «Come in!»

She rushed to close the door, after pulling her friend inside.

«What's wrong? Why are you acting like that?»

«Sssht, lower your voice! They mustn't know that you're here.»

Jordan furrowed his eyebrows.

«Is it against the rules?» he whispered.

«I... don't know? In any case, it's crystal clear that they're doing everything in their power to keep us busy enough not to meet! Or something like that. I guess they wouldn't be pleased to know you're here – unless you already told someone?»

He shook his head.

«Those of the Red Stone don't know I'm here, I told them I needed the bathroom. I reckon I don't have much time.»

«Holy Olympus, you even lied!» Anna passed a hand through her hair, as she always did when she was nervous «If they catch you...»

«What could they ever do?» Jordan cut her off.

«I don't know, enclosing you in your room for the rest of your life?»

«That's rubbish. We're not kids anymore, how could they punish us? We're living in an air bubble, if you haven't noticed!» Jordan let out all at once, surprising even himself for his words.

Anna slightly widened her eyes, observing her friend warily.

«That doesn't mean we can break rules at our pleasure» she began with caution, trying to bring Jordan back to his senses. «It takes a moment to blow up an air bubble.»

Jordan knew she was right. He had no idea where those words he blurted out really came from. As he locked his eyes with hers, blue mixing with green, his agitation faded away and he found a renowned sense of peace. He sighed and reluctantly looked away, sitting on a chair.

«Listen, let's not waste time. Did you and Yan check the computers?»

«I did, but they nearly caught me. Whereas the computers in the Hong Se De Du have been patrolled for the entire sol and Yan couldn't even approach.»

«And so? Did you find anything?»

The girl slightly tilted her head on a side, lowering her gaze.

«There are some secret files that I can't open, they request codes of every kind.»

Jordan sighed, frustrated.

«Obviously.»

«I have a bad feeling. Or rather than a bad feeling, it's a certainty. Those files have been blocked recently, Jordan. The block they entered is very recent, there wasn't anything like that before. You know what that means?»

«It means they know we know. Or at least, they think so.»

«Exactly. And now they're controlling us.»

«But what could it ever be...» Jordan whispered bringing his hands to his face.

He thought deeply for few moments, then he lowered his hands and stood up.

«I got to talk to Yan.»

He headed to the door but he was suddenly stopped by a hand that closed around his arm and yanked him backwards.

«Forget about it!»

Jordan turned and found himself sinking in the abyss of two concerned, celestial eyes in front of him.

«It's important, Anna. We can't wait any longer.»

He lowered his gaze and sighed, noticing she wouldn't let him go.

«Listen» he continued, «I know it's dangerous and they can't know we're here. But if I can't go to Yan, let's make Yan come here.»

The girl moved her gaze to the laptop laying on her desk.

«If you're thinking of sending him a message, I don't think that would be a good idea. They could intercept it, or rather, they surely will.»

The boy stepped towards the laptop and switched it on, sitting at the desk.

«Of course they will. But we'll send something that only Yan could understand, something that could sound like a joke to the others and so they wouldn't suspect anything.»

«It's stupid» Anna pointed out.

«We're kids, we do stupid things.»

«Didn't you claim quite proudly that we're not kids anymore like two minutes ago?»

Jordan shrugged.

«Well, it did fit my speech pretty amazingly indeed.»

Anna rolled her eyes. She approached the boy to look at the screen as he opened a chat-room with Yan's personal computer.

«Come on, help me think» Jordan hid his face in his hands, thoughtfully.

«Mmm, it has to be something that makes him come here, but without being seen, that's very important.»

Few moments of silence passed, when suddenly Jordan almost jumped on his chair, thunderstruck.

«Of course! Of course!» he exclaimed aloud.

«Sssht!» Anna warned him and he lowered his tone again.

«His videogame, Anna! In the enemy mother spaceship you have to reach the refuelling station without being seen!»

The girl widened her eyes.

«Brilliant» she commented, unbelieving, while Jordan was already typing on the keyboard.

From: Anna Taykeeva; To: Yan Heng
Hello, Nunki. I was thinking about how cool your game is. Most of all when you move on the enemy spaceship. I think I saw a refuelling station somewhere here. Ah, be careful, the countdown is over. You know what to do... after all, you developed it! The situation is urgent.

«Well, we have nothing to do but wait and hope» Jordan said, after pressing the button "send".

«You think he'll understand?» Anna asked.

«I'm sufficiently confident that he will.»

All of a sudden the message passed from a grey colour to light blue.

«He has already visualized!» Anna exclaimed, Jordan held onto his chair with his hands and swallowed.

Seconds passed, feeling infinite, the two guys stared intently at the computer's screen. Then suddenly the reply appeared.

From: Yan Heng; To: Anna Taykeeva
No problem, the situation is under control.
I feel victory is close.

Jordan and Anna exchanged looks. They reflected intently on those simple words, but in the end everything was clear already.

«Hope he won't get caught» Jordan said.

«Let's be ready at the door» she added and the boy nodded.

They moved to the sides of the entrance that, after various minutes of frustrating wait, opened. Jordan grabbed the boy badly and threw him into the room, while Anna closed the door right away. Yan had ended up with his stomach on the bed. He got up as his friends approached him.

«So? Did they see you?»

«Mission completed, I'm still invisible!» the boy exclaimed, fixing his t-shirt. «Guys, that message was the most brilliant finding of the century! At first I thought Anna had gone totally crazy, but then I thought Anna cannot go crazy (I mean, she's too serious to be someone who goes crazy), and so I realized it was an urgent situation and, well, here I am. So, what is it all about?»

Yan had spoken so quickly that the two guys struggled to follow the whole speech. Jordan leaned absently against the desk in front of the bed and crossed his arms.

«Nunki, your time has come» he said.

«Cool. What do I have to do?»

«You're a hacker, analyst and super computer scientist, right?»

«And programmer, don't forget that. But yes, however, I'm all of these things. Effectively I've never told anyone, but I could easily access and modify at pleasure the entire computer web of the Aresland» Yan specified, all full of himself and with a big smile on his lips. That suddenly disappeared though, as soon as he realized his friend's intentions. And so he resumed to speak before Jordan could say anything.

«Hey, pal, wait wait wait! This does not mean that I can actually do it, you got it? I'd end up in a storm of troubles, you understand?»

«And do you understand the importance of the issue?» Jordan retorted.

«Yes, but...»

«Jordan, come on, Nunki is right! Think of what would happen if they found out we've hacked the web to download some secret data!»

«But I am sure Nunki would be able not to leave signs of the activity online and for what concerns the people, well... We need a plan.»

«This is madness» Yan commented to himself, «You're right, though. It isn't impossible, but it's extremely risky.»

«That's exactly why we all have to agree. And if we decide to act, we have to be united, until the end, for better or worse» Jordan declared.

An inevitable moment of silence followed during which they fell deep in thought, wondering if it was going to be a good or terrible idea. Finally, Yan was the first to raise his gaze on Jordan with a smile of someone who's up to no good.

«Count me in. I can't leave all the fun to you!» he gave him a wink.

They both turned to look at Anna, who was staring at the floor. She had always obeyed the rules with discipline and rigour. This was going to make her break a good amount of them. In the end she raised her gaze on her two friends who were waiting for an answer and hid her face in her hands.

«We'll get ourselves into infinite troubles, won't we?» she asked with a defeated tone.

«Definitely» Jordan replied crossing his arms.

«That's right» Yan added.

The girl lowered her hands and smiled slightly.

«Fine, I'm with you.»

«Group hug?» Yan suggested and they laughed all together, finally hugging tightly and exchanging looks that spoke volumes.

«So, I must run back to the Red Stone now. Tomorrow is sol saturni therefore we'll surely have more free time. We'll plan and act» Jordan said.

«Ah, yes! Tomorrow no lessons nor work. We could meet after breakfast» Yan proposed.

«Yeah, try to come to me at about nine, okay?»

«Okay» Anna agreed and Yan nodded.

Finally they greeted and wished each other a good night before Jordan and Yan left her room together and took two different corridors.

FIVE
~ *190 sols before* ~

It was almost 7:30 am, Jordan was laying with his stomach on his bed, partially covered by a light sheet, the red blanket was completely pushed and rolled up at the bottom of the bed while a dangling hand grazed the floor. He slept blissful and safe in his messy room. All of his clothes from the previous sol had been gathered on the chair in front of his desk and one of the blue socks had fallen on the ground. There was a book on the table, surrounded by scribbled papers, full of thick writing. It was still opened on page one hundred and ninety-six, *"Proteins, enzymes and vitamins"*. In a corner of the desk there was a high tower of other volumes, the one on the top was entitled *"Physics: relativity and quantums"*.

The peaceful silence was suddenly interrupted by the Aresland's morning bell that resounded in every dome. Jordan turned around in his bed and stretched, before getting up while yawning widely. He loved sol saturni. Of the whole week, it was the sol when he could allow himself to do nothing. Except for the gym, the hour and a half of workout had to be done every single sol. After putting his clothes on and going to the bathroom, he headed to the Main Base, where he found his father, George, Klara and Hans having their breakfast. As soon as the four of them turned to look at the boy, he tried to figure out if they knew anything of how things had actually gone the night before.

«Good morning» he greeted smiling innocently and taking a seat next to Hans.

Everyone greeted him back and Jordan felt relieved, it really seemed they had bought it. He helped himself to some pieces of toasted bread and spread some peanut butter on them, then he prepared a bowl of muesli, that was a mixture of cereals and dried fruit, moistened with some fresh water and raspberry juice.

«You slept well?» Hans asked him with his kind manners.

«Yes, very well, thanks» the boy replied before biting his toast.

«Good. Anyway, I was saying» the man turned back to Klara, sitting at his right and Jordan listened «I officially start my work tomorrow. I have to test the little Audax, check the functioning of its solar panels and robotic arms, then I'll drive it remotely, to the South Pole, where it'll collect some ice and then come back.»

«Gosh, I didn't know we have such a rover. Is it like the good old Curiosity?» Jordan interjected.

Hans turned again to the boy on his left.

«Yes, we can say they're cousins.»

«Or rather, Curiosity is the great-grandpa» Klara added with a giggle.

«True» Hans agreed cheerfully.

«But the South Pole is pretty far, what if it breaks or falls down a hill?» Jordan asked.

«Well, my job is about trying to avoid it. If it breaks on its own, there's not much we can do. We try to find the problem and make sure that it won't happen again during the next mission.»

«Cool. Good luck.»

«Thanks, Jordan» he smiled.

The boy tried to eat as fast as he could because he couldn't wait to meet Anna and Yan in his room. He filled his mouth with spoonfuls of muesli and, once it was finished, he grabbed the second toast with peanut butter and left the table.

«Jordan, how many times have I told you not to eat away from the table?» his father ranted .

Alexander always kept an eye on his son.

«I'll be careful!» Jordan shouted back from the corridor, with the toast between his teeth.

Trying not to leave a track of breadcrumbs on his path, he reached his room. He decided he had to do something, like for example, reordering. But this time seriously: Anna and Yan hardly ever came to his room and theirs were always well kept.

He slipped the last piece of bread into his mouth and then started from the desk, he folded in a half every flying paper and put it into the biochemistry book, that he closed and placed on the top of the pile. He threw away all the papers that he didn't need anymore and finally put all his pens into a pencil case. Then he passed to the bed, he fixed the blankets and made it presentable, placing the pillows and the various plushes one next to the other against the wall. Finally he lifted the bunch of abandoned clothes from the chair using both his arms and, without seeing where he was going, he left the room, heading to the bathroom of the Main Base: he was going to put everything in the laundry.

When he reentered his room, he had ten minutes left before 9:00 am. He sat in front of his computer and switched it on, to check if all the lessons he followed had been registered on his personal profile. Anna and Yan had their own profiles as well. It was all about an online platform on which the three of them could see the progresses they made with their education. It contained all the materials that they studied during the lessons, some tests and a section dedicated to the practical skills. Everything turned out to be fine, so he played a list of his favourite music and waited.

Few moments later his door slid open and Anna and Yan entered his room.

«'the hell of music you listen to, pal?» was the first thing that Yan blurted out.

A cheerful, rhythmic melody resounded in the room, with solos of mandolin and banjo.

«It's called country, folk, or something like that. You don't like it?» Jordan replied calmly, shrugging and turning to his friends.

Anna looked around herself as if that was the first time she entered his room.

«I'll be damned, man, you got to be kidding me! Turn it off!» Yan almost threw himself at Jordan's computer, but he managed to turn it off before the boy could put his hands on it. «Oh, finally. I'll have to teach you some things I guess.»

«Look, I have no intention to listen to your eardrums-breaking stuff, honestly, that's barely music.»

«How dare you?»

«I dare as you appeared in my room to destroy my peaceful moment with my music. I have all rights to dare.»

«You want me to leave?»

«Guys, stop now» Anna spoke up, «Let's focus on our goal.»

«And here comes the eternal serious...» Yan commented in a low voice.

Jordan let out a giggle.

«Yan Heng!» the girl ranted, furious.

«Sorry, sorry, sorry, I didn't mean it really, you're right» Yan excused quickly, bringing his hands in front of his face in a defending manner.

Jordan definitely burst out laughing.

«What are *you* laughing at?!» the girl snapped to Jordan «You two would go nowhere if I weren't here to keep your feet on the ground, are you aware of this?»

«Yeah, come on, you're right. Now let's everyone calm down. Don't worry, Anna. Yan and I were simply joking, we've got more serious stuff to focus on at the moment» he sent a final warning look at Yan, who simply sat on Jordan's bed and sighed.

Anna took an abandoned chair and sat with the two.

«So» Yan began, now seriously «I'm about to jeopardise my quiet existence for a just cause. Jordan, you have a computer but it isn't linked to the general web, right?»

«I think so, I can only send and receive messages, but that's an independent system, is it?»

«Yes, indeed, I imagined. Well then, I'll need a computer here in the Red Stone or in the Krasnij Gorod.»

«Nunki, but aren't your computer or handheld linked to the web?» Anna asked.

«They were. They disconnected me when they realized what I could be capable of, just to be safe. Anyway, accessing the computers in the Hong Se De Du is impossible, as a matter of fact, there are always at least two persons there. So?»

«The Krasnij Gorod's computers are in the hall, so it's very risky, whoever could pass there for any reason, being the main room» Anna explained.

«At this point I'd say the least worse situation is the Red Stone» Jordan concluded «Here we have a separate room for that purpose only. The problem is that to go to the gym you have to go through the office. We have to act when there's absolutely no one though. The risk must be reduced to the minimum.»

«Then we have to check the sol's activities and move when it's free. Do you have the table with all the names, times and sol's tasks?» Yan asked.

«Yep, I should have it here.»

Jordan turned back towards his laptop and amongst the various folders he found the file he needed. He clicked on it while his two friends approached him to have a better look. They observed carefully the intersections of columns with times and rows with names.

«It seems the only certainly free moment is from four fifteen pm to five pm» Yan stated, following a column on the laptop's screen with his index.

«Do you think forty-five minutes could be enough?» Anna asked.

«Well, I don't know exactly. It depends on how many bytes I have to download. However it's already a good time. Let me see...» the boy leaned towards the screen once more to observe more carefully, then he tapped on the screen with his fingertip. «At five pm the only danger is George Jenner's imminent arrival, he will want to go to the gym.»

«Gosh, just why him...» Jordan commented, rubbing his forehead with a frown.

«In case we need more time, we'll have to entertain him somehow» Anna sat back on her chair.

«It's a terrible plan» Jordan muttered to himself.

«I'll stay in the office messing about with the computers while you two stay outside and stop people from entering.»

«Yeah» Anna thought aloud «Jordan, you and I could sit at the top of the ladder, in front of the office door and if someone wants to enter, we entertain them.»

«Of course!» Jordan exclaimed ironically, with his hands behind his head «Like it's perfectly normal that you and I sit on the top of the ladder in front of the Red Stone office!» he shook his head, lowering his hands «Wouldn't it arouse suspects?»

The girl returned to think deeply and silence reigned for the following minute.

«According to this table, it seems you'll have to deal with Dounja Douglas who should pass in front of you at four thirty pm... and then with Jenner» Yan said, still observing the screen. «But we also have to count the possibility that anyone could pass there at any moment in order to simply go to the bathroom or the greenhouse, for example.»

«Come on, Jordan, don't worry. We just have to look natural and go into an interesting conversation in case it turns out necessary» the girl tried.

«You can always talk about my super interesting videogame, that would surely be entertaining!» Yan suggested.

At those words Anna let out a frustrated, animal scream. She grabbed the first thing that happened at arm-length (a pillow from Jordan's bed) and began to whack Yan, who couldn't stop laughing, hitting him at the rhythm of her words:

«When – will you – stop – with that – stupid – game?!»

The boy seized a star-shaped plush with a hand from behind his back and threw it at the girl to defend himself, but she deviated it with a twist of her arm and it ended up against Jordan's face.

«Hey!» he exclaimed, readily grasping another big pillow from his bed.

And that was how all the struggles to make his room presentable became useless. After twenty minutes, his room was submerged in complete chaos. They stopped suddenly when the door opened and Alexander appeared.

Yan was standing on Jordan's bed, holding a pillow up in the air. Anna was using a chair as a shield and Jordan had just thrown a plush at Yan, that bounced on his head and fell on the floor. They stood still like in a photograph, staring at Alexander.

«Hey, dad» Jordan said with a big, guilty smile.

Alexander narrowed his eyes at the three.

«I heard noises. What are you doing exactly, may I ask?» he pronounced slowly.

«We're refurnishing Jordan's room» Yan answered matter-of-factly.

Alexander raised an eyebrow.

«In a Martian style» Jordan added.

His father looked puzzled.

«What?»

Jordan shrugged.

«What?»

It was 4:15 pm. Jordan, Anna and Yan walked in formation at a deliberate pace through the corridor that linked the Hong Se De Du to the Red Stone. They had passed by Yan's room to take a removable memory support on which they were going to download all the data. And after repeating the whole plan once again, they were ready to act. They climbed up the ladder that brought to the office. No one was around.

«Go, Nunki. Do your work» Jordan encouraged him, patting him on the shoulder «Anna and I will do the rest.»

The boy nodded, sighed and slipped into the office. The doors closed right away behind him. Jordan and Anna exchanged looks and went to sit with dangling feet above the ladder. It was quite high up there, three meters from the floor, they were basically sitting on the roof of Klara Nowak's private room.

«Okay, we've got fifteen minutes to make up something to talk about» Anna declared.

«Mmm... Let's see, do you remember when I was a child, one of the first times that I exited from the base, I risked to run out of oxygen because I would reenter only if I was to bring inside some sand?»

«No, really? I don't remember that, maybe I was elsewhere. How could I miss such a scene!»

«Yeah, it was exhilarating! I was so stubborn that they had to drag me inside and you can imagine the struggle with the old EVA suits!»

«Really. And then?»

«They grounded me at the hall's table, I had to write down for one hundred times the sentence "I must obey the rules". It was awful, one of my worst memories.»

«From what I can see the message hasn't gone deep yet» Anna commented with a chuckle.

Jordan passed a hand through his hair.

«Yeah, well... It won't certainly be a sentence repeated one hundred times to make me change» he replied thinking again to the words that Frank had told him *"You haven't changed a bit, Jordan"*.

Anna began to tell the boy about the strong rigour and discipline that had always been imposed on her in the Krasnij Gorod and how she wasn't allowed to step out of line in the slightest way. She told him of all the time she spent reading, it seemed she had read every single book in the Aresland and the one she had now, she had stolen from Jordan's room.

After a while, as they foresaw, Dounja Douglas passed in front of their position but, seeing them, she simply smiled and continued on her path. They were very lucky, in fact no one else passed for a long time. Few minutes after Dounja's passage, Yan's head had come out from the office to warn his friends that he had succeeded to access the web and he had just begun the transcription of the data. It was going to take thirty-five minutes in total, which meant the process would end exactly five minutes before 5:00 pm.

Jordan was getting more impatient as time passed while Anna who, for her part, always managed to keep calm and concentrated, was trying to reassure her friend.

«What's the time?» Jordan asked for the umpteenth time.

Anna huffed and glanced once again at the watch she had in her hand.

«Four fifty-one.»

«Holy Olympus!» Jordan shrieked jumping on his feet and throwing himself to the door of the office, that opened.

He leaned inside.

«What's your status? George could arrive at any moment now!» he exclaimed.

«Few minutes, Jordan. Few minutes and we have it all.»

«Hurry up!»

«But it's not up to me, I can do nothing to accelerate the process.»

«You hurry up anyway!»

Jordan returned to the girl scratching the back of his neck nervously.

«Anna, if *he* catches us we're screwed, gone, all of us.»

She opened her mouth to reply, but a deeper voice stopped her.

«Catch you doing what?»

Jordan was petrified. His gaze fixed into Anna's eyes where a worried spark shone briefly, before it was replaced by a warm smile addressed to someone who arrived from the corridor. The boy closed his eyes and swallowed. He felt his hands icing and sweating at the same time. He had no idea of what face he had, but he tried to turn as well, trying to look as natural as possible.

«*Zdravstvuy,* George» Anna greeted, with her charming attitude.

«*Privyet,* Anna. *Rad vidyet' tebya zdyes*[19].»

He smiled sincerely before moving his gaze on Jordan.

«What are you doing?» he asked.

«Not much, chitchatting a little bit» Jordan shrugged.

---

19 Rad... zdyes: from Russian, "Good to see you here"

«And where did you leave Yan?»

«Uhm, he is...»

«He's gone to his room one second, he should be back soon» Anna replied sharply, with a tone that convinced even Jordan.

He found himself staring at her and unable to look elsewhere, wondering how could she be so confident every time.

«And why are you staying up there?» George's voice dragged Jordan out of his trance.

«Well, it's...» he cleared his voice «It's a cool place. There's a good view.»

It was too late when he realized there was no view at all, as they had the wall of the main geodesic dome in front of them. He felt sweat forming on his forehead, that was a terrible excuse.

«Uh-huh, I understand» George briefly glanced around himself. «Well, I'm now going to the bathroom. Then you'll let me pass, right? I got to go to the gym» he smiled.

«Yes, sure. We're about to leave in any case. We change location» he said, trying to mock a chuckle.

George nodded and left. When Jordan heard the bathroom's door closing with a "clack", he turned to Anna with a worried frown.

«I'm an awful liar» he said.

«Yes, you are!» she confirmed, before they both jumped to their feet and rushed to the office.

«Go, go, go, shut it down! Immediate evacuation!» he ordered to his friend who was sitting in front of a monitor where pages of codes and programming language kept opening and closing.

«One minute, one minute!»

«We don't have a minute, we have a second!»

«One more moment!»

«Do as he says, Yan!» Anna interjected.

In that moment, a small green text saying "Download completed" appeared on the screen.

«I've got it, I just have to cancel the tracks.»

Yan's hands moved quickly and precisely on the computer's keyboard and in thirty seconds, all the windows closed and the computer was switched off.

Without another word, the three flew out of the office and rushed down the ladder, to suddenly find themselves standing in front of George Jenner.

«Are you quite alright, guys?» he asked, «You look like you have just run for miles without stopping.»

«Everything's fine, really, we were just going» Anna said calmly.

Yan hadn't managed to raise his gaze from the floor yet. Jordan looked around himself.

«Good gym» the girl added smiling before resuming to walk, Jordan and Yan trailed behind her.

George didn't say anything else. The mission was completed.

It was 9:00 pm when Jordan and Anna showed up in Yan's room. After leaving the office, that afternoon, they both had their gym session, while Yan had gone to his room to begin the conversion of the downloaded files, in order to make them readable. Jordan had met George again in the gym, but luckily the topic of what happened wasn't brought up.

The two went to sit in front of Yan's laptop, at the boy's side.

«So, are you ready to discover the truth?» he asked, moving the mouse's cursor to the button "Open".

«Do it» Jordan urged.

Yan clicked and a text file opened. A title towered over a list of numbers and words, followed by a thick text.

«*Autonomous space base on Mars, Rubentes Terrae*» Yan read aloud, «Wow.»

Jordan shook his head, furrowing his eyebrows.

«How nice of them to keep such things hidden from us, really.»

Anna leaned closer to the screen and stroked it with a fingertip.

«But keep reading: *built and activated in May 2049 (Sagittarius 239). Location: Huygens Crater, diameter of four hundred and fifty-six kilometres, in the area of Iapygia Quadrangle, bla, bla... Number of hospitable people: six. Future launchpad for... for the Nostoi Mission*» the girl paused.

«Launchpad for a mission?» Jordan repeated, unbelieving.

Yan scrolled through the text on the screen.

«These are basically all the technical and practical guidelines of the base, a kind of package insert.»

«A launchpad» Jordan insisted, «Why would they put a launchpad out there and why not to use the usual one, few kilometres from here?»

«Nostoi Mission... Nostoi» Anna thought aloud.

«And what a name! What the heck is this Nostoi supposed to be?» Yan asked.

«I have no clue» Jordan shook his head, staring at the screen.

«I... I think I know» Anna admitted shortly after.

Jordan and Yan swirled their heads towards her.

«Well?» Yan pressed.

«I had read something in a book of History of Earth, time ago. It's about a very ancient language and I believe Nostoi means... *return*. Because this particular term refers to the return of the Greeks to their homeland after they destroyed a city called Troy and they were seen as heroes for this.»

«Should any of this make sense?» Yan asked, raising an eyebrow.

«It must. The names of the missions are never casual» the girl replied.

«So it is the "Mission of Return" or something like that?» Jordan tried.

The girl nodded, thoughtfully.

«But I don't understand the reason why this mission should be kept in the dark from us three, I mean, we've always known who left and who arrived, we've never done anything bad» Yan frowned.

«It's strange, effectively» Anna commented.

«There isn't even anything about when and how it will start» Yan continued, reading the introduction again.

«Nunki, search for some pictures, maybe at the bottom» Jordan suggested.

Yan obeyed and scrolled the document to the bottom, where he really found some attached images. He clicked on the first one, opening a detailed map of the Huygens Crater that showed the exact location of the Rubentes Terrae with the coordinates. The second attachment showed a 3D computer-made model. The structure was more or less a parallelepiped and, a little further on, the model of a rocket standing vertically could be seen.

«Cool» Yan commented, without emphasis. «Well, the Aresland is way more cool anyway.»

Anna shook her head and rolled her eyes at the boy.

«Well, then. Nunki keep all of this stuff safe» she said, «I must go now, they wait for me early at the Krasnij Gorod.»

«Okay, everything will be kept more secretly than they did.»

«I must go too now» Jordan said «But this isn't over.»

«No» Anna convened «This was the first step only.»

The three greeted each other and then went to bed.

Jordan knew that that evening he had taken a step forward. Yet his ideas were now even more confused than before.

SIX
~ *189 sols before* ~

Jordan, Anna and Yan entered the classroom at 8:00 am and took their seats, now with only a paper, a pen and a calculator. The dim sunlight illuminated the beginning of a new week inside the Aresland. Tain Tseng, who lived inside the Hong Se De Du like Yan, entered shortly after and switched on the computer and the multimedia whiteboard. That small man was skinny and scrawny, with short, dark hair and tremendous bangs that covered half of his forehead.

«*Zaoshanghao*[20]» he greeted quickly.

«*Zaoshanghao*, Tain» the three answered in unison.

He grabbed the special pen to be used on the whiteboard and turned to look at his listeners.

«So, I'm going to write some limits on the board. Solve them quickly and precisely. Afterwards we'll start the differential calculus» he instructed with a serious tone.

He waited for a sign of consensus, then he quickly turned and began to write on the whiteboard with his bony hand that looked like it could drop the pen at any moment. The three immediately began to write down

---

20 Zaoshanghao: from Chinese, "Good morning"

the texts of the exercises and to solve them. As usual, Yan finished his work much earlier than Jordan and Anna. Maths really was his strong point and often he offered to do his friends' homework while they would write his essays of History of Earth and Survival in exchange.

After about an hour and a half, Tain Tseng had filled the whole whiteboard with calculations and graphs and he had thrown himself into a long explanation, thorough and detailed, with so much passion that he didn't even notice George Jenner appearing at the entrance, followed by Ling Yu, the Hong Se De Du commander. It wasn't difficult to guess that also Viktor Taykeev was standing just outside the door. At the sight of them, Jordan lost a heartbeat and froze on his chair, while a hand closed tightly around his wrist. He turned in a spin, Anna had clung to him involuntarily and, as soon as she noticed, she let him go.

«Tseng» George called, gravely.

The man stopped and turned suddenly, surprised.

«Jenner, good morning» he said, not understanding his presence.

Jordan, Anna and Yan observed the scene, petrified like cement, fearing the worst.

«You'll excuse me for the interruption, but I've got something to say.»

Jordan had never heard George speaking with such an austere tone and he began to feel more and more nervous, his heart pounding.

«Of course, go ahead» Tain replied, moving aside.

George's gaze scanned carefully the pale faces of the three guys and finally stopped on a pair of dark eyes.

«Yan, I'll be clear and direct. We need to check all your digital devices» he announced with authority, his tone didn't admit replies.

Jordan was crossed by a chill. He couldn't imagine how his friend was feeling.

«Wh–why?» Yan stammered.

«No questions. Give us the passwords to access your laptop and handheld.»

«What? No! It's a private thing!» the boy complained.

«Not for us, Yan. Come on.»

«And what if I won't tell them?»

«You won't be allowed to keep them anymore.»

Yan swallowed and glanced over to Jordan and Anna to look for some support, but their eyes were iced on George's figure. He sighed.

«Alright» he sighed again, «The laptop's password is *mimi renwu*[21] twenty-four. While the handheld's one is two, zero, two, two, six.»

«Excellent» George said, then he nodded at Ling, who was standing with an expressionless face and her arms crossed «Let's go.»

They exited and the door closed again. In that moment Jordan and Anna turned to look at Yan, whose miserable gaze was now lost on his paper covered in calculations.

«Very well. So, we were saying...» Tain Tseng turned again to the whiteboard and continued his lesson, like nothing had happened.

But the three weren't following a word of what he was saying anymore.

21

   Mimi renwu: from Chinese, "Secret mission"

At 11:00 am Tain Tseng dismissed the three guys. They got up from those chairs with a heavy load on their shoulders and a twisting stomach. They left the room unable to say a word and walked silently until they passed in front of the bathroom, when suddenly Anna whirled to open the door and dragged everyone inside.

They found themselves locked up into the bathroom, in the darkness.

«What are you doing?!» Yan screamed in a whisper.

There was a click and the bathroom's lights were turned on. Anna threw herself at Yan like a tornado.

«WHAT AM I DOING, *I*?! YOU INSTEAD, WHAT HAVE *YOU* DONE, YAN?»

Jordan had to seize the girl from behind before she could jump on Yan and turn him into mush.

«Calm down, Anna, chill out» he told her.

She breathed deeply and swallowed. Then she turned slightly to see Jordan out of the corner of her eye. He still kept her tight.

«Jordan, let me go» her gaze was fierce.

«Cool your jets» he repeated once again, before slowly freeing her.

She crossed her arms and glanced at Yan with a feline gaze. The boy was pressed against a shelf, he wore a ridiculously scared face.

«Now, Yan» Jordan began, bringing his hands to his head, «Tell us exactly the percentage of trouble we are in.»

Yan seemed to return to his senses and pulled away from the shelf. He swallowed.

«First of all I would like to make something clear» he began, «Do you really think I would give away my passwords like that if I knew that they could find the data? I would rather give up everything! So, don't worry too much. The data is safe and I'm quite certain they won't find it. The percentage of trouble is twenty percent. Seventeen of which is because the fact that they've decided to check means they highly suspect. The remaining three percent is the probability that they'll find the data.»

Jordan observed Yan carefully, then smiled.

«Ah, I knew it! I always trust you!» he reached out and high-fived with him.

Then he turned to look at the girl. She sighed, slightly embarrassed for her prior reaction and nervously passed a hand through her hair.

«I'm sorry, you know, I feared the worst» she said with a low gaze.

Yan smiled.

«Hey, come here» he told her, opening his arms.

The two hugged. Jordan observed that scene from a corner of the room, while a pain in his stomach returned. But it faded away as soon as the two pulled away.

He just couldn't understand why he felt that way every time he saw Anna and Yan together, every time he saw her smiling to him or every time he knew they had been together without him. Those situations always led him to feel a sort of hate and repulsion towards his friend, something he had never felt before.

«Jordan, are you here?» Yan brought him back to reality,

«Eh? What, why?»

Yan shook his head, laughing.

«I asked if we can go to my room, so we check if everything's alright.»

«Uhm, certainly, let's go.»

As they walked down the corridors, all the people they met gave them strange looks. Some observed them with curiosity, some smiled uncertainly, some wore an indecipherable expression. As they exited the Krasnij Gorod, they walked under Viktor Taykeev's hard gaze who squared them from top down. Jordan could say Anna had inherited that same gaze at some level. The three didn't even dare to raise their head and they quickened their pace towards Yan's room. When they entered, they found everything was in its place. His laptop was off and his handheld laid next to it.

«If they had found something, now we wouldn't be free to wander around like this, don't you think?» Yan speculated, sitting in front of his laptop and turning it on.

«It's a possibility» Jordan replied, «But was it only me, or you too noticed the way everyone looked at us?»

«Sure, that's because we're glorious» Yan explained, mocking a snooty look.

At those words, Anna let herself sit heavily on Yan's bed and held her forehead with her hands, like in the grip of a painful headache.

«Yan, I beg you» Jordan pleaded, «Every time you talk shit, Anna loses a year of life.»

The girl raised her gaze on Jordan as a chuckle escaped her lips.

«HOLY OLYMPUS!» Yan shrieked suddenly.

Jordan whirled his head towards him and swore to himself that he had never seen such terror in his friend's eyes before.

«What's wrong?» he asked right away, approaching him.

The boy seemed unable to speak.

«Holy Olympus Mons» he repeated in a whisper, his hands trembled.

«Wh–what?» Jordan stammered, staring at the screen.

«What's going on?» Anna asked, immediately returning to her seriousness and approaching too.

«Oh» she added in a whisper, after seeing.

On the laptop's screen, a red text said "Wrong password".

«What does it mean, Nunki? Try again» Anna suggested.

Yan shook his head weakly.

«No way. I've already tried three times» he murmured and swallowed «It's been changed.»

He brought his hands to his hair and sighed profoundly, closing his eyes.

«Keep calm» he said to himself.

He grabbed his handheld and tried to access, but the result was the same.

«I can't access my laptop nor my handheld» Yan observed, almost talking to himself. «And I have a theory for this. I'm sure they haven't found the data because, as I already said, we wouldn't be here now. But... They know we know everything and at this point I think they also know we have the data. How? I have no idea.»

«And so, taking away our access to the laptop, they've taken away our access to the data. That's brilliant, we must say» Jordan said with bitterness.

«That's right» Yan confirmed.

Anna didn't say anything. She was thoughtful. Yan leaned his elbows on the desk, in front of his laptop, and held his forehead just as Anna did before, with the difference that the pain was quite real now. Jordan sat down on Yan's armchair, next to him, staring at the floor. Anna laid down on the boy's bed, hiding her face in her hands. They remained like that, silently, for a long time. Reflecting, thinking about a possible solution. The questions in Jordan's head were more numerous than the answers and they continued to increase. After several minutes, it was Yan's voice that broke the silence.

«If they think they won...» he began, without moving «Well, they're wrong.»

Not receiving any answer, he raised his gaze and turned. Jordan and Anna were looking at him expectantly.

«I think I know how to get the data back.»

«Explain yourself» Anna urged.

«It's kind of complicated to explain. Because now it is different than before, now our data is inside this computer» he placed a hand on his laptop in a tender gesture «And this isn't linked to the general web, but rather to the independent one that puts it into communication with yours.»

«So, you might be able to take everything back through my computer or Anna's?» Jordan assumed.

«Perhaps. I can, or better, I must try. But it's going to be tough.»

«I'll be busy after lunch till six pm.»

«I have a break of forty minutes at four pm» Anna spoke up.

«Alright. I'll have free time after four thirty. Therefore as soon as I finish to study, I'll run to you and in ten minutes I try everything» Yan addressed the girl.

«Fine» she agreed.

Jordan didn't say anything, he simply sighed, observing Yan.

Then the lunch bell resounded in the Aresland.

When Jordan left the gym, exhausted, it was 4:30 pm. He thought about Yan, who at that moment was probably reaching Anna in the Krasnij Gorod to perform the emergency rescue. He took a deep breath and headed to his room at a deliberate pace, in order to change clothes and quickly rinse off. For the entire sol he had been reflecting on how much a simple image, that maybe had remained on that computer due to someone's oversight, had shaken up his whole world. After all, though, he was expecting it. No matter how strange it could sound, he perceived within himself that, sooner or later, some-thing was going to upset the intransigent repetition of his quiet sols. Wake, breakfast, class, lunch, study, gym, work, dinner, every sol, all the same. Every month the order of the activities changed, but they remained al-ways the same, except for some rare exchange of tasks or promotion.

Often Jordan observed Dounja cooking or George and Hans sitting for hours and hours in the office to work at the computers or Frank spending the majority of his time in the greenhouse to take care of the plants or everyone making turns to clean up every corner of the bases and he asked why. *Why all of this? To what end? Is there one?* He observed Klara repairing the ma-chines of the Life Support System when they didn't work and pondered the fact that his life depended only on them. If the water recycling system broke, they could continue with the supplies for some time, plants would die and they would too eventually, from dehydration. The carbon dioxide absorber broke? Everyone would die from intoxication. The oxygen generator broke? Everyone would suffocate. The temperature regulator broke? Hibernation. And the airlock? Suppose it didn't seal well. The entire Aresland would explode. Jordan was used to repress those thoughts and to focus on his duties. But lately they were taking him over and he couldn't ignore them anymore.

That time as well he tried to get rid of them with a deep sigh while heading to his father in the storage room. Alexander was ready and was waiting for him, holding his biosuit and helmet.

«You alright, tosol?» he asked, while the boy began to suit up.

Jordan simply nodded and smiled slightly.

«You seem different lately» he continued.

The boy pulled his biosuit up and slipped his arms into the sleeves, then he met his father's gaze.

«Really? No, it is always I. Jordan never changes, right? Come on, help me seal the suit» he urged, turning around.

«Are you sure you have nothing to tell me?» Alexander did as he was told, then Jordan returned to look at him and took his helmet.

«More than sure. And you?»

Alexander didn't answer right away, a worried spark shone in his eyes. Jordan was serious, his gaze was hard and determined, almost challenging.

«No» he replied shortly after, shaking his head.

Jordan smiled bitterly, but still trying to hide his disappointment.

«Splendid» he said, then he headed to the exit patting Alexander on the shoulder. «Let's go, I can't wait to stay on a pressurized rover.»

Jordan exited the Red Stone with the Life Support System backpack on his shoulders. He headed to the garage, followed by his father.

«Good, let's start from here» Alexander said, while observing a big rover «Come, have a closer look.»

The boy found himself in front of a huge vehicle, taller than him by at least four feet. It had three series of wheels on each side and it was almost four metres long. On the front, through a transparent glass, two seats were visible for the drivers.

«This is a small-sized pressurized rover» Alexander began to explain, «It can carry a maximum of three persons and cannot go on long trips because it works with electrical batteries. Usually we take this rover to go pick up the astronauts that land few kilometres from here. George and I went to pick up Hans with this one, for example, and both the Krasnij Gorod and Hong Se De Du have one.»

Jordan observed the rover in silence, studying every single detail.

«So, shall we go for a ride?» Alexander asked then, opening the hatch.

The boy jumped onboard without hesitation. The cabin was very small and his helmet almost grazed the ceiling. In a corner there was a chair for a passenger, while in an isolated compartment there was a small place for the hygiene facilities. His father entered the vehicle behind him and sealed the hatch. After pressing some buttons and pulling some handles on the wall next to the hatch, a "bip-bip" resounded in the whole rover. Alexander turned and took off his helmet. For a second Jordan thought his father had gone crazy, but then he reminded himself that they were on a pressurized rover, so he calmed down and removed his helmet as well.

They entered the cockpit and Alexander motioned for Jordan to take the driver's seat.

«We could take our suits off» Alexander said, «But since we won't stay long, we'll keep them on.»

«Fine» Jordan replied, giving his full attention to the console in front of him.

In the end the commands turned out to be very similar to those of the unpressurised rovers where he worked the previous week. The only differences were the indicators of temperature, pressure, humidity and air composition. And more than that, there was a compass whose lancet now pointed at South-West. The driving sensation was a bit different, it felt like everything had become heavier and there was much less turbulence as it went up and down the dunes. After making a couple of rounds around the Aresland, they returned to the garage and Alexander explained to Jordan the functioning of the onboard Life Support System, teaching him to regulate each level at pleasure.

They put their helmets back on and got down from the rover, when a question arose in Jordan's mind.

«What's the biggest rover in the whole Aresland?»

«It is...» his father glanced around himself after sealing the hatch, then pointed at a corner of the garage behind Jordan's back «That one.»

Jordan turned and widened his eyes. He approached the rover with a quick pace and observed it from top to bottom with his mouth agape. It was three meters tall and six long at least. It had four big wheels, a little less tall than him. A flamboyant red text popped out from the ashy white side.

«Atenavan» Jordan read in a whisper.

«That's right» his father commented, behind him «The Atenavan is currently the largest pressurized rover at the Aresland. It hasn't been used yet. And there's just one: this.»

«Why hasn't it been used yet? What does it serve for?» Jordan asked without moving his eyes away from that flaming word.

«Simply because it hasn't turned out necessary yet. And well, you would use it to cross long distances for sure.»

«*How* long?»

«Mmm, well... I'd say you could approach the Promethei Terra, that's it. Obviously with all the supplies and resources calculated in detail, you don't joke with such ventures.»

Question after question, with his exuberant attitude, Jordan extrapolated from his father all the information he needed to develop the idea of a new extraordinary plan that had slowly slithered into his mind. He tried hard to keep all those explanations in mind. He needed to see Anna and Yan as soon as possible.

After dinner, Jordan took the corridor which led to the Krasnij Gorod almost running. He came out on the other side in the same moment when Yan came out from the other corridor coming from his base. They exchanged looks and ran to each other.

«What a timing, pal, we're basically telepathic!» Yan commented with his usual, contagious euphoria.

Jordan smiled sincerely.

«So, how did it go?» he asked lowering his voice.

Yan tucked a hand into a pocket of his trousers and took out a USB pen, showing it to Jordan and holding it like a piece of crystal.

«Everything's here, safe and sound, in our hands. In my hand, actually.»

«Ah, wonderful!» Jordan rejoiced grabbing Yan's shoulders and shaking him, «Wonderful! You're a genius, Nunki.»

«Thanks, thanks. Yes, honestly it hasn't been easy» Yan pretended to wipe an invisible dust away from his t-shirt.

«Shut up» Jordan laughed, before returning serious «Let's go to Anna. I need to talk to the two of you.»

«Oh, lord. Whenever you say so I get chills. I feel your fatal mind is elaborating something dark.»

«And you feel right» Jordan convened, grabbing his friend's arm and dragging him away «Get a move on, you crackpot.»

«No, no, no and no. That's not gonna happen!»
Anna paced back and forth, measuring her room with big steps, nervously. Yan had burst out laughing, as if he had just heard the best joke of his life, then he suddenly stopped and looked at Jordan with an expression that was both curious and flabbergasted. Jordan frowned at his friends' reactions.

«Jordan, you've lost your mind, that's the thing» Anna snapped, continuing her measurements, her gaze fixed on the floor. «I mean, until we act in here is one thing but...» the girl stopped suddenly, in front of him «Going *out there!* Do you have any idea of what it means?!»

«Well, Anna, if you allow me: Jordan is the only one who effectively has an idea. I mean, he works out there and, on top of that, he works with the rovers!» Yan said with caution, after recovering from the previous shock.

«Thanks, Nunki» Jordan nodded, grateful.

Anna sighed profoundly and shook her head, frustrated. The green-eyed boy observed her for few moments, then stood up to face her.

«Listen to me» he ordered and Anna looked at him, crossing her arms. «We can do it. With the Atenavan we can easily go and come back. We go on a trip, a little adventure and then return here right away. This way we find out what this damn Nostoi Mission is and the others realize what mistake they made keeping all of this hidden from us, having not the slightest right!»

Jordan's words came out clear and decisive. Anna and Yan stood still, listening and studying him silently.

«Trust me» Jordan added, addressing both of them «Let's trust ourselves. I mean, I work with the rovers, I use them every sol!»

Anna's eyes were as sharp as blades while she looked at him.

«This could be your life's greatest mistake» she murmured.

Jordan found the strength to give her that same determined look.

«"Earth and life", page one hundred and sixty-four: the birds leave the nest for the first time. This is not a mistake.»

Anna lowered her eyes, letting out a deep breath. She passed a hand through her hair while Jordan observed her, hoping his words would have the right effect on her.

«You know, I hate...» she began, shaking her head «I so hate that you're capable of convincing me so easily. I can't let you two go on your own. Because if you die, what am I to do here alone?»

As the girl spoke, Jordan's face was illuminated with delight and pointed a finger at her.

«Excellent point!»

All the three of them laughed together.

«It's gonna be fun» Yan commented.

«We've got plenty of things to organize and think about» Anna said.

«Yeah, we need a detailed plan. But I suggest to work on it from tomorrow on, what do you think? I'd be just a little tired right now» Jordan admitted, keeling over an armchair.

«Same» Yan laid down on Anna's bed and closed his eyes.

«Well, then get out of here. I'd like to sleep too, my sol wasn't easier than yours.»

They both slowly got up again.

«Yes, boss» Yan said.

«Hey, I thought I were the commander? What is it, you've already taken the title away from me?» Jordan asked with a cunning smirk.

«Oh, right. Sorry, commander Miles. Mrs sub-commander. Good night» Yan continued, seriously.

«Get out!» Anna shrieked, after bursting out laughing.

Jordan exited laughing, sincerely amused. Yan followed him, pushed by Anna, and the room door closed behind their backs.

SEVEN
~ *182 sols before* ~

A week had flown away and the dim light of the sun began to delineate the silhouette of the Aresland. It was the first sol of the twentieth month, Kanya.

When the clock struck 8:00 am, Jordan was heading to class. He was trying his hardest to look serene and ordinary but within himself, such excitement thrilled and such an enthusiasm that he feared he could catch fire at any moment. Throughout all those past sols, Anna, Yan and he had planned in detail all their moves, step by step, in order to reach the Huygens Crater and return. And just that night they were going to simulate the departure. At a certain time of the night, that was yet to be established, they were going to reach the Atenavan inside the Red Stone garage in order to check and fix all the necessary. They were going to break a billion rules and, actually, Jordan was awfully afraid to get caught before they could carry out the whole plan. He considered their venture so secret that he even tried not to think about it, as if fearing that someone could read his mind or could figure it out by simply looking at him in the eyes.

When he reached the classroom in the Krasnij Gorod, he found Anna and Yan were already sitting at their desks, switching their laptop on, while Klara Nowak was placing on her table some small transparent containers that enclosed some curious, colourful rocks.

«Good morning» he greeted before taking his seat.

«Bright and early, Jordan!» Anna spoke up without turning.

«I'm two minutes late only and it's sol solis, spare me your comments» the boy retorted.

Yan chuckled and greeted him with a nod of his head. Klara moved the desk in front of the three guys and finally leaned on it, crossing her arms. Her cold eyes lingered on the three for few moments, before she spoke.

«So, geology of Mars. In the last lesson we've discussed the planet's inner structure, briefly: metallic core of iron and nickel, surrounded by a less dense mantle mainly composed of silicates and finally the crust, whose composition is derived by the iron oxidation. Everything's clear so far?»

The three nodded.

«Fine. Tosol we'll talk about the chemical composition of Mars' surface and about the minerals that can be found, I've got some here that you can take a look at. So, the most abundant elements on the surface are silicon, oxygen, iron, magnesium, aluminium, calcium and potassium, which compose the minerals of the magmatic rocks. There's also some hydrogen that can be found in iced water and in hydrate minerals, which we'll talk about later. You must know that Mars is an igneous planet, igneous means magmatic, in fact the superficial rocks are mainly composed of minerals that have crystallized inside magma. Now let me show you three minerals that are very common.»

Klara collected three transparent small boxes from the desk and gave them to the guys, who were meanwhile finishing to type their notes on their laptop keyboards.

«Tridimite» she announced, giving a small, pale gold rock to Anna, who began to observe it carefully.

«Silicon dioxide. It is formed at temperatures that go from eight-hundred and seventy to one thousand four-hundred and seventy degrees Celsius.»

Then she gave Yan a small green rock with occasional darker spots.

«Lizardite. It's a phyllosilicate and usually forms inside impact craters.»

Finally she gave Jordan an elegant black, lucid rock and the boy admired it, fascinated.

«Magnetite. It's the ferrous mineral with the strongest magnetic properties existing in nature.»

While they were observing and exchanging the rocks, Klara turned to the desk.

«Then, let me see...» she picked up a pair of boxes and addressed the guys, «Here I have a couple of primitive basalts, they are very similar to the komatiites on Earth. These in particular were found by the rover Spirit, inside the Gusev Crater.»

Hearing the word "crater", the three exchanged looks before immediately returning to focus on the minerals, not to arouse suspects. Fortunately Klara didn't seem to notice and kept explaining.

«Furthermore, on Mars there can be minerals that were produced through hydrothermal alterations and by the action of atmospheric agents, even though in minor quantity. If you want to get closer, here I have some small minerals that are very interesting: hematite, goethite, jarosite, opaline silica, iron sulphate, chalk and other phyllosilicates.»

They got up from their chairs and reached the desk to observe a series of small, colourful rocks.

The class proceeded calmly until 11:00 am. They studied in detail the inner structures of the minerals and their way of crystallizing. Finally they also learned how to recognize them on their own, a new practical skill that they were going to register on their personal online platform.

As the hours went by one after the other, the countdown inside Jordan's mind continued. He was by now focused on his goal and the only thing that really mattered to him was reaching the Huygens Crater, one way or another.

However, just like every sol, he completed his normal activities: he studied geology, went to the gym, went out with his father on the pressurized rover and made sure the Atenavan was still there, he took a hot shower, considering that for a good while he wasn't going to have the chance to take another, he dined with the members of the Red Stone and everything could have been perfectly normal, a sol like another, if only there wasn't a secret escape plan.

At 8:00 pm, the door of Jordan's room slid open, letting Anna and Yan in. The two sat down on his bed without a word and Jordan took a seat on an armchair in front of them.

The boy sighed observing the floor, then raised his eyes on his friends.

«Anna, Yan» Jordan began with a serious and concise tone, «Sol number zero. Tonight we are going out there to fix everything for tomorrow's departure. It's not going to be an easy operation, nothing of what expects us is going to be easy. Therefore we must have everything under control or, at least, as much as we can.»

Anna and Yan both nodded comprehensively.

«So, let's review it all for one last time» Jordan suggested, «Nunki, you do it.»

The boy got up from the bed and reached Jordan's laptop to enter his USB pen. Since he couldn't access his digital devices anymore, he kept everything safe in that pen-drive and updated, edited or removed using his friends' computers.

He opened a map of the Hellas Planitia and the Huygens Crater, followed by a list of passages that were the various steps of the plan.

«Alright» the boy began turning to his friends again and only occasionally glancing at the document, «We'll leave in the night between sol lunae 2nd and sol martius 3rd onboard the rover Atenavan, travelling North-Westward at a speed of twenty-five kilometres per hour for eight-hundred miles till the Rubentes Terrae, located in the Huygens Crater. Considering that we'll stop for six hours every sol, of which four by night and two in the sunlight, the estimation for this trip's duration is of approximately three or four sols, but this measure could vary because at the moment we're not aware of all the obstacles that we may meet on our path, except for the minor impact craters to circumvent.»

The boy stopped to breathe and scroll down the document on the computer screen.

«Tonight» he resumed, «We'll bring to the Atenavan the necessary supplies to survive. Although the trip will last four sols, we'll bring enough supplies for one week. More than that wouldn't fit in, materially. For the return we're covered as the base's guide assures the presence of water and food supplies, therefore we'll use those. For that which concerns the energy, the Atenavan uses fuel cells...» Yan stopped and glanced at Jordan, who spoke up.

«Nope, I thought so, but I've talked about it with my father and he says it uses a radioisotope thermoelectric generator with uranium two hundred and thirty-two.»

«Wait wait wait. Say it all over again ten times slower!» Yan interjected.

Jordan sighed and rolled his eyes, amused.

«All you need to know is fuel cells use liquid hydrogen that has a high risk of explosion. While the RTG with uranium is much less risky, it weighs less than a kilogram, lasts sixty-nine years and provides us with an energy of two thousand watts.»

«And how does it work?» Anna asked, curiously.

«The radioactive decay of uranium produces heat that is turned into energy by a thermoelectric converter.»

«Cool. So, I suggest we now plan tonight's operation. Time?»

«We have to make sure everyone's asleep» Yan underlined.

«I say we act between three and five am, maximum. But if we finish before, it's better because I know that in the Red Stone a couple of persons wake up at five, sometimes» Jordan proposed.

«In my opinion one hour is sufficient. I say we act between three and four, nobody will be awake at that hour» Yan shrugged.

«I agree» Anna spoke up.

Yan suddenly turned to her with wide eyes.

«You agree? That's crazy! Jordan, did you hear her?» he snapped to his friend, «She said she agrees on something I say at the first try!»

Jordan laughed, shaking his head.

«Yeah, life's great achievements!»

Anna glared daggers at them both and that was enough to make them stop immediately.

«So, we were saying» Jordan resumed, «At three in the morning we'll meet in front of the Red Stone airlock, already with the biosuits and ready to exit.»

Anna and Yan nodded once, showing their understanding.

«Now, I know it sounds terrible, but you have to kind of raid your kitchens, storage rooms and greenhouses.»

At those words Anna stiffened and Yan smirked.

«Come on, don't make that face, we have already talked about it. Alright, maybe I used the wrong verb. It's more a "borrowing for the purpose of our survival". Is that better?»

«Definitely» Yan giggled, glancing at Anna.

«Jokes aside, we seriously need enough food supplies not to starve, as matter of fact. Nunki, do you have everything written there?»

The boy turned to the computer and scrolled through the document.

«Yep, so: with sixty-three portions of food we survive for seven sols. The Atenavan is spacious, but these portions are an awful lot, so they must be reduced to the essential. Everyone of us must take care of their own twenty-one portions, of which seven breakfasts, seven lunches and seven dinners. Theoretically we need two thousand calories per sol, but if our intake will be less I promise you we won't die. We're free to choose what to take from our kitchens. I have sent a table to your laptops with some guidelines if you want to have a look at it. Just to be sure we take the right stuff for every meal, without waste.»

«Very well» Jordan breathed passing a hand through his hair and the room fell in silence for some moments.

That was the plan. And the moment was approaching. Jordan glanced at the clock on his nightstand.

«It's nine ten» he said, «In order to prepare and take everything, we need to wake up at two at least, then I'd say we better go to sleep. The night's gonna be long.»

«Yeah we got to rest» Yan stretched and stood up.

Anna did the same silently and they headed to the door.

«Good night, bro'» the boy waved his hand dismissively before definitely leaving Jordan's room.

Anna was about to leave as well, but she stopped by the door and turned again. She studied the floor of Jordan's room with an uncertain expression and he observed her behaviour curiously. Finally she raised her gaze on him and spoke.

«And what if tonight or tomorrow night we get caught?» her tone was uneasy, her cerulean eyes shone with worry.

Jordan didn't answer right away, he simply looked at her for some seconds, his lips softly curved up.

«We'll be in huge trouble» he finally replied lightly.

The girl stood still and silent, staring at the boy who finally opened up in a wide, reassuring smile.

«At least we won't have the regret of not having even tried. I'm sure it will be worth it. Trust me.»

Anna sighed and lowered her gaze briefly, before her eyes met his again. A corner of her mouth hinted to a small smile.

«Good night, Jordan» she murmured before disappearing from the room and the boy didn't even have the time to reply.

Red sand under his feet, a beige sky spread to the horizon, without boundaries. A high rocket threw a huge shadow on the ground and Jordan couldn't even see the top of it. There was a signboard badly stuck into the sand next to the rocket. Jordan got closer in order to read. It said, "One-way trip to Earth". He looked around himself, confused, a strong sandstorm was about arrive and rain down, it was going to make the rocket fall. Jordan was overwhelmed by anguish. The signboard flew away with the wind and suddenly everything went black, while a continuous bip-bip seemed to drag him far away.

And suddenly he woke up. He was breathing fast, he sat up and looked around himself, his small alarm-clock was ringing. The screen showed "2:00 am". He quickly reached out and shut it. He strongly hoped it hadn't rang long enough to wake up Alexander or Dounja. He sat still for one minute in order to capture any movement or noise from the two rooms next to his, but nothing came. Then he sighed, turned the light on and began to put on his clothes, trying to forget that weird nightmare.

About ten minutes later, his head came out of his room. He could perceive nothing but the buzzing of the Life Support Systems which gave a sinister atmosphere to the darkness, only slightly illuminated by some LEDs on the ceiling. He swallowed and started down the perimeter of the dome, he took the corridor for the Main Base and then headed to the storage room, discovering that his sneakers made absolutely no noise on the floor. For the time being everything was going fine. He slipped into the storage room and, with delicate movements, trying to make the least possible noise, he emptied a small metallic container that he decided to use as his supplies collector. In a dusty corner of the storage room, in the alimentary section, he found a tower of boxes with a label indicating "For emergencies". *This is the case,* he thought to himself. The light was very dim inside there, but it was enough for Jordan to do what he had to.

He opened one of the boxes and tucked a hand inside to take out a small, transparent bag, airless, which contained what at first sight looked like a greenish mush. A sticker on it said, "Broccoli au gratin, 100 mL of hot water, 5-10 min". Jordan turned his nose up in a disgusted expression. He hated broccoli, but on the other hand he knew he had found what was going to keep him alive for the following sols. He began to fill his metallic box with some of those foods that had been prepared who knows how much time before and then had been put in a condition of long conservation. He also found some snacks and decided to take a bunch of

119

them, as they might always come in handy. When he thought he had taken enough, he seized the box with both his arms and left the storage room, heading to the kitchen. He took a jar of dehydrated fruit, an entire package of muesli, he filled four bags of different kinds of legumes and in another container he put some pieces of crunchy bread.

He was about to leave the kitchen and head to the greenhouse, when he suddenly heard the noise of a door sliding open and he froze. He quickly backed off, noticing out of the corner of his eye that it was Frank Larsen's door, and he disappeared again into the kitchen. His heart was pounding so heavily he almost feared it could be audible. He softly placed the box on the ground and then approached the door, to try and close it very slowly. It was one of the few doors that had to be closed manually. He couldn't leave it open, if Frank had passed in front of it he would surely check since it was always closed when there was nobody inside. But when the door closed, a loud "clack" seemed to propagate through the entire Aresland. Jordan was crossed by a freezing chill while cold sweat began to appear on his forehead. At first he stood rigidly, unable to move. When he heard some steps approaching the kitchen, he felt his knees weak, he had his heart in his throat. He began to back away from the door. *That's how I end,* he thought. *Please, go away. Please, go away.* But he didn't go away, he was always closer. Jordan was by now sure Frank was standing right in front of the door. He was pressed against the cabinets at the bottom of the room, almost as if he wanted to disappear inside them. The last thing he saw, before he closed his eyes, was the door's knob moving.

But all of a sudden he heard a noise. Far, like coming from the corridor of the Krasnij Gorod, it sounded like a pen falling on the floor. He swallowed and dared to open his eyes, fearing what, or rather, who he could see in front of himself. He saw the door was open by a crack only, and it was closed again. He heard the steps going away, probably in the direction of that new sound. He remained pressed against that shelf. The danger wasn't over yet. Shortly after he heard the steps once again, but they passed the kitchen and went on to the bathroom.

He heard Frank's voice as he mumbled to himself

«Man, I must be losing my mind.»

After that, he heard the bathroom door closing, soon opening again and finally Frank seemed to disappear in his room. He took a sigh of relief and only then he realized he had been holding his breath till that moment. He remained closed inside there for another ten minutes, in order to calm down and make sure he didn't risk too much.

His last stop was the greenhouse, where he took seven potatoes, one per sol, he collected some tomatoes, asparagus and blueberries. When he felt he had gathered enough supplies for his survival, he sealed the box and went back to the storage room to suit up. Since some sols he had learned to seal it on his own, so he met no problems. He finally left the room with the box in his arms and his helmet placed on top of it. He found that Anna had already arrived and Yan joined them shortly after.

«You okay?» Jordan mouthed.

The two showed him a thumb up. Jordan helped Anna and Yan to seal their suits and wear the helmet, then put his own helmet on. After running a quick verification to check the functioning of every system, they entered the airlock, that fortunately wasn't too noisy.

«You should thank me» Anna's voice resounded in Jordan's helmet.

He turned and saw she was looking at him through her helmet's visor.

«Was it you who saved my life?» he asked, thinking back to the noise that pulled Frank away from the kitchen.

«Yes, Jordan. That door closing was well audible even from my base storage room, I ran to check on purpose» she scolded.

«Olympus, thank you so much!»

«I'm not Olympus» the girl snapped.

«You should be» Jordan talked back and for a moment they all three laughed lightly.

When suddenly the airlock's hatch opened on the dark of the night in front of them and their cheerful moment died instantly. At first Jordan didn't even believe such a dark could be possible.

«Hell» Yan cursed in a breath.

The three exchanged looks and Jordan found himself wondering if it still was a good idea. But then he simply took a breath and returned to look in front of himself with determination.

«Let's go» he encouraged.

And he moved forward first.

They proceeded until they stepped on the sand and the hatch closed behind their backs. As soon as they were outside, some automatic torches on their helmets were switched on in order to show them the obstacles on their path.

Some intermittent red lights surrounded the entire Aresland. Jordan had never noticed them before. It looked almost beautiful in the night.

«Follow me» he ordered to Anna and Yan and started down to the garage.

The three moved in compact formation, overwhelmed by the black of the night, with their boxes of supplies in their arms. The Atenavan was parked in its usual place, waiting for them.

«What a beast of a rover!» Yan exclaimed as soon as they arrived in front of it. «And you would be able to drive this thing?»

Jordan smirked slightly while moving to the back of the Atenavan, where he was supposed to find the main hatch. And in fact it was there.

«We'll find this out tomorrow.»

He turned, Yan was behind him so he left his box on top of the one the boy was already carrying (making his friend curse due to the weight) and returned to focus on how to open the hatch.

«Jordan, are you kidding?» Anna's sharp voice bounced in his helmet, but he ignored her.

The hatch opened and Jordan got onboard the rover.

«Hurry, come on here.»

And for the first time they were finally and officially inside the Atenavan. It was pretty spacious and quite empty. In a corner there was a small compartment of no more than one square metre, that contained the hygiene facilities reduced to the essential. Alongside a wall there were four seats one next to the other, while on the opposite side there were some metallic cabinets. The anterior part of the rover, with two driver's seats, was separated from the rest through a section that left less than one metre of space to pass.

Jordan moved forward to observe the cockpit, Yan placed the boxes on the ground and Anna left hers on the top of the pile, then the boy approached the cabinets and, after studying them carefully, he decided to open one.

Anna was observing the small bathroom, while Jordan was sitting at the driver's seat and studying the controls to figure out how to turn on the main engine. When suddenly an acute shriek broke the silence. Jordan's head came out of the cockpit and Anna whirled around. Yan was wiggling convulsively under an unshaped brown shroud, one of the cabinets was wide open. Anna furrowed her eyebrows in front of that disarming scene, but then she shook her head and approached her friend, who seemed in the grip of panic, while yelling "I've been attacked, I've been attacked!". She grabbed with a hand his "aggressor" and freed him.

«It's a cover, dumbass» Anna said aloud.

Jordan simply shook his head and returned to focus on the controls of the Atenavan.

«A co–, a co–cover?» Yan stammered, glaring at what Anna was holding in her hand.

«What a drama queen» the girl commented, continuing to shake her head at her friend, still wearing a confused expression.

«I wanted to see if that thing flew on you, you could never know! Then, what's the point of putting covers in a place without beds...»

«We'll sleep on the floor» the girl hypothesised, folding the cover and placing it on a seat. «I guess we'll use these things as beds. What else is there?»

«Ah, you look, I've had enough of aggressions.»
The girl shook her head and decided to check herself.

Shortly after the entire Atenavan was crossed by a tremble and all the lights were suddenly turned on. Everything was followed, one minute later, by a series of "bip bip".

«Yeah!» Jordan exclaimed, and finally came out from the cockpit. «It works splendidly. From there you can monitor all the levels of the Life Support System, the speed and trajectory. There's also a kind of computer, but I still don't know what it serves for, I'll leave it to you» he addressed Yan.

«Ah, and all levels are nominal, therefore we can take the helmets off» he concluded removing his.

«You know» Jordan began. He was sitting at his driver's seat, Yan was next to him and Anna was leaning against the entrance of the cockpit. They had just finished to check every corner of the rover and finally Jordan had explained to them the functioning of the main driving commands, so that during the trip they could take turns. «Few hours ago, while sleeping, I had a dream» he said vaguely, his gaze lost on the console buttons.

«Well, tell us» Yan said turning by three quarters towards him.

Anna observed him with curiosity.

They used to tell each other what they dreamed at night anytime it was particular or bizarre.

«I was in the Huygens Crater, I guess. There was a big rocket» at those words, Yan and Anna gave him their full attention, without blinking. «And that rocket was going to leave for Earth, a one-way trip to Earth.»

«And you got on it?» Yan asked.

«No, no. The alarm rang before I could decide what to do» the boy answered, giggling nervously, but he stopped at Anna's question.

«Would you get on it?»

A moment of silence followed, Jordan stared into space while Anna and Yan stared at him.

«Well... I don't know, a sandstorm was coming, I guess, it didn't look that safe.»

«Rockets are projected to stand and resist against the sandstorms for emergency lift-offs, Jordan. This wasn't the point, I—»

«Yeah, I know what you meant» Jordan interrupted her. «And... come on, I don't know, there are many things to take into account. Why, though, would *you*?»

Anna remained silent for some minutes, observing the boy intently, as evaluating whether to speak or not. Jordan was certain that Anna was going to say no. Let alone, an all-laws-and-discipline such as herself would never imagine to push so far.

But unexpectedly...

«Yes» Anna replied with determination, «Yes and without thinking twice» Jordan and Yan widened their eyes at the same time, the girl continued. «I mean, haven't you ever wondered who you really are? What are we? Here, far from everyone, because yes, they're all out there, whether you accept it or not. Well, I have been wondering about it, but I haven't found an answer yet and it's frustrating! I read, I read books on books. Why? Because I look for answers. But the truth is that the more I read, the more I discover that actually all the answers are out there, on Earth.»

It was the first time that one of them had spoken so openly about that topic. Usually it was always avoided or bypassed, but neither they knew why. Jordan found himself being perfectly mirrored in Anna's words. He didn't read that much, he didn't look for answers, he just wondered. He thought his questions would never find an answer. Evidently his friend hadn't given up yet.

«But what do you mean?» Yan asked, scratching his forehead. «I mean, I know who I am. My name's Yan Heng, I was born in the Hong Se De Du of the Aresland on Kanya 24th, 226 and on top of that, I'll shortly turn nine years old.»

«Those words describe you, Nunki, but they don't say who you are» Anna explained with a strangely sweeter tone. «Instead of asking what's your name,» she continued, «Ask yourself what's your purpose in life, ask why were you born right here.»

Yan found himself staring into space with narrow eyes.

«Okay, I've got a headache now.»

«Exactly. It hurts thinking, doesn't it? And yet, I want to know.»

«Me too» Jordan interjected and Anna moved her attention on him, «I happen to think about it too, but effectively I've never tried to go deep into the issue. Then, you never know, maybe there's no purpose. It's just the way it is.»

«I think there is one. You just need to be patient.»

«Uh-uhm» Yan mumbled, catching the attention of the two. «I don't mean to disturb your mind twists but it happens to be four fifty-two, therefore I'd suggest an immediate evacuation, since our risk probabilities are increasing by ten percent each minute that passes by.»

Even before Yan had finished to speak, Anna had already run to put on her helmet and Jordan had turned the engines off, throwing himself behind Anna. The three sealed their suits, ran quick verifications, then Jordan turned the Life Support System off and they left the Atenavan to rush towards the Aresland.

EIGHT

~ *181 sols before* ~

When the Aresland general bell rang in every dome at
6:30 am, the following morning, Jordan had fallen
asleep just one hour before. He was heavily dragged
away from his blissful, dreamless sleep, but when he
opened his eyes he realized how much his brain refused
to stay awake. He laid still in his bed for the following
ten minutes, with the red blanket pulled up above his
eyes, trying to make a point of the situation. He mentally recapped that little time before he had been onboard the Atenavan with Anna and Yan, that he had
taken a bunch of food from the kitchen, from the storage room and from the greenhouse and that everything
was ready for the departure.

Then he thought that it was almost seven by now and
that at that moment he should have been preparing instead of laying hidden under the blankets and finally he
also considered that he couldn't absolutely go late to
breakfast or class and he couldn't show that he had lost
some hours of sleep that night. He breathed profoundly,
slightly blowing the sheets above him, then he got up.

Once in the bathroom, he looked at himself in the
mirror. His hair was dishevelled and his face still sleepy,
underlined by a pair of dim shadows under his eyes. He

felt his eyelids heavy. He washed his face with cold water and tried to make himself presentable.

When he arrived in the Main Base, everyone was already sitting at the long table, one next to the other, eating and chatting. He entered nonchalantly, but when he noticed that the only remaining free place was right next to Frank Larsen, his stomach twisted. For a moment he froze where he was, but then he resumed to walk right away; luckily enough no one had noticed it. Effectively they saw him only when he took his seat at the table and they greeted him cheerfully, as nothing new. He felt relieved and began to eat a little more peacefully. But that peace faded away as soon as he caught some words of what Frank was saying while chatting with George and soon he felt like he could throw up everything he had just ingested. He stopped with a blueberry stuck in his fork, half-way from the plate to his mouth.

«I swear, it was the noise of the door closing» Frank was saying. «I don't think I imagined it, I'm sure I heard something.»

«Old age plays tricks on you, Larsen» George chuckled.

«Oh, speak for yourself, Jenner! I say there was somebody.»

«But please, anyone of you yestersol night was hungry maybe?» George asked aloud, keeping a hint of sarcasm.

Jordan was still immobilized with the blueberry half-way to his mouth and his gaze stuck to his plate. Some chuckles were aroused from the table.

«Yes, I'm wondering the same» Klara intervened above the other voices with a serious tone. «This morning was my turn to prepare breakfast and I noticed the lack of an entire package of muesli and a jar of dehydrated fruit.»

Jordan, that for a single moment had believed he could get away with it, stiffened even more.

«Told you» Frank mumbled.

«Oh, now this! Come on, we're all adults here, who went to the kitchen yestersol night?» George asked more seriously.

«We're not all adults» Frank commented with a sharp hint and only then he turned to look at Jordan. Everyone turned to look at Jordan.

All that the boy managed to do was bring the blueberry to his mouth and begin to chew it slowly, his gaze still stuck to the plate, ignoring everything that was happening around him. Shortly after he raised his head and turned to look at all those eyes fixed on him. He lifted his eyebrows, mocking a questioning look and swallowed the blueberry.

«What? Is it my hair?» he asked, as nonchalantly as possible.

«Jordan, be serious» George intervened, «Do you know anything about the disappearance of some food from the kitchen?»

«Wha– really? I know nothing» Jordan frowned, it was his last chance of salvation. «Perhaps you were just confused, maybe that package and that jar have never existed» he said, shrugging, before resuming to fill his mouth with scrambled eggs in order to make it clear that he had finished to participate in that discussion. His opinion seemed to convince them, or at least, it was convincing enough to move their attention from him.

He had escaped big trouble. He wanted to leave that table as soon as possible, despite he hadn't finished everything. His hunger had faded away already.

Once in the Krasnij Gorod he was happy to see Anna and Yan. They had a quite relaxed look. It meant that nothing had gone wrong. The three exchanged meaningful looks and entered the classroom together, where Nastya Ivanova was ready for the hour of chemistry. That was going to be his last class before the departure, Jordan thought. He meditated on what would happen once everyone discovered their night escape. Probably nothing was going to be like before. Nobody had ever taken the initiative to go away from the Aresland before and Jordan had no idea of what future was going to expect him, once they would leave.

They sat silent for the entire lesson, paying very little attention to Nastya who was explaining a new kind of chemical reaction, because more urgent thoughts roamed in their minds. Jordan could say that Anna and Yan were tired as well for the hours they had lost that night. They both had a sleepy expression, a dead look in their eyes and a little too many yawns escaped their mouths. But Nastya seemed not to notice them.

Once the lesson was over, at eleven, they decided to return to their rooms and try to sleep for one more hour till lunch. They absolutely needed to get rid of that heavy sensation or they would never bear waking up in the middle of the night a second time.

The sol proceeded placid and peaceful as usual in the bases of the Aresland, it could be a very normal sol like any other. Jordan, Anna and Yan didn't see each other after class, too busy in their daily activities of the sol solis. Apart from that morning at breakfast, the escape plan didn't meet other risks and Jordan was about to convince himself that everything was going to be fine. All was ready. It was just a matter of hours.

After dinner he was about to head to his room, happy he had gotten through that sol of pretty frustrating wait when, before he could enter the corridor, George Jenner's voice stopped him.

«Jordan, a word» he said to call him back.

The boy turned to the man with silver hair who had just swallowed his last bit of dinner and was cleaning his mouth with a paper tissue. «Have you got anything urgent to do or we can talk for a moment?»

«Uhm no, nothing. I'm available» Jordan replied while countless thoughts crossed his mind and his heartbeat accelerated, sensing something was wrong.

He stood still and silent until George got up and reached him, placing a hand on his shoulder. From his body language, Jordan understood that he wanted to walk, so they started down the perimeter of the dome, bypassing the entrance for the corridor which led to his room and continuing alongside the zone with the Life Support Systems, with a slow and thoughtful pace. Jordan didn't understand what he had to tell him so urgently right now that he longed for nothing but going to sleep.

«You know, you seem changed lately» George began, bringing his hands behind his back. Jordan breathed deeply, thinking "There, we're at it again". «But do not misunderstand, not in a bad way. Often changes bring to improvements. You grow up, you change.»

«You're not the first one who tells me, George. But I don't understand, I am always me. I don't feel changed.»

«Eventually you'll understand» the man answered, then a minute of silence passed. «Recently I've noticed a certain chemistry between you and Anna Taykeeva and, you know, I couldn't help but think that something could have been born between the two of you, more than a simple friendship.»

At those words, Jordan's feet glued to the floor. That was the last thing he expected to hear.

«What!?» he exclaimed, his cheeks flushing slightly. Also George stopped, they had surpassed the airlock and they were almost in front of the greenhouse. «No, no, no. I mean, Anna is an extraordinary girl, I admire her intelligence, but we're friends. Friends» he repeated as to convince even himself, despite within himself he knew he wasn't telling the whole truth.

He felt a weird heat surrounding him. He absolutely wanted to change topic or rather, he wished that topic had never been brought up. In that moment he would rather talk about the escape plan than what was there with Anna.

«Oh, well. It was just a thought of mine» George assured with a smile.

They resumed to walk.

«Was it all you had to tell me?» Jordan asked, a bit more sharply than he intended too.

But his nerves were too tense. He took a silent, deep breath to calm down.

George didn't answer right away, the boy felt a bit uneasy.

«Jordan, you know you can trust me and everyone else in the Aresland, don't you?»

«Yes, I know.»

«And that if anything's wrong, you got to say it right away…»

«Yes, sure.»

They kept walking silently until George stopped and the boy did the same. Few meters after they would already reach the table, completing the round of the dome. Jordan leaned slightly to see, but it seemed there was no one sitting by now. He noticed that they had stopped in front of George's private room. He raised his gaze and found a couple of clear eyes observing him with a strange glint.

«Is there anything you have to tell me, Jordan?»

The boy looked at him feeling even more uncomfortable. That twinkle in his eyes made him wonder how much did he really know about everything that was secretly happening. He had never lied to George before. It turned out more difficult than he imagined. But he couldn't betray the plan. He clenched his jaw and shook his head.

«No» he forced himself to say, «Nothing» he added, hinting a reassuring smile.

George looked at him intently for some more instants, like trying to read his mind, but then he simply nodded.

«Very well. Then good night» he said smiling and moving a step towards his room

«Good night» the boy replied smiling back briefly.

He turned and was about to leave, when George's voice called him again.

«Ah, Jordan?»

He turned, giving him a questioning look. The man seemed hesitant at first, but then he spoke with decision.

«Do not forget the Red Planet's Law.»

And with that he disappeared in his room, leaving Jordan astonished.

Jordan returned to his room staring into space. He kept wondering what was George trying to tell him with that last warning and albeit the answer seemed right in front of his eyes, he did his best to avoid it. The Red Planet's Law said that Mars doesn't forgive. Jordan fell asleep promising to himself that he wasn't going to give Mars any reason to punish him.

But his body was crossed by so many adrenaline rushes that he woke up at two in the morning, just one minute before his alarm rang. He didn't even need to change as the evening before he hadn't bothered to put on the comfortable clothes he used to sleep. He didn't even stop by the bathroom, he didn't need it and then he would have made too much noise. In that case, he was going to do everything on the Atenavan, once they would leave. He felt a certain nervousness that made his stomach sting, but he ignored it. He found that some trepidation was normal, after all he was about to flee from the Aresland and no one knew anything.

Or at least... He kept hoping so.

He didn't take his laptop because he knew that there was already one on the rover and it was going to be enough. He put on his sneakers, fixed his bed covers just a little bit and then, after turning the light off, he approached the door. But before leaving, he turned back once again. He couldn't tell why, but looking at his room, he felt a weird sensation. Was he going to leave it like that? He didn't know for how long was he going to stay away exactly. His eyes landed inevitably on the framed picture on his nightstand. The darkness hid what it portrayed. He breathed deeply, staring at it. Then he decided. He went to slip the picture out of its frame, he folded it in a half and tucked it into an inner pocket of his hoodie. That was the only picture he had with his mother. It had always been there with him in the Aresland and now he was going to take it with him. He felt that maybe, somehow, it was going to protect him.

And so he left his room for the last time. Actually he was going to return, but in his mind it kept feeling like a *last* time and he didn't know why. He walked away from his father and Dounja, he passed for one last time through the corridor which led to the Main Base, he went to the storage room for the last time in order to slip into his biosuit. The night was peaceful and calm. Although that darkness gave him chills, he found that all in all everything was quiet. Ready, with his helmet under his arm, he walked around the central cylinder until he reached the airlock. There was still no one, but shortly after he heard some light, stealthy steps arriving in his direction and then Anna and Yan appeared. The three didn't say a word, their eyes spoke volumes. They nodded their heads once before putting their helmets on and running all the safety procedures. They entered the air-lock without looking back and a door definitely closed between them and the Aresland.

«Sol number one» Yan said in a breath.

His words spread in Jordan's and Anna's helmets.

«Sol number one» they repeated in unison.

They walked out into the deep darkness, intermittent-ly illuminated by the red lights surrounding the station. They walked among sand and rocks, now black, now reddish. They reached the garage in silence and got onboard the Atenavan. It was as if they feared someone could hear them. Jordan and Yan headed to the front to sit on the driver's and the passenger's seats. A tremble crossed the Atenavan and the lights were turned on as well as all the indicators in front of Jordan. After a "bip-bip" had spread in the whole rover, the three took their helmets off.

Soon Anna's voice came from the central body of the vehicle.

«Air levels?» she asked.

«Nominal» Jordan replied right away, «Twenty per-cent of oxygen, eighty percent of nitrogen.»

«CO_2 uptake?»

«Nominal.»

«Temperature?»

«Seventy-two degrees Fahrenheit.»

«Pressure?»

«One atmosphere.»

«Relative humidity?»

«Sixty percent. Zero point O three atmospheres of wa-ter vapor.»

«Everything's okay» the girl stated, approaching the cockpit. «We can go.»

«Fine. We start to move» Jordan declared wielding the hand control and pushing it forward.

Moving that vehicle was quite another story, Jordan thought while bringing the Atenavan out of the garage.

«How is it?» Yan asked.

Jordan nodded weakly, he was too focused on what he was doing.

«Huge and kind of heavy» he observed, «But feasible.»

The rover's headlights illuminated the Martian desert as soon as they were outside.

«Trajectory... North-West» Jordan said slowly while turning the vehicle until it pointed in the right direction, keeping his eyes on the digital compass.

Then he raised his gaze in front of himself, to the horizon.

«Direction... Huygens Crater» he continued, «Journey time... I have no idea.»

«Here we go» Anna sighed.

Jordan nodded without moving his eyes away.

«Say goodbye to the Aresland.»

The boy didn't turn back, he saw the continuous intermittence of the red lights on the sand in front of him fading away as they moved further.

«Goodbye big fella, I'm gonna miss you» Yan whined.

In other circumstances they all would have laughed at his words, but that time they only managed to smile slightly. Anna turned back without saying a word, in order to see a piece of the base disappearing from the lateral window.

And Jordan accelerated. He increased the speed until the indicator showed twenty-five kilometers per hour. The whole rover wobbled as it moved. The Red Stone, Krasnij Gorod and Hong Se De Du bases were getting further and further away. Their light faded slowly, until the Aresland became nothing more than a red dot. In the end, the only source of light in the darkness came from the rover's headlights that showed any obstacles to get past. Jordan was serene, but at the same time he felt something within himself that, as he moved further on, seemed to wake up. He felt alive.

He knew, deep down, that sooner or later it would happen. He didn't quite know how, but somewhat the horizon called him. He wanted to explore, he wanted to know the reality outside the safe boundaries of the Aresland.

He realized that, since the first time he had stepped foot outside his little world, he hadn't longed for anything but to make another move and then another and another to go on and see what was waiting for him just over the border.

And now it was finally happening.

He was taking those steps.

NINE
~ *180 sols before* ~

Jordan woke up at the alarm ringing. He wasn't really sleeping actually. It was more a kind a of rest, he was half-asleep, that status when you're always ready to react. And then it wasn't that easy to fall deeply asleep in those conditions. They had found out that the covers were actually inflatable mattresses, but the situation wasn't so comfortable anyway. The continuous loud buzz of the engine and the Life Support System together with the jolts of the vehicle as it went up and down dunes and rocks weren't really helping.

Jordan shut the alarm quickly, the digital clock showed 7:00 am. He yawned and narrowed his eyes at the cold light of the LEDs on the ceiling, that couldn't be turned off. He stretched to get rid of his numbness and discovered that the shoulder he had slept on hurt. He massaged it briefly with a hand, but he didn't bother much about it. He turned. Anna was laying on a mattress next to him and looked completely absorbed in a deep sleep. He sat still, looking at her for some moments while George's words flashed back in his mind.

Her face had gentle features, framed by a bunch of red waves that reminded him of the sand dunes in the Martian landscape. She wore an innocent and relaxed expression. A lock of hair had fallen on her face and Jordan found himself repressing the impulse to move it away. He didn't want to wake her up. Therefore he got up and reached Yan in the cockpit.

He didn't exactly know how long he had been driving. Jordan had driven for an hour and a half, then he had left his place to the girl to go rest. And now it was Yan's turn. He trusted his friends. After all they simply had to make sure that the rover moved constantly in the right direction. They had agreed that if they noticed something wrong, anything really, they would wake him up right away. They had decided to go on for the entire night, without the four hours break.

«Good morn – woah!» Jordan couldn't complete the sentence when his gaze landed over the window of the cockpit.

«Incredible, isn't it?» Yan asked, without moving his gaze away from the path.

They were proceeding in a North-Western direction, but looking Eastward, outside a lateral window, very far just above the horizon, a white marble was raising slowly, defining the difference between the ground and the sky, one black, the other light blue.

«Say, Nunki, had you ever seen it before?» Jordan asked, captured.

«Mh, what?»

At that obvious question, the boy turned to look at Yan and only then he realized how tired he looked.

«The sunrise» he replied, returning to look outside.

«No, never.»

Jordan let himself fall sitting on the passenger seat next to Yan and yawned a second time.

«How long have you been driving?»

«An hour and ten minutes more or less.»

«Can you resist for twenty more?»

«Yeah, yeah. Never mind.»

«For how many kilometers have we travelled so far?»

«Nearly eighty-three.»

A moment of silence passed and the noises of the rover took over.

«Do you think they've noticed our absence by now?» Jordan asked.

He wanted to make conversation because his friend seemed on the verge of falling asleep at any moment.

«Nah» Yan waged in a croaky voice, «Right now they'll be having breakfast and thinking we're late or still sleeping. Then, in my opinion, at seven thirty they'll begin to worry and they'll look for us in our rooms. They'll discover we're not there, they'll rush to alert one another and then I don't know, they may come after us.»

Jordan was thoughtful. And what if they actually already knew? After all, that was what George seemed to tell him by his last warning. But if it were true, they would have stopped them before, wouldn't they?

«I don't think they'll come after us. They don't know where we're heading» Jordan said, almost hopefully.

«Ah, I think they do» Yan objected.

«Even if they do, they couldn't. There's only one Atenavan in the whole Aresland. And only this very vehicle can handle such a trip» Jordan observed.

Yan didn't answer anymore and Jordan gave up that topic.

They were proceeding upward, the altitude indicator occasionally increased the meters as they went on.

Fifteen minutes later, they saw what looked like the end of the ground taking shape in front of them. As if there was going to be a jump into nothing. Yan narrowed his eyes and Jordan leaned forward to have a better look.

«What...?» Jordan began, but no one said anything else until they reached the edge and stopped. «It's a canyon» he observed.

A long, deep valley cut through the Martian surface and extended for several kilometers.

«Yeah» Yan agreed, «It must be Hellas Chasma. I didn't imagine it like this. Should we wake Anna and show her? Maybe she wanted to see it as well.»

They both turned back to look at the girl sleeping deeply. Jordan pursed his lips.

«Mmm, we'd better go on. We can't waste time.»

Yan nodded once and returned to study the canyon.

«We got to get around it» he looked right and then left. «We bend Westward» he stated.

And the rover resumed movement.

One hour later, when both Anna and Yan had woken up with more energy, there was Jordan at the wheel. They had circumvented Hellas Chasma and were returning on their path. Since it was eight in the morning, it was clear that by now everyone at the Aresland was officially aware of their escape. The sun was higher in the sky, the soil was regaining its usual rusty coloring and the sky its habitual mustard yellow. In the distance, Westward, they could spot the high ground of the mountain range called Hellespontus Montes.

«How about we eat something?» Yan proposed.

«Yup, have your breakfast, I go on here» Jordan conceded. «I'll eat once you relieve me.»

Anna entered the cockpit with a box in her arms and camped there with Yan to keep Jordan company. Yan opened it.

«This container is not mine» he commented.

«I reckon it's yours, Jordan, let's see what you brought» the girl said beginning to dig through.

She took out some potatoes and tomatoes that were the last foodstuffs Jordan had taken.

«Want a tomato, Nunki? Here, bon appétit» Anna joked, handing a tomato to Yan, who waved it away with a hand.

«For Olympus's sake!»

«Uhm look at the bottom for breakfast» Jordan instructed, keeping his eyes on the path. «You should find some muesli. I almost got caught for that.»

«For how many other things you almost got caught, venture-boy?» Anna prodded him and Jordan rolled his eyes.

«Ah, there it is!» Yan exclaimed taking out a package of cereals and dry fruit.

The girl went to fill two bowls with some water. They had brought enough water supplies for seven sols if the one produced by the Life Support System wasn't enough. The two ate silently, sharing the passenger seat next to Jordan and trying not to drop their meals at every turbulence of the vehicle.

«This silence's so sad» Yan commented few minutes later.

«And on top of that» Jordan added, «Your continuous chewing doesn't do much but increase my hunger and sufferance.»

Yan burst out laughing.

«We go in the back if you prefer» Anna said, drily.

«No, stay here. Instead… I think I have a solution.»

Jordan tried to push some small buttons on the console and soon a rhythmic mandolin music spread throughout the entire Atenavan, the same Jordan was listening to in his room. Following Yan's example, he had filled up a pen-drive with his favourite music and had taken it with him. And the night before, when they had gone onboard for the first time and he had holed up in the cockpit, he had entered it without being seen. Because he knew that his friends weren't going to like his idea and, in fact, he had the confirmation when the music started.

«Noooo!» Yan shrieked, closing his eyes.

«You cannot do this, Jordan!» Anna raised her voice in order to be heard. «I charge you with high treason to the members of the crew!»

All the three of them burst out laughing. With that music in the background, everything felt more enjoyable and cheerful, even the jolts, even the placid Martian desert and the discolored sky.

The trip proceeded quietly while the sun seemed to chase them on its path through the sky. Four hours later they had found themselves circumventing a large crater and when the clock struck 1:00 pm they stopped for the first time. The last one at the wheel had been Anna, but anyway all the three of them were quite tired and bored. After all they didn't have much to do during the trip, apart from looking at the landscape, listening to Jordan's music and chitchatting. They had promised to themselves that they were going to get out of the Atenavan after lunch, in order to wander a little bit in the area. Jordan was thrilled about that idea.

They discovered that in the central body of the vehicle, in a corner next to the closets, there was a little hatch hiding two metallic plates which served for heating up the dishes. They tried it right away with a tin of rice and beans. When it was ready and they opened it, the appearance was distasteful. Of course there was no comparison with what they were used to eat at the base. When they tried it, they realized that if they had no way of warming it up, they would have never managed to eat it. It was quite tasteless, but despite everything they scraped the floor of the tin. They needed energy to go on, just like the rover, no matter if their propellant wasn't so pleasant. What mattered was having it. Then they tried to heat up three potatoes and ate one each and, after some blueberries, they agreed that as a lunch it could be sufficient.

They slipped up their biosuits and, once all the three of them were certain they had sealed their helmets well and the atmospheric pressure had decreased, Jordan could turn off the rover's engine and the Life Support Systems. They opened the hatch and jumped down on the dark sand.

Jordan couldn't keep himself from crouching down with a knee on the ground, he gathered some sand in one hand and let the grains stream between his fingers. He observed them falling slowly. He loved that feeling since he was a child.

«What's Jordan doing?» Anna's voice spread in his helmet.

«Advanced mental communication with Mars» Yan replied with confidence «Aren't you?»

Jordan raised his gaze and saw his friend was addressing him. He got back up on his feet and clapped his hands to wipe the dust away.

«Yes, exactly» he confirmed, playing his game. «Mars and I talk often.»

«Did he tell you anything? Like, I don't know, if we'll make it alive to the Rubentes Terrae?»

«Mmm, I think he mentioned something about it.»

«Come on, ask him again, be more precise» Anna encouraged him with an amused tone.

«No...» he waved it away with a hand «He doesn't want to speak anymore.»

«He can't stand you already» Yan commented.

«Possibly» Jordan laughed. «So, shall we take a look around?»

«Where are you going to go?» Anna asked, returning serious immediately.

«Let's just go for a walk. I think I saw a small crater over there» Jordan pointed somewhere in the distance.

«You're not thinking of going so far? It's not a good idea.»

«Then you stay at the rover. If anything goes wrong, speak. Let's not lose the contact.»

«Still looking like a terrible idea to me.»

«Everything looks like a terrible idea to you. Nunki, you're with me?»

«You got it, bro» the boy replied cheerfully.

The two started down in the desert.

«I'm offended» Anna's voice mumbled.

«It'll pass» Jordan talked back.

«I'm about to describe you with an adjective you wouldn't enjoy, Jordan.»

«I imagine, but you're not bold enough anyway.»

«Do not try me…» she hissed threateningly.

«Never mind, I'm not even trying.»

«… asshole…» she murmured in a barely audible whisper.

«What? I didn't quite catch what you said»

«FUCK YOU, JORDAN!» she yelled in the helmet's microphone.

The two boys burst out laughing from satisfaction. Jordan turned back and realized how much they had already pulled away from the rover. Anna was leaning with her back against the Atenavan and had her arms crossed. Jordan was too far to see what expression she was wearing. As soon as she noticed the boy was looking at her, she untangled her arms to give him a middle finger. He replied laughing even louder and lifting his arms to show a double thumb-up. Finally he turned again and resumed to walk behind Yan.

Looking around himself, he saw no boundaries. The Martian desert with its dunes, craters and rock formations, seemed to extend endlessly. Jordan had never felt so free before.

«I can't believe you really did it» Yan commented, talking about what had happened shortly before.

«It's been easy» Jordan shrugged.

«I HEAR YOU!» Anna's voice shrieked.

Yan froze for a second. Evidently he had forgotten he was still connected to the both of them. Jordan giggled smugly.

Then they walked silently for several minutes in the same direction, but the crater Jordan had seen seemed to pull away as they tried to approach it. Then he stopped and Yan did the same.

«Let's drop it, it's too far» Jordan admitted.

«Ah, pity. You're right though, look how much we've walked!» Yan exclaimed after turning back.

Jordan turned as well and spotted the Atenavan as a far dot.

«Alright, I say that's enough. Anna, are you there?»
They received no answer. The two exchanged a look.

«Anna, do you copy? *Otvyeti, pozhàluista*[22]» Yan tried.
But also that time nothing happened.

«She might be pulling a prank on us to retaliate» he assumed.

«No, I don't think so» Jordan said seriously, «You don't pull pranks with this stuff. Especially if you're a Martian named Anna Taykeeva. I guess she's returned onboard the Atenavan, she took off her helmet and left it somewhere.»

«Mh, yeah, it might be so.»

«Listen, let's take a look around here, but then we reenter.»

«Roger, commander.»

After roaming the area, they focused on a stone which showcased some interesting patterns. They tried to speculate about what minerals it could be composed of, remembering Klara Nowak's lessons. Meanwhile they tried to crumble it with their hands in order to bring

---

[22] Otvyeti, pozhàluista: from Russian, "Answer, please"

away some pieces as souvenirs, but soon they realized that gathering some rocks from the ground would have been easier and quicker.

After several minutes of peace and tranquility that felt almost unrealistic, an odd rustle, a disturbance that came and went, spread inside their helmets.

«What the… Nunki, you hear it too?» Jordan asked bringing a hand to his helmet as if he could touch his ear.

«Yes, but…» the boy didn't manage to complete the sentence as a voice interrupted him.

«Atenavan to Jordan and Yan. Do you copy? I order an immediate reentry!» Anna's voice sounded tense even though she tried to keep it firm, the two boys perceived a distressful hint.

«Anna, we copy you. What's the matter?» Jordan replied trying to keep calm.

He stood up and turned to look in the rover's direction, but everything seemed as calm as always.

«I repeat, emergency reentry! There's a str…» the communication was suddenly cut off by an intense buzz.

«What? Redo, I can't hear you!» Jordan raised his tone of voice as he felt restlessness taking over him.

He thought he had heard Anna's voice chopped up, but then the rustle resumed, stronger. He felt Yan touching his shoulder, he was turned to the other side, but Jordan ignored him, continuing his attempts to get in touch with Anna. The communication returned all of a sudden and when Anna spoke, her voice came out loud and clear.

«There's a strong sandstorm coming from South-East, winds at ninety kilometers per hour, you have little time, come back right away!»

«Coming a… a what?!» Jordan stammered, still unable to ponder properly Anna's words, feeling panic overwhelm him. He began to look around himself «South-East?»

«J–Jordan» Yan mumbled and only then he turned around completely.

All his muscles paralyzed. A powerful sandstorm was running in their direction, engulfing everything it met on its path.

«… we're d–dead…» Yan whined helplessly.

«GO! MOVE!» Jordan shouted before grabbing his friend's arm and starting to run in the opposite direction.

«Anna, we are… inbound» he panted, trying to breath.

He mentally thanked the suit's flexibility allowing them to move quickly. He hoped Anna had put on her biosuit again and had turned everything off in order to open the hatch avoiding explosions.

However quickly they ran, the blizzard seemed closer and closer, the rover still far and the struggle helpless. Despite an excruciating pain to his spleen and a shortness of breath, Jordan didn't slow down, his gaze fixed on the Atenavan. He began to perceive strong air movements and the sand under his feet was lifted to obscure his sight. They kept running without turning back.

When suddenly, at about thirty meters from the rover, Jordan heard a cry in his helmet. He slightly turned his head, Yan wasn't by his side anymore. He stopped immediately and looked back, the boy was on the ground, trying to get back up. Breathless and in pain, he ran back to him and tried to lift him by his shoulders.

«I tripped» Yan panted, «My foot hurts.»

«Stand up, stand up, there's no time!» Jordan shouted, glancing a couple of times behind his back and noticing that within few seconds they were going to be absorbed into the storm.

«It hurts» Yan repeated between his teeth once he was on his feet again.

Jordan, at the end of his strength, let his friend cling to him and, limping, they continued to move one step after another, at the mercy of the gusts of wind. Visibility kept decreasing, sand hurled violently against their visors. They were at about fifteen meters from the rover when it disappeared into the blizzard. Jordan kept going, hopeful.

The storm was taking them over and suddenly, a small rock lifted by the wind moved fulminous towards them. When Jordan noticed it, in that chaos, it was too late. He felt his helmet's visor being hit violently and, taken off guard, he fell on the ground with Yan. It took him few seconds to realize what had happened and to recover. He barely perceived a stinging pain on his forehead. There was a quick air movement in front of his face, he felt like coughing, a continuous bip-bip resounded in his helmet. He opened his eyes and looked around himself, confused. Everything hurt more than before.

«Holy shit, Jordan! Shit!» he heard Yan scream in an alarmed tone. «How are you?! Say something!»

Jordan brought into focus Yan who was kneeling next to him and blinked.

«Let's… go» he coughed, his head hurt as he took one last breath.

He seized Yan and stood up with him. Visibility was almost zero, the blizzard covered the sun and everything seemed darker, at the point that their automatic torches turned on. He tried to ignore the small hole and the crack that crossed his visor. He was aware of the danger, he knew how much oxygen he was losing.

He did the last thing he thought logic. He held his breath and started down in the rover's direction. Now they were both clinging to each other, fighting the storm. He wasn't aware of what happened shortly after. The Atenavan's hatch opened in front of them, he felt someone pulling him inside and he ended up on the floor. The last thing he saw was a third figure wearing a biosuit.

Then he passed out.

After what felt like one second, he opened his eyes slowly, blinking, blinded by the LEDs on the ceiling.

«Jordan? Jordan, can you hear me?» he heard a female voice calling him.

He knew that voice. Someone shook him slightly, therefore he tried to reopen his eyes. A very strong numbness overwhelmed him. He wasn't sure he could move at all. He made out a mass of reddish hair in front of him and narrowed his eyes to bring it into focus. Anna was observing him with a frown.

«Can you hear me? For Olympus's sake, say something!» the girl begged him.

But everything Jordan managed to do was filling his lungs up with air and letting it all out a couple of times. Then he decided to get up. With slow, painful movements, he turned on a side and eventually pushed himself up with his arms. He saw Yan sitting on a chair. He had a worried look too, but as soon as he met his gaze, he smiled widely in order to hide his concern.

«You saved my life, pal. I owe you one» he told him.

Jordan shook his head weakly and briefly waved his hand dismissively.

«I could hardly leave you out there» he answered in a raspy voice.

«Then you can speak!» Anna squeaked, relieved.

Jordan trudged until his back found a wall of the vehicle and he leaned onto it. He felt everything hurt.

«What happened?» he finally asked, closing his eyes and leaning his head against the wall behind him.

«An errant debris got through your helmet» Anna began to explain. «You lost a lot of oxygen and then you fainted.»

«For how long?»

«Twenty minutes.»

«Yan, how are *you*?» he asked after some moments of silence and reopening his eyes to look at him.

«Ah, I twisted my ankle, but I don't think it's broken. I've now taken a painkiller and I've wrapped my foot with what I found in the bathroom. Hope for the best.»

Jordan nodded weakly.

«Where's my helmet?»

Anna, as if she were ready for that question, handed it to him. Jordan took it and observed it attentively, almost with affection. A crack crossed vertically the visor on the left and, aloft, there was a hole of few millimeters. He suddenly perceived a stinging on his forehead and raised a hand to touch it. He found he had a cut, probably provoked by the debris. He brought that same finger to touch the crack from top down, careful not to cut himself with the sharp glass.

«The Red Planet's Law» he whispered almost to himself.

«What?» Yan asked, he hadn't heard well.

But he didn't want them to hear. He slightly shook his head, then raised his gaze on his friends with a frown.

«What am I supposed to do now?» he asked.

Yan frowned and pursed his lips, unsure, Anna observed his helmet with twinkling eyes.

«You're not leaving the Atenavan until we reach the Rubentes Terrae» the girl said.

«Yeah, *if* we reach it...» Yan commented, but Anna ignored him.

«Meanwhile we think of some way to cover the crack and the hole. There has to be some duct-tape or something, it should be enough. Afterward we can only hope that there will be other helmets at the base.»

Jordan nodded and sighed.

«What time is it?»

«Half past two» Yan replied.

«The storm?»

«Persists» Anna replied.

Jordan sighed again, thoughtful. Then, without another word, he stood up and moved to the cockpit. Anna and Yan, limping, trailed behind him. Despite the headlights being on, the visibility was void. Nothing could be seen at two meters away from the front of the rover. The sand enraged before them, the front glass was splintered, but it was way thicker and more resistant than their visors.

«Listen, Jordan» Anna began, taking the passenger's seat next to him. «Yan and I wanted to tell you something.»

The boy turned curiously and motioned for her to continue. The girl raised her gaze to Yan who was leaning against the doorjamb of the cockpit entrance. He continued Anna's speech.

«I'm speaking seriously now. Whatever we are doing, well… it's an expedition, a mission, after all. And every mission with a crew needs a commander» he paused dramatically, «We want you to be our commander, Jordan. You'll lead this mission till the very end.»

Jordan stared at Yan with wide eyes, trying to figure out if they were kidding him. He slowly lowered his gaze on Anna, questioningly.

«No joking» she assured seriously.

Jordan sighed and passed a hand through his hair.

«But guys, I… I can't» he murmured.

«Yes, you can» the girl objected with confidence. «You proved it. No one would be better than you.»

Jordan swallowed and looked his friends in the eyes. Their gazes were sincerely convinced. He glanced outside the window, at the enraging storm. He nodded slightly.

«Very well» he said. «Then we start again. We'll proceed in a North-Western direction at only ten kilometers per hour. We won't stop till sunset. We must pull away from this monster.»

«Yes, commander Miles» the two replied at unison.

Jordan turned to look at them, amused, and the two let out a brief laugh.

And so Jordan had risked his life, he had a cut on his forehead and his only source of safety and survival was that rover that he couldn't leave anymore. Yan had twisted his ankle and even walking had become a challenge. The only one who had remained healthy was Anna, thanks to whom the two of them were still alive.

Jordan took the controls and eventually the Atenavan resumed to move forward, slowly, in that disarming, powerful and unpredictable blizzard.

TEN
~ *179 sols before* ~

They travelled at ten kilometers per hour through the storm. For a straight seven hours they didn't stop, taking their turn every two hours until they reached the border of a huge crater whose limits couldn't be seen. They decided to stop and rest for the entire night. So, after having something for dinner, they went to sleep. They had figured out a way to cover the LEDs on the ceiling tying and setting up their biosuits in order to enjoy some darkness and facilitate the sleep they needed. And this way they fell asleep, despite the turbulence of the wind that occasionally shook the rover.

When the first sunrays illuminated the horizon and filtered through the glass of the Atenavan's cockpit, reaching the central body of the vehicle, the three eventually woke up. Anna got up slowly, Yan yawned and Jordan stretched one arm, happy to find that all the pain from the previous sol had worn down significantly.

«How are you?» the girl asked in a low voice.

Jordan got up to sit and yawned.

«Way better than yestersol» he replied.

He raised a hand to touch his wound on the forehead and found it had scabbed over.

«Your foot, Nunki?» Anna still asked.

«Mh, yeah… it looks better as well.»

After they ate something for breakfast, they returned into the cockpit to evaluate the situation. They found that the visibility had improved as the sunrays managed to find a way through the floating dust. Anna switched on the computer on the console in front of the passenger seat, dazzling both Jordan and Yan, and a false-colors image of the Martian zone they were crossing appeared on the screen. A whitish mass moved glitchy showing the sandstorm's trajectory.

«How did you...?» Yan began, but the girl cut him short.

«I'll tell you everything later.»

Yan sent Jordan a questioning look and he replied shrugging and shaking his head. After spending several moments observing the screen, the girl spoke again.

«Oh, great. The winds' speed has decreased to sixty kilometers per hour. I'd say we'll be completely out of it in fifty kilometers, give or take» then she raised her gaze to Jordan. «Commander?»

«Amazing» the boy nodded, «We resume at the usual twenty-five kilometers per hour and we won't stop till this evening, we'll have lunch in rotation.»

And so Jordan started the rover again and they left toward the Huygens Crater.

«I remained there looking around myself for some time, but in the end I was just getting bored» Anna began to tell, «Then I remembered there was this computer onboard the Atenavan, so I decided to go back inside to try switch it on and see what it was for. Anyway you two weren't going to return for a while and everything looked just fine, so I thought there was no problem in taking my helmet off. So I switched the computer on and this image opened right away, showing our location. It took me a while to realize that it was a kind of satellite image in real time and that the white mass was a storm on the go coming straight for us. So I took my helmet again and began to speak inside of it so that you could hear me, but the communication wasn't so good. You know the rest.»

«Okay, it went well» Yan commented, he was at the wheel.

Jordan was sitting in the passenger seat and Anna was standing behind them. They were getting around a couple of craters that crossed each other, the wind's speed decreased and visibility increased.

«So, if you didn't get the idea to try switch the computer on, maybe we wouldn't be here now» Jordan thought aloud.

«Maybe not.»

«It really went well» Yan added.

«But I told you!»

«Oh, don't start…» Jordan passed his hands through his hair.

«No, I do start!» the girl objected raising her tone of voice in a scolding manner «If you would just listen to me occasionally, maybe we could avoid these troubles! And the same goes for you, Yan!»

«But Jordan had communicated with Mars shortly before, I was trustful!» he argued, mocking an innocent expression.

«You shouldn't joke when there's your life at stake» Anna suggested with bitterness.

After some moments of silence, Jordan spoke again.

«Anna's right. No more terrible ideas from now on.»

Time passed inexorably slowly in that narrow space of six meters by four. Jordan's excitement for that trip was fading away kilometer after kilometer. He didn't exactly know why he expected it to be something grand. After all, the Martian landscape repeated quite uneventfully and eventually everything became usual, ordinary.

He had lunch with Anna and finally relieved Yan at the wheel.

His gaze was lost on the horizon, still confused and hazy due to the floating sand. They proceeded uphill, the altimeter counted meters as if it was a chronometer. The Hellas Planitia was the lowest point on the Martian surface therefore they were going to go on like that till the Huygens Crater. He remained alone for at least one hour. Yan had gone to eat something and rest, while Anna had crouched in a corner with a book she had secretly brought. There was nobody else, only Mars and he. He tried to drive as best he could, avoiding every rock too big, as fearing to destroy that quietude that was returning. He wasn't going to challenge the Red Planet again, he wouldn't repeat that mistake.

«Commander Miles, I ask your permission to inspect the on-board computer» Yan said at a certain point, leaning into the cockpit.

«Proceed» Jordan conceded, keeping his friend's tone, despite all of that still sounded fun to him.

The boy entered and took the passenger seat. Jordan observed him out of the corner of his eye because he didn't want to move his focus away from the path. Yan turned the computer on and as always the satellite image with their position opened, while the white cloud pulled away in a corner.

«This computer is more interesting than we might think» Yan commented pushing some buttons, «Because if it's linked to the satellite, as suggested by this image that saved our lives, then there should be the possibility to communicate with... well, I don't know, the Aresland I guess.»

«You say we can contact the Aresland?»

«It's a hypothesis.»

«And usually your hypotheses are confirmed?»

«Mmm, sometimes.»

«But we don't want to contact it.»

«Of course not. But I just want to see if this possibility actually exists.»

The boy continued to operate on the computer until Jordan saw the image disappear. He noticed some weird blue texts on a black screen. He saw Yan type some words or numerical codes, he wasn't sure, he couldn't look at him. Then a quick list of codes scrolled down the screen and finally all the texts disappeared but a flashing dash. In that exact moment, Yan sank back on his seat and raised his hands in the air with a gasp, but Jordan didn't understand if it was from happiness or scare.

«What have you done?» he asked.

«I don't know» Yan replied, still breathless.

«Of course…»

«Okay, technically I've created a chat-room with a computer of the Aresland. A satellite-based link.»

In that moment Anna appeared at the cockpit's entrance.

«Really?» she asked before approaching and crouching on seat next to Yan, who moved aside to make room for her.

They observed the screen attentively and also Jordan turned briefly to glance at it, but returned right away with his gaze in front of him.

The dash kept flashing.

«How about we write something?» Yan proposed, raising his gaze on Jordan.

«No, do not write anything.»

«Why?»

«Mmm, I don't know actually. But I think we'd better avoid creating a contact with them. You never know, they might manage to take a distance control of the rover and bring us straight back and we would see not a whiff of the Huygens Crater.»

«I don't think this rover was programmed for such a thing. Also, taking distance command of a rover by simply using this kind of link is very complicated, almost impossible. I don't think I myself would be capable of it.»

«Okay, whatever, we better not risk.»

«Uhm... guys...» Anna mumbled at a certain point, she hadn't moved her gaze away from the screen yet.

«What?» Jordan asked.

Yan lowered his eyes on the computer.

«What?!» he gasped.

«Too late» Anna commented between her teeth.

«What? What's that?» Jordan urged impatiently, after glancing quickly at the screen.

A brief text had appeared at the top.

«Fine, let's calm down, everyone. I think the Aresland has just sent us a message» Yan explained.

«Come on, read it» Jordan encouraged him.

«There's a sequence of numbers and then it says *"Shan Fang here, sending this message from the Hong Se De Du base of the Aresland station, are you receiving me?"*. Holy Olympus, Shan is someone who knows about computer science almost (I say almost) like me in the entire Aresland!»

«How did she know that you opened a chat-room?»

«Consider that over there they'll be monitoring everything since we've left, I bet they're following us with the satellites, I wouldn't be that surprised» Anna observed.

«What do we do, Jordan?» Yan asked, eagerly.

The boy sighed profoundly.

«We'll answer, but first: Anna, come here. It's your turn.»

«Alright» she said standing up.

Jordan stopped the rover and went to sit next to Yan. They restarted right away. Yan typed quickly on the keyboard and, after receiving Jordan's approval, he sent.

[12.04.317.9]: Yan, Jordan and Anna here, onboard the Atenavan. We're receiving you.

They sat silently, waiting for an answer, unsure of what would happen. But it didn't take long to arrive.

[73.88.503.2]: Fine! It's a relief for all of us here being able to talk to you. We request updates about your state of health. Did you get through the storm unharmed?

«They know about the storm!» Yan exclaimed after reading the message aloud for Anna too.

«Well, what did you expect?» she talked back.

«I expected them to be mad at us or to ask explanations» Jordan spoke up.

«I believe they have some more important things to tell us before being mad at us» the girl assumed.

«What do we answer? The truth?»

«No, we'll say that we're unharmed.»

And so they sent a new message. Jordan felt his hands trembling from agitation. He feared they would fail to carry out that mission completely. A long time passed before they received a new message.

[73.88.503.2]: Excellent. So, we know where you're heading, but you won't find anything at the Rubentes Terrae. It's nothing more than an experimental base. You're risking huge danger, therefore we request you to turn the tide and come back immediately to the Aresland, we'll come to you with other vehicles. Requesting confirmation.

Jordan and Yan exchanged looks. Anna inevitably slowed down the speed of the rover until it stopped and she turned to look at her friends.

«She's lying» the green-eyed boy stated.

«Jordan…» Anna begged, as if trying to bring him back to his senses.

«It can't be so, she's lying! It's not true that there's nothing, we've read the instructions together, there's everything that six persons need! And still, why would they keep it hidden from us three?»

No one answered.

«We got this far and we will reach the end» Jordan continued, very seriously. «Do you agree?»

Yan nodded.

«I agree.»

«Okay, Jordan» the girl raised her determined gaze on him. «We go on.»

The boy reached out to the computer and quickly typed an answer that he sent right away.

[12.04.317.9]: Negative.

«Go, shut everything off! Remove the link!» he urged.

Yan hurried to do as he was told and shortly after the usual satellite image reappeared. Anna started the rover again.

Everything returned as if nothing had happened.

* * *

NASA Headquarters

It was March 19th in 2060 and at the NASA Human Exploration and Operations department the stakes were high. Despite it was night and darkness seeped through the windows, the director Claire Dennis, in office after

Robert Walmore and Thomas Elliott, kept watch over the huge screens of the Control Room.

She was older, her face was crossed by more wrinkles, but her energy hadn't faded away. John Torres, the director of the Ad Martem program, had retired, leaving his place to James Walker. Amanda Lynch had been a spaceflight psychologist for more than twenty years by now and she was still holding her role inside the Ad Martem program. Terry Coleman, former vice-director, now worked at one of the consoles in the Control Room, while his previous place had been taken by Leonard Kelley, a former astronaut. Claire Dennis' associate director now was Tom Reynolds, an aerospace engineer. Although they covered different roles, all of them were characterized by the same worried twinkle in their eyes. All the angles showcased on the monitors portrayed the Martian surface, more or less zoomed, in false-colors or real. One in particular kept changing image every ten minutes, showing the progression of a small dot on the surface. The only person who didn't look genuinely concerned was Eugene Townfield, a journalist who was sent by the NASA Office of Strategic Communications and Public Affairs, in order to publish about the developments of Ad Martem 12. Since he had arrived, he hadn't managed to stay silent for a moment, continuing to ask questions and complaining about how much the Office and the public stressed him, requesting more news. He was a round-faced little man with a pair of thick, rectangular glasses that made him look like he was constantly surprised. Only in those last minutes they had miraculously managed to pacify him.

But soon silence was interrupted again, this time by Terry Coleman, sitting in front of one of the many computers of the Control Room.

«The Aresland has sent a new message» he said aloud.

«Pass it on the main screen» Dennis instructed.

«Right up, Claire.»

And so, in front of everyone, instead of one of the images of the Martian surface, a chat-room opened showing three messages sent from the Aresland and two answers from the Atenavan.

«Okay, we just have to wait and hope» the director commented after reading it.

«Doctor Lynch, do you think they're telling the truth?» Reynolds asked, referring to the message sent from the Atenavan where the three guys said they were fine.

«Hard to tell from simple written messages, I'm inclined to believe them. But if I think of what James said before...»

«They've stayed still for more than an hour in the same place until the storm literally ran over them» Walker explained. «Why? They could have avoided or circumvented it in time if they had left right away.»

«Maybe they didn't see it coming» Reynolds guessed.

Amanda Lynch nodded thoughtfully.

«Maybe they got out of the rover to explore the area. It would be totally normal and comprehensible. They've been living for more than fifteen years inside the Aresland. The instinct to explore and discover is proper of human beings and we cannot nor we have the right to suppress it.»

«If they've really come out unharmed from the middle of a storm of such intensity... ah, I don't know! It sounds like a miracle, honestly» Walker continued.

«But this way they're running towards great dangers» Reynolds shook his head, addressing the psychologist. «If they reach the Rubentes Terrae...»

«They got in touch with the Aresland right halfway to the Huygens Crater, it's probably been a causality. But only now they can go back» Kelley observed with caution, joining the conversation.

At the bottom of the room, sitting in a corner, there was a woman who had been staying there with her eyes on the screens for hours (some said for days), vigilant of everything that happened, everything that was said. She had long, dark hair partially gathered up with a clip, soft features, high cheekbones and visible grey shadows under her eyes, suggesting she hadn't been sleeping in a while. She wore a black hoodie with NASA's patch on the upper left. The fear portrayed on her face was different from that of anyone else in that room.

«If they reach the Rubentes Terrae alive, they would inevitably discover the truth on the mission. It's what they want, after all» Kelley continued.

«What if they decide to...» Reynolds began, but Kelley cut him off.

«Impossible. Let them decide what they want, they wouldn't be capable anyway, they're just kids. And if they have a little bit of common sense, they'll go back.»

«My team and I have analyzed their skill levels registered on the platform and, actually, if they wanted to, they could. It wouldn't be impossible for them» Lynch stated.

Kelley sighed, uncertain.

Claire Dennis listened in silence. The whole situation had taken a turn that neither she nor anybody would have ever imagined.

«We've got the answer from the Atenavan!» Coleman announced, suddenly.

Everyone turned at the same time towards the screen to read the answer that was composed of one single, very clear word. Tom Reynolds went pale, Leonard Kelley found himself with his mouth agape, but tried to recover quickly. Amanda Lynch was nodding slightly, as if she was expecting that answer. Claire Dennis stood serious and stoic, Eugene Townfield sprang to his feet. The woman in the corner hid her face in her hands before standing up suddenly and leaving the Control Room, followed by a couple of people.

«Negative? What does it mean, negative?» Kelley mumbled.

Reynolds passed a hand through his hair.

«It means they're going to proceed» Dennis explained, «They must be stopped, tell the Aresland to keep trying to convince them.»

Suddenly, the smartphone that Dennis kept for work began to ring in her pocket.

«But ma'am, time we get in touch with them and send a message, they won't read it before fifteen minutes!» an analyst at another computer complained.

Dennis ignored him as she saw on the screen of her smartphone the name "Roman Garibov". He was the director of the Russian Space Agency, Roscosmos. She sighed and answered.

«Claire Dennis, tell me.»

«Oh, you think she doesn't know? She's NASA's administrator, for God's sake!» Kelley talked back right away, exasperated.

«Of course, I'm sorry. You know, the agitation... I'll do it immediately.»

«I don't know what's happening!» Dennis exclaimed in her phone. «Yes... No, there's nothing we can do at the moment... Of course I know! ...»

«Broken link» Coleman mumbled to himself all of a sudden, then he repeated it aloud.

«What?!» Dennis exclaimed before hanging up the call, ignoring an increasingly nervous voice on the other side.

«What's that supposed to mean?»

«The Atenavan has broken the link with the Aresland. They've cut all the ties, we have no possibility to contact them from the Aresland, let alone from here.»

«*The Rebellion of the Martians*, it would make a perfect article!» Eugene Townfield squeaked cheerfully, appearing in front of Dennis. «Director, have you got anything to say?»

«Oh, yes, I've got plenty of things to say. And the first of all is that you must get out of the way, we have no time for this rubbish!»

«Rubbish!? Ma'am, this is journalism! People want to know!»

«They'll know at the proper moment!»

«When? Tell me when, so that I'll settle down the Communications Office!»

«We'll wait for a couple of days to see how the situation evolves, then we'll publish. At the moment we are all powerless in front of what's happening. We can do nothing but look and cross our fingers and may God be with us and with them, even though they're two hundred million kilometers away!»

ELEVEN
~ *178 sols before* ~

When Jordan woke up at 6:00 am and headed to the cockpit, the darkness was beginning to lose its imposing intensity as a light blue spot grew larger towards the East. Anna had been driving for two hours probably.

«Hi» she greeted him with little voice.

Jordan read the tiredness in her eyes. He answered with a nod of his head he knew she would see out of the corner of her eye. He sat at the passenger seat while Anna decreased the speed until she stopped in order to let him drive his turn. She didn't leave right away though, she left the controls and sat back in her chair. Jordan lost his gaze outside the window, studying the horizon, looking for nothing in particular.

«What's going to happen now?» he murmured.

That question wasn't solely directed to Anna, but also to himself, even to the Atenavan and to Mars too. The girl turned to look at him

«What do you think?»

Jordan was taken off guard by those words and raised his gaze to her eyes, finding the same light of the sunrise. He had to look elsewhere again in order to be able to talk.

«We escaped in secret» he began, «We lied and we foreclosed any possibility of communication with anyone.»

Out of the corner of his eye he saw the girl nodding slightly and returned to look at her, noticing her eyes had remained firm on him. He began to feel warm.

«And now we're alone» she stated simply.

«We're alone» Jordan convened. «Does it make any sense to you?»

«What?»

«What we're doing.»

«You mean this journey?»

The boy nodded. Anna glanced outside.

«Maybe not, for now. Just think about it! What are we doing lost in nowhere, inside a metallic box of six meters by four that's the only thing keeping us alive? It makes no sense in itself. But...» she returned to look at the boy, «It's a journey, in fact. And maybe that's the best part: we'll find a meaning only at the end, at the touchdown. And if we don't find it, we'll give it one.»

Anna smiled and Jordan smiled back. A good minute of silence passed and when Jordan thought all of that was getting too awkward, he spoke.

«Go rest» he said, «I'll keep driving, we cannot waste time.»

Their eyes met briefly before the girl stood up.

«Aye, commander» she replied before leaving.

Jordan took her place and restarted right away. As he looked outside he noticed some dim glows in the sky and briefly raised his gaze. They were stars. The truth was that he had never seen them in person. He had never left the Aresland by night and in any case the flashing red lights would have probably concealed their soft luminescence. He promised to himself that he would spend some time gazing at them, before going back, once they would arrive at destination. He wondered how could it be to stargaze without any visor or glass between the eyes and the sky. He also said to himself that probably it was never going to be possible as he would die. He frowned at the thought, but then he simply pushed it away, as he always did, returning to focus on his work.

He drove in complete tranquility and peace for about an hour and a half, enjoying the far sun rising and illuminating his world, as red as a firebrand, yet frozen.

At a certain moment, all of a sudden, he began to feel a weird sleepy sensation descending on him. He thought it was strange as he had slept enough hours to feel fine. And yet he felt heavy, even the hand control seemed more resistant to his movements. Or was he weaker? He tried to sit straighter on the chair, realizing he had slipped down a little bit. In the grip of exasperation, he slapped his own face, but by doing so he didn't pay attention to the path and ran straight into a big stone, making the entire vehicle jolt violently. He regained control of the situation and the rover returned to be steady, but suddenly he felt a stinging pain in his head that slowly faded away. Then returned. Jordan realized he was struggling to keep his eyes open every time that pang arrived and thought it was best if he stopped the rover. He had no idea of what was happening. He took a deep breath, but it didn't help. He felt the pain increase and coughed a little bit. Then he stood up and stumbled towards the central body of the rover where Anna and Yan slept peacefully. He fell on his knees and began to shake them.

«Wake up, please» he almost begged.

«What... What happens?» Yan mumbled opening his eyes.

Anna got up yawning.

«I don't feel good» Jordan said bringing a hand to touch his forehead.

«What is it?» Anna asked right away, alarmed, but as if she herself was blocked by a pang, she brought a hand to her own head.

«I feel tired, strong headache» Jordan panted, «You feel it too?»

The girl nodded weakly, squeezing her eyes. Yan got up to sit with a lost look and passed a hand through his hair.

«Hey, I also feel... I feel like» he took a deep breath and coughed, bringing his hands to his temples, «Like I can't breathe.»

At those words, Jordan widened his eyes.

«Oh, no» he whispered before standing up suddenly, despite the pain, and flying into the cockpit.

He threw himself on the driver seat and scanned the indicators of the Life Support System, looking for a leak. He watched many times again and again until suddenly his gaze stopped on the level of carbon dioxide. He went pale.

«Three point eight percent! Holy Olympus!» he shrieked, rushing back to his friends and coughing.

«The CO_2 level in the air is extremely above normal, three point eight percent and seems to be increasing. Just know that at five percent we'll die from intoxication!» he said in a hurry.

«How's it possible?» Yan asked, panicking.

«I don't know!» Jordan yelled back, heading to the back of the rover where there were the Life Support System machines. Jordan was certain the problem laid in the carbon dioxide absorber, a machine that looked like a big canister on the outside. He opened a hatch and found himself in front of all the machines, including the absorber. But the truth was he had no idea of what to do, nor where to start. And he didn't have a lot of time. Anna reached him and looked up, where there was a receptacle. The system absorbed the rover's air from there in order to purify it. But it didn't seem different than the usual.

«Jordan, you're the expert in this field» Anna admitted shortly after, «Where might the problem be?»

Jordan reemerged from the hatch and turned to look at Anna with a dishevelled look. With the tiredness and the pain in his head he didn't know how long he was going to resist.

«The thing is I really have no idea!» he exclaimed, «The absorber is the last one I expected to create problems. I mean, it's an automatic system that absorbs, purifies, frees the purified air and expels the CO_2 outside and goes on like that! Absorbs, purifies, frees, expels; absorbs, purifies, frees, expels...»

«Stop it! Focus! We have no time!» Yan shouted to interrupt him.

Jordan was crossed by an angry rage, but tried to repress it. Maybe too much carbon dioxide went to his head. He leaned with his back against the closets and, overwhelmed by an inexistent weight, he thought. He wondered what could be the reason that brought that machine not to purify the air. He felt his mind more and more foggy, sincerely he had no idea. He wondered if it really was going to end so and on the other hand he began to feel guilty for not really thinking about a solution. But he felt defeated, lost. He saw out of the corner of his eye Anna keeling over against a wall and sitting on the floor with her head in her hands, Yan had curled up on one of the chairs. Suddenly, a continuous bip bip began to spread in the rover. He imagined that the percentage had already exceeded the four.

«Jordan, do something!» he heard Anna's voice, far away.

He began to lose his mind among various thoughts, apparently random, as if he was about to fall asleep. And inevitably the storm came back to his mind, the sand enraging around the rover and... and suddenly a light turned on at the end of the tunnel, an intuition, a hope. He realized he had his eyes closed and opened them immediately, pulling away from the wall.

«The storm!» he said aloud, as trying to wake his friends up again. «It's obvious, isn't it? The debris must have blocked the expulsion of the carbon dioxide on the outside and the system couldn't purify the air anymore!»

«Of course» Anna acknowledged, struggling to get up again and beginning to gather the biosuits that had been piled up in a corner.

But suddenly she stopped and turned to Jordan. One glance only was enough and they both understood. His helmet was broken and in order to get out of the rover he had to shut down the Life Support System. The truth of the matter was clear to all the three of them without the necessity to speak it aloud: Jordan was going to die both with or without the suit. The boy swallowed, feeling his throat suddenly dry and looked at the suits Anna held in her hands.

«Come on, let's move!» he ordered reaching her and grabbing his own biosuit.

«Jordan, you can't!» the girl cried.

Jordan stopped and looked at her straight in the eyes without blinking.

«I can. It's the only way. I'll find something to plug the hole.»

After slipping into his suit to his waist, he headed to the Atenavan's bathroom, ignoring Anna's twinkling eyes. He heard Yan encourage her to move on, he was grateful to him.

In the bathroom there was a small toilet, a little sink and a closet above it. Jordan opened it and began to dig through, looking for some duct-tape or anything that could serve for plugging the hole in his visor, ignoring several packages of tablets, bandages and patches that kept falling into the sink and on the floor. Finally he found some cotton and a roll of thin masking tape. It wasn't the best, but still better than nothing. He wriggled out of the bathroom and saw Anna and Yan were ready with their suits on.

«Did you find anything?» the girl asked in a hurry, rushing to him with his helmet in her hands.

Yan reached them.

«Yes, help me» Jordan urged, beginning to rip some pieces of cotton.

They placed it on the floor and inserted some cotton in the hole before sticking the tape both on the inside and the outside all the way down the crack, until they created a thick layer.

«Thanks» Jordan uttered quickly and, without many compliments, he put on his helmet and sealed it.

Yan passed Anna her helmet and they did the same. Jordan took a deep breath of good oxygen, provided by the tanks of his suit, and reached the cockpit to turn off the engine and the Systems. Eventually the pressure decreased to the Martian atmosphere level and Jordan observed the white tape on the visor before his eyes with some fear, hoping it would hold. It didn't allow sight from his right eye. It seemed to hold, but he still didn't feel so safe. He wanted to solve all of that soon.

«It works?» Yan asked.

«Yes, for now» Jordan replied firmly and all the three of them got off the Atenavan.

They began to walk around it. The way it had come out of the storm was surprising. On the roof there were at least two centimeters of reddish sand and the sides were covered by a tiny layer of dust. Even the fierce inscription "Atenavan" didn't seem so vivid anymore. Jordan reached the back of the rover and began to scan it, looking for a possible vent. Anna and Yan were right away at his sides and did the same. Everything was so dirty that they could barely make out the external hatch that hid the Life Support System. All the three of them

177

got closer and began to clean the surface with their hands. Jordan knew that if they didn't solve the problem, their life was going to end there. Returning onboard would be useless because the absorber would intoxicate them and sooner or later they were going to run out of oxygen in their suits. At that thought, Jordan froze. Speaking of oxygen, after the extravehicular walk, in the confusion of the storm, they had forgotten to change their tanks with the new ones that they had found in the closets! It meant that…

«Are you okay?» Anna asked suddenly, noticing he was standing still.

Yan turned to look at him too.

«No, I'm not okay» he urged, lifting a flap with velcro on his arm, «I'm not okay» he repeated before observing a small digital screen. He winced. «Yan, how much oxygen do you have left?»

At his words, he noticed his friend stiffening like he did before. Through the visor he thought he had seen him going pale.

«Oh, man» he mumbled, before controlling his right arm as well.

«Don't tell me that…» Anna began, but her voice died in her throat.

«Holy Olympus, only fifteen minutes!» he admitted helplessly, fear in his voice. «What about you?»

«Eight» Jordan replied and as soon as he finished to pronounce that word, the usual bip bip started off in his suit.

But this time it wasn't indicating a loss of oxygen, rather an almost total exhaustion.

He had less oxygen than Yan because he had lost a lot due to the hole, while the girl had returned onboard almost immediately so she still had a good amount.

«Why haven't we thought about it before?» he heard Anna's voice interrupted by a sob.

She was behind him, he turned.

«It doesn't matter now, we got to find the vent!» Jordan tried to encourage both himself and his friends.

Oxygen or not, they were going to die anyway.

They spent the following three minutes scratching the dusty surface with their hands before Anna spoke breaking the silence.

«Here! Here there's something!» she exclaimed.

Jordan and Yan turned quickly to her and got closer. At the bottom, in the dust, a rock was leaning out of apparently nothing.

«Yeah, it has to be the right one» Jordan commented approaching and beginning to clean all around it.

«Jordan, I've got only ten minutes left!» Yan whined.

Without the need to check, the boy figured he had only three.

«Shut your mouth up and help me out here!» he shouted.

He decided not to remind his friends how many minutes of life he had left, he didn't want to scare them. Anna, who had already understood his intentions, began to help him to crumble the rock and soon Yan joined the efforts. It was a fight against time. With six hands everything was quicker, the rock was ripped up and they quickly cleaned up the pipe with their fingers, dropping on the ground all the debris and the dust. Without another word, they rushed to the entrance of the rover. Jordan was by now keeping his breath and inhaled slightly once every ten seconds. They threw themselves inside, but he felt like he wasn't able to do anything else. He keeled over against a wall in a corner and took a deep breath. With his last forces, he managed to look at the screen on his arm and realized it had been his last breath of oxygen. He imagined that Anna or Yan had gone to turn on the engine because he perceived the floor quivering under him. He still had to wait for the Life Support System to be fully reactivated, he had to wait for all the air to be breathable again, with the right levels of CO_2. When he began to perceive a pain in his lungs and the need to breath became unbearable, he seriously thought that time he wasn't going to make it. He didn't know why, but his thoughts converged to the picture of his mother and he in his pocket. He was still wearing it. His mum was with him. He tried to imagine her face, her reassuring smile, and subconsciously asked her to help him. But he wasn't afraid anymore.

He felt like he was about to fall into a deep sleep when something shook him violently and he breathed. He breathed because he didn't want to give up just yet and he clung to his life. Realizing he wasn't dead yet, he opened his eyes and noticed he wasn't wearing his helmet anymore. Anna and Yan were kneeling next to him, still wearing their suits, their helmets were scattered on the floor. He coughed a little and breathed deeply once again. They smiled to him.

«You did it, commander Miles» Yan announced jokingly, but finally calm.

«I did it?» the boy repeated, unbelieving, feeling euphoria growing inside of him. «It's working?»

«Perfectly» the girl confirmed.

Jordan turned to look at her and saw a tear running down her cheek and meeting her lips, curved up in a smile. A smile opened up on his face as well, inevitably. He shook his head.

«Ah! Come here you two!» he exclaimed smiling widely and holding out his arms.

The three hugged tightly, aware of having just escaped a deathly trouble and happy, extremely happy, to be still there and to be able to continue their journey. Anna's cheeks were beaded with tears of joy, of faded fear, of past danger.

Jordan felt his eyes lucid as well, but he put all his efforts not to let out a single tear. He would never cry, he never cried.

They continued to move in the same direction for six more hours, as always taking turns of two hours each. The optimism, as well as hope and enthusiasm, became part of breathable air inside the Atenavan when on the satellite map of the on-board computer they saw the Huygens Crater appearing and getting closer. Yan made a quick calculation and declared they had only three hours left before reaching the crater and four more to park the rover definitely at the Rubentes Terrae. They had a break from 12:00 am to 1:00 pm to have lunch together and then they restarted right away.

Time seemed to pass as quickly as the meters that increased on the altimeter, with the rhythm of Jordan's cheerful music which, at last, began to please even Yan. Anna was at the wheel when the rover stopped. They had arrived at the edge of a crater, so immense that all the others they had met on their path looked like puddles in comparison.

«Ladies and gentlemen, the Huygens Crater» Jordan announced solemnly in front of that breathtaking view.

«We made it, after all» Anna commented rubbing her hands, probably sweaty, on her pants.

«It was worth it, after all» the boy added and turned to her.

Their eyes met. Jordan thought they looked even bluer than the usual, he felt mesmerized.

«Keep your comments for when we'll be safe at the Rubentes Terrae, please» Yan spoke up and he almost winced, dropping his gaze to the floor and huffing silently. «We have four hours of descent left and then ascent again, anything could happen. Anything really, like, I don't know, we could be hit by a meteor or something.»

«Don't jinx it!» Anna exclaimed laughing and switching seats with Jordan, who was going to drive.

«Honestly, I wouldn't be impressed at this point» Yan resumed, amused.

Jordan simply chuckled.

The altimeter showed 2853 meters, probably they had never been so high. And as soon as Jordan restarted, the number began to decrease.

They travelled peacefully for the following four hours, enjoying the sunset right in front of them. With the passage of the hours, everything became greyer, darker, more unified. Eventually there was no more difference between the land and the sky.

And the far sun, white and perfectly round behind the dusty haze, surrounded by a light blue blaze more and more intense, disappeared, swallowed by the horizon, as well as its every celestial glow.

TWELVE
~ *177 sols before* ~

Actually nothing else happened. By now the nocturne darkness reigned. It was almost 8:00 pm and they hadn't had dinner yet because they were sure they were close to the Rubentes Terrae. And in fact it didn't take much for Jordan, Anna and Yan to find themselves struggling to make out an obscure building that blended in with the night.

«I reckon we've arrived» Jordan said after several minutes of silence.

«It gives me chills» Yan commented while driving.

«What did you expect? Obviously everything's shut down since it's unoccupied» Anna pointed out addressing Yan.

Jordan himself perceived a chill running down his spine. Silence returned until the headlights of the Atenavan illuminated a wall of the Rubentes Terrae and they didn't stop until they were right in front of it.

«Who knows where's the entrance» Yan wondered, frowning.

«Surely there has to be an airlock on another side, Nunki» Jordan assumed, «Let's get off the rover.»

Anna sent him a cross-eyed look and Jordan noticed it. He knew she was still worried for his helmet and that he still risked. But Jordan was quite sure that that plug of cotton and duct-tape would hold at least until the airlock. All the three of them moved to the central body of the vehicle to put on their biosuits for the umpteenth time.

«Are we bringing those?» Yan asked, nodding his head at the containers while slipping an arm into a sleeve of the suit.

One of the three had been completely emptied, the second was still half full, while the third hadn't even been opened.

«Not for now, they would hinder us in case of emergency» Jordan replied, «And anyway the Rubentes Terrae's instructions said the base is provided with supplies, isn't it?»

«Yeah, kind of» Yan scratched the back of his head.

Once they were ready, they turned off the engines and got off the Atenavan. They walked around the structure with rectangular sides of Rubentes Terrae until they found a sort of cubic room leaning outside from a wall. They opened manually the external hatch as well as the internal one. The inner pressure was the same as the outer one because it was inhabited by nobody and all the Life Support Systems were turned off. There was no electricity and so all the doors, usually automatic, didn't open on their own. Luckily enough they had automatic torches on their helmets.

«Interesting» Jordan commented sarcastically once they were closed into that dark base. «Now what?»

He looked around himself with a lost expression until he suddenly heard a noise that reminded a loud yawn and eventually he noticed all the lights were turning on. He turned. Anna was pressing buttons and pulling handles on a console right next to the airlock. When she finished, she turned to her friends.

«What, you don't read? Page three of the instructions for the Rubentes Terrae, part one» she shrugged.

«Blimey, Anna. What would we do without you?» Yan asked, mocking a worried tone.

Jordan shook his head slightly and returned to look around himself.

«I wonder the same» Anna replied. «However, all the levels are stabilizing, within a couple of minutes we'll be able to take off the suits.»

Right in front of the airlock there was a big staircase, built with the same material of walls, leading to an upper floor. In the cupboard under the stairs, a little room hosted the hygiene facilities. In front of it, a bigger room was the kitchen, with a small table in the center, directly linked to a dorm with three couples of bunk beds. Jordan and Yan were in the kitchen inspecting the various containers, similar to those they had brought, looking for something to eat for dinner. Anna arrived removing her suit.

«It doesn't look bad» she commented casually.

The two boys noticed her and took their suits off as well.

They ate a couple of bags of lyophilized food each and remained at the table of the kitchen some more time to talk about the Rubentes Terrae and still wondering why would they keep that place hidden from the three of them. When they entered the dorm to spend the night, after making turns to wash themselves, they felt totally exhausted.

«I sleep here» Jordan declared throwing himself on one of the first lower beds.

Anna picked the one on the other side of the room and sneaked under the sheets without another word. Yan appeared at the entrance of the dorm lastly and sent a calculating look firstly at Jordan and then at Anna. Finally he spoke.

«Mmm, I'll sleep on Jordan» he decided.

185

«You what!?» the boy exclaimed, stopping the fitting-out of his pillow to make it more comfortable and turning to Yan with an unbelieving, amused expression.

A giggle raised from Anna's bed. Yan, who was approaching Jordan's bed, stopped frozen and burst out laughing.

«What did you think!? I mean on the bed above yours!»

Jordan glanced at the sky and shook his head, returning to his work with the pillow.

«You want me to sleep with you, Jordan? I might change idea» Yan continued mocking a mischievous tone, Anna laughed in the background.

Jordan turned to him sharply with a look that was shocked, amused and furious at the same time.

«Yan Heng, off to your damn bed immediately!» he shrieked before bursting out laughing, «It's an order!» he added.

«Aye, commander» Yan obeyed, after glancing at him from top down with a superior look, still unable to repress a laugh.

«I'm going to die with the two biggest idiots on this planet!» Anna complained.

When eventually all the laughs died down in the darkness of the room, Jordan was laying on his back, his gaze was lost on Yan's bed above him. He felt extremely relaxed. It felt like an infinite time had passed since the last time he had laid in a real bed. As tired he was, it seemed sleep had forgotten about him. He was slowly realizing that he had really made it to the mysterious base of Rubentes Terrae. He didn't know what to expect exactly, but everything there seemed just as normal as at the Aresland. In his distant mind he wondered why there were six beds and why in the kitchen there was a table with six chairs. Who were the six persons to whom those beds and those chairs were destined? But in the end he didn't manage to find an answer because sleep took him over.

The following morning he felt like he had woken up too early. And yet, since the moment he opened his eyes, there was no way that he could fall back asleep. He thought it was probably because it wasn't his bed in his room, the one he had always been used to. It was very similar of course, but it wasn't his. Not even Jordan could really tell why, but finally he just got up to sit, stretching and being careful not to hit Yan's bed with his head.

He noticed Anna wasn't in her bed, probably she had already gotten up. Maybe she felt that same magnetic repulsion as well. Yan, on his behalf, snored loudly. He imagined Anna had gone to the kitchen or to the bathroom. He thought of going to her, but that idea aroused a pain in his stomach. He began to reflect on the fact that every time Anna and he were alone, something weird happened, as if the air pressure decreased and temperature increased and their conversation took an unusual turn. And on top of that, he always perceived a kind of tension, a static electricity that was probably going to provoke a lightning if they got too close. On one hand he was eager to feel that happen again, but on the other he was terribly afraid of it. He decided to wake Yan up. He stood up on the edge of his bed and began to shake his friend.

«Hey, wake up» he shouted in a whisper not to scare him and continuing to shake his shoulder.

Eventually the boy stopped snoring and turned heavily to Jordan with a goofy expression.

«What – what's the matter?» he asked trying to get up in a fidgety way.

«Nothing, nothing» Jordan reassured him, «Time to get up.»

«What time is it?» Yan mumbled.

«I have no idea.»

Yan frowned, but Jordan couldn't see him because he had already turned to leave.

«How can it be time to get up if you don't know what time is it?» he asked aloud then.

«Just get up!» Jordan snapped before disappearing into the kitchen.

As he imagined, he found the girl sitting at the table, busy chewing a dry energy bar.

«Morning» he said before sitting as well.

Anna had her mouth full, so she simply waved her hand in acknowledgement of his presence, meanwhile Yan entered too, still looking sleepy.

«And since how long are you awake exactly?»

«Nearly an hour» she replied casually, before slipping the last bit of the bar in her mouth and leaving the wrapping crumbled up on the table.

«At least you know what's the time?»

«Almost seven thirty.»

«How come you got up so early?» Jordan investigated.

The girl shrugged.

«I woke up and didn't fall back asleep. However, I have good news» she announced. «Beyond that door there's a storage room» she said pointing at a door next to the dorm which Jordan had been too tired to notice before. «There are some new biosuits and then three more suits that… I don't know, they look like the usual sort of suit that the new arrived ones wear, but it looks, how can I say, less bulky. But at least, Jordan, you can take a new biosuit.»

Yan nodded.

«Only three?» Jordan asked instead.

The girl raised an eyebrow at him.

«Yeah, why?»

«It's weird. There are six beds, six chairs. There should be six suits of that kind. Or not?»

The girl drummed her fingers on the table, thoughtfully.

«I didn't think about it» a moment of silence passed. «I don't know.»

After Jordan and Yan had finished their breakfasts too, they decided to change their clothes with some new ones that they found in the storage room. They hadn't changed them for three sols, not even to sleep. Jordan found himself wearing a black t-shirt with a text saying "Occupy Mars" in the center and a brownish circle that he assumed being Mars. Then he had a pair of dark grey trousers, quite comfy, and finally he kept his usual hoodie because he couldn't abandon the photo with his mother and he had no idea where to hide it otherwise. Anna had a t-shirt similar to his, but with the text "Mars or Bust" while Yan's one said "Get your ass to Mars".

«What the hell?!» Yan exclaimed, looking down at his t-shirt. «My ass was born on Mars already!»

They decided to venture on the upper floor. They took the mysterious stairs, but at the end they didn't find anything of what Jordan had imagined the sol before. The whole floor was a single hall containing three long tables, one in front of the other, with at least four or five computers each. In front of the three tables there was a huge offline screen and on the entire perimeter there were closets and drawers.

«Alright, I didn't see this coming» Yan admitted, mouth agape in front of all those computers.

Jordan was beginning to think that his doubts about the mysteriousness of that base were confirming.

«It kind of looks like a... an office» Yan continued, but his voice was drowned out by Anna's.

«A Control Room» she said. «I know on Earth they control missions from places like this.»

«How do you know?»

«Oh, well... There always are in literally any novel about space.»

«So there has to be a kind of mission controlled from here. The Nostoi Mission, for example» Jordan thought aloud.

«It has to be so. Do you remember? In the images that Nunki downloaded there was a rocket not too far from the base. I read the guidelines for the Rubentes Terrae from top down, but there are not even hints. I suppose we can only find all the answers... in this room» she said moving her gaze around herself.

«Fine. Let's get to work, then» Jordan prompted.

For nearly two hours, all the three of them spent the time exploring that Control Room. Mostly, Jordan and Anna inspected and dug through all the shelves and drawers on the perimeter of the room, while Yan jumped from a computer to another trying to turn them all on and figure out their function.

Jordan found plenty of plastic folders containing endless papers, documents, calculations, data, some of them showed orbital trajectories, others explained the slingshot effect and then many many manuals concerning life in space, how to live in microgravity for six or nine months and so on. Tired and by now quite resigned, he was absorbed in reading a paragraph explaining that you can't take showers in space, but you can only wash yourself with wet wipes, when suddenly he heard a loud crash. He came out from his reading and raised his gaze towards the source of the noise.

There was Anna, standing next to an open drawer, she was holding a white plastic folder in her hands open on the first page, a bunch of papers and books had fallen at her feet, probably she had dropped them. He wasn't touched by all that chaos though. What impressed him was the expression on her face. The way she was looking at that page. He couldn't decipher what she was feeling, he had never seen her like that before. Her eyes were wide in a mixture of surprise and fear, her lips disclosed, her face paler. He thought he had seen her been crossed by a shiver. Also Yan had remained blocked looking at her, as fearing what she could say.

Jordan hurried to reach her.

«What is it?» he asked with worry. «Did you find anything?»

The girl raised her gaze on him and Jordan read in her eyes a storm of emotions that had fallen upon her. Jordan felt anxiety mounting up inside of him. If something was able to upset Anna Taykeeva so much, it was nothing good. She swallowed hard.

«You r–read it» she stammered, before handing him the folder.

Jordan took it, confused. Before he could lower his eyes to read, the girl added: «It wasn't only a dream, Jordan.»

The boy tried his best to ignore her last words and tried to calm his mind down, although it was already running to find a sense to Anna's statement. He wasn't sure he wanted to know the truth. He took time sighing and closing the folder to observe the cover. Despite the black text in the center, "Nostoi Mission", accelerated his heartbeat, it was nothing of enthusing: it was all flatly white with the small NASA blue logo in the upper left. He happened to see it anywhere very often. But it was probably all that seriousness, so rigid and technical, that made him realize he was holding all the answers in his hands. Then he opened it, cleared his throat and began to read aloud.

«Kennedy Space Centre, United States. February 13th, 2056. Nostoi Mission. The robotic building of the base

Rubentes Terrae, inherent in the mission, is automatically concluded in the year 2060 and the interiors are manually set up by the already present astronauts at the Aresland station in the Hellas Planitia. Ad Martem 14 brings the Odysseus spaceship in a Low Martian Orbit and the Argus ascent vehicle in the Huygens Crater, three miles away from the Rubentes Terrae, control centre» Jordan stopped to breath and briefly raised his gaze on Anna and Yan.

The girl was staring at her feet, the boy hung on his every word. Then he resumed.

«The Nostoi Mission, with purposes of medical research, has the goal to analyze the effects provoked on the human body by...» the boy stopped, reading silently what followed and, as if certain of having misunderstood, he kept scanning the same sentence with his eyes.

«Go ahead, continue. You're almost there» Anna encouraged him.

Jordan was crossed by a shiver and continued.

«... by being born in different conditions from those of Earth. As such, with this mission, Jordan Arcturus Miles, Anna Yesfir Taykeeva and Yan Heng, as the first human beings ever born on planet Mars, inside the Red Stone, Krasnij Gorod and Hong Se De Du bases of the Aresland station, will be brought back to Earth for further medical studies. On January 18th, 2056, the Nostoi Mission is approved. It will start in the year 2064 from the Huygens Crater on Mars and will end, after six months of trip onboard the Odysseus, in the Kazakhstan desert on Earth. Signed, Claire Dennis, Alger Wolff, Roman Garibov and Wong Fui.»

Jordan understood immediately the reason why everything had fallen from Anna's hands shortly before: he felt like even his legs could give up at any moment. He stood still, staring at that page and reading and re-

reading it, until someone took the folder out of his hands.

«Oh, please!» Yan's voice exclaimed. «Good joke, you two. What is it, you made a deal?»

Both Jordan and Anna raised their shocked gaze on Yan in time to see him read the page and change expression. He whirled his head back up with wide eyes.

«It wasn't a joke?!»

«Not really, Nunki» Anna answered coldly, she was slowly recovering.

Jordan was in a kind of trance. He felt his mind foggy as he let that information sink in. It was hard to accept. Like if it was a nightmare: you wake up scared, but you don't remember why.

«No, wait a second, hold on... WHAT?!» Yan shrieked and returned to stare at the folder with wide eyes. «You are telling me that... For Olympus's sake, this Nostoi Mission is for *us*?»

«Yes... The Return Mission. Our return» Anna replied thoughtfully. «This mission should start in two years, in 241. Sooner or later they would've told us.»

«Now that's why there are only three suits of that sort» Jordan began, addressing his feet. «They're for us, for the launch. Six beds, six chairs, because clearly someone would have accompanied us, we weren't supposed to come on our own. And that's why they've been keeping it hidden. Probably they feared a wrong reaction on our behalf, like, if we had known of a rocket that would bring us to Earth we could have escaped alone, driven by curiosity or something. And in fact they were right» the boy added after a moment, raising his gaze on his friends. «I want to go.»

Anna sighed.

«I've been studying rockets and spaceflight so far. I know the launch procedures. On top of that, Mars and Earth are still in good positions for us to leave, at the moment. If you think about it, three new people arrived at the Aresland nineteen sols ago. This means that if we don't leave within eleven sols we'll have to wait for five hundred more or the trip would be so long that such an exposure to cosmic and solar radiation would be devastating. Hereby I'd agree to leave, if it wasn't that… it's impossible» she stated.

Jordan sent her a questioning look, furrowing his eyebrows.

«Why?»

«Look around yourself. Where are we?»

«In a… Control Room?»

«Exactly.»

Jordan's expression eventually darkened as he got the point of the issue.

«It's impossible to launch without a ground control.»

They remained in silence for several minutes, reflecting. Nothing but the far buzz of the Life Support System could be heard. Until silence was broken by Yan's firm voice.

«I stay.»

Jordan and Anna fixed their eyes on him and he continued.

«I'll stay here. I managed to switch on all the computers, I've seen that all the trajectories and everything are automatic. I'll be your ground control. I'll take you to Earth.»

«Forget about it» Jordan established even before Yan could finish the sentence. «I'm not leaving you here.»

«It's not about leaving me, Jordan. It's a choice. My choice. I knew from the beginning, like you, like Anna, that this trip would have a purpose in the end. And this is it. Look, it seems this was meant to be so! You're a rover expert and we got here thanks to you, Anna is expert of launches and spaceships so she'll know how to handle the situation up there and I'm a computer expert, we wouldn't be here if I hadn't downloaded the data and you couldn't reach the Earth if I weren't here.»

His words lingered in the air. Jordan felt his heartbeat resounding in his ears.

«We cannot leave you here alone» Anna intervened with caution.

«Yes, you can. And then, however, I'm certain that by now someone is coming for us from the Aresland. You leave tomorrow morning or it'll be too late.»

Jordan swallowed and searched Anna's gaze for support. The girl seemed to do the same.

«We can't take hasty decisions. If we've been risking our lives so far, in case we decide to leave, our probabilities of making it would be maybe a little more than fifty percent. A trip in space for so many months is hard. Frustrating. It would be all about living in minimal spaces and conditions that are barely sufficient to stay alive. It would be a huge sacrifice and an even bigger risk» Anna considered.

«But in the end it would be worth it» Jordan said, Yan nodded. «And then... If I think that I might have even the slightest possibility to see my mum again, I'd be ready to risk anything.»

«Jordan...» Anna's voice sounded moved.

«That's my biggest motivation» Jordan confirmed «Anna, if you want to take this risk, you need a motivation as well. What is it?»

The girl seemed taken aback, she dropped her gaze to the floor.

«I...» she shook her head, «I have a very good one, that's all you need to know» she admitted quickly, then she returned to look at the boy. «But... I don't know if you understand the matter, Jordan. We're talking about potentially never coming back. If something goes wrong we might not even make it out of this atmosphere. Or we could survive the entire trip and then die at the landing!»

«Anna» Jordan stopped her and moved a step forward, their eyes locked. «I'd rather die trying than not trying at all and living the rest of my remorseful life in a box» his last statement came out almost like a growl.

Anna was slightly startled by his words but her expression hardened right away.

«That's quite selfish of you, considering that if we leave, Yan would be destined to that» she pointed out bitterly.

That statement hit him. His expression softened as he turned sharply to look at Yan. He hadn't thought about that. If the two of them left, there was going to be no other chance for Yan to leave. His gaze was apologizing.

«No, Anna, Jordan is right» Yan assured, he had his arms crossed. «I'm fine here, I have my parents and all. If I were Jordan I would do the same. I want you two to go. I haven't come so far for nothing. Everything would change at the Aresland, if we just went back. I mean, we've broken all of the rules basically and maybe they'd cancel this mission. No guys, you cannot lose this chance. It's now or never.»

Silence returned, time seemed to stop. Jordan looked at Yan in the eyes and read his determination. He felt the weight of Anna's eyes on himself.

«Now or never» she repeated in a low voice. «And at this point I say now.»

«Then it's settled?» Yan asked firmly, still holding Jordan's gaze.

He swallowed.

«Nunki, you're my brother» Jordan's voice almost broke.

He saw Anna walking at his side out of the corner of his eye and nodding once.

«It's settled» she declared.

The darkness of the night was much more intense in that corner of the Huygens Crater. Probably because they had figured out a way to turn off all the external lamps of the Rubentes Terrae. And so the only source that illuminated the Martian desert was the starry sky. The stars were endless, even more than the grains of sand. The sky was clear and free from any threat of storm. Jordan, Anna and Yan were laying on the Martian sand, some meters away from the airlock, enjoying that spectacle. It was their way of spending their last night together.

For the entire sol, Anna had been closed inside the dorm to analyze all the manuals she had found about the Odysseus spaceship and the ascent module. Yan had spent the sol studying how to move correctly between the computers and keep an eye on every parameter. While Jordan had returned to the Atenavan to take the containers and bring them into the base, meanwhile checking if every System on the rover was still functioning. Then he investigated on how to reach the ascent vehicle that was at about five kilometers from there. They had already had dinner and everything was ready for the following sol.

Among all the stars, a brighter, slightly oval object slowly crossed the sky above them.

«This is the first time I see Phobos» Yan considered, observing that bright ball. «Actually this is the first time I gaze at the stars. Incredible, isn't it?»

«Yeah» Jordan replied calmly, captured by that sky.

«I wonder how it is like to see the Earth's Moon from the Earth.»

«I will tell you» Jordan said, but Yan ignored him.

«Then, what a name they gave it! I mean, how can you call a moon, Moon?! So why didn't they call the

Earth, Planet? It's nonsense. They should give it a better name. Even all the sixty-seven moons of Jupiter have a name! Also it's so lame to have one Moon only. At least we've got two. Who knows, maybe we're lucky enough to see Deimos as well.»

«This was honestly the best speech I've ever witnessed» Jordan joked.

«Thank you.»

«I'd like to point out, Nunki, that the meanings of the names of our two moons are "fear" and "panic"» Anna chuckled.

«Still better than not having a name at all.»
Finally all the three of them burst out laughing.

«Talking about the Earth, look over there» Anna raised an arm and pointed at something above the horizon where the sun had just set, followed by its sapphire glow.

Among many twinkling dots, there was one, slightly bigger than the others and brighter. There was no need to underline what planet it was. They observed in silence.

«It looks like nothing more than a bright dot among many» Jordan commented.

«That's how it is, in fact. That's what we are. Nothing more than bright dots» Anna said.

«I wonder if they're looking back at us now» Yan admitted. «Will you look at me?»

«That's for sure. And we'll wave to you» Anna answered.

«However it will be like you're still with us and we with you. Even if we are two hundred million kilometers apart» Jordan was crossed by a shiver as he pronounced those words.

Yan sighed.

«I will miss you.»

«We'll miss you too, Nunki» Jordan replied softly on behalf of Anna too, who evidently wasn't able to speak anymore, probably fearing her voice would falter with emotion.

Yan was laying between the two and suddenly he reached out on the sand until he found Jordan's hand and grabbed it. When he lifted it up towards the sky, Jordan noticed he was holding Anna's as well.

«We are so cool» he said. «Just look, look! It's all ours, all of it! We are the voyagers of space!» he exclaimed.

Despite those words touched him, Jordan couldn't keep himself from bursting out laughing. Also Yan chuckled for his own words, while Anna let out a sound that was halfway between a giggle and a sob, then she decided to return to her silence. Jordan couldn't blame her. Even he himself realized his sight had become slightly blurry.

His eyes twinkled like the stars.

THIRTEEN
~ *176 sols before* ~

At 5:00 am silence reigned inside the Rubentes Terrae. There wasn't much to say. It was only necessary to stay focused because a single mistake could be fatal. Anna had reached the top of her seriousness, Jordan thought. Since she had woken up, she had performed every single activity, even brushing her teeth and putting her clothes on, with such a rigor that it looked like she was already carrying out the launch procedures step by step. Jordan and she were putting on two of the three suits of the other type that they had found in the storage room, Yan was helping them. They were very different from their biosuits, completely blue and thicker.

«How's it?» Yan asked as he finished to close Jordan's suit, breaking the silence.

«A little heavy» he replied, making his friend smirk.

«Ah! I don't envy you» he said, walking around him to double-check if everything was fine.

«Of course» Jordan remarked, ironically.

Yan returned in front of him and Jordan saw an octave of smile on his lips, but it didn't reach his eyes. Yan patted him on an arm as to encourage him.

«You're ready» he announced, looking at Anna too, who stood near there with her helmet in one hand and the Odysseus manual in the other.

Her red waves fell on her suit. They returned to silence because the truth was that they didn't know what to say. What were their last words going to be? They wished for those last words to never come. Maybe they weren't going to speak till their return, Jordan thought. Then Anna moved a step forward and, despite the intrusion of her suit and the things she held on her hands, she managed to squeeze Yan in a hug.

«Be careful» she said after pulling away and looking him in the eyes.

«Okay» he simply said in a low voice, then turned to Jordan.

«See you, commander Miles» he nodded his head once, «It's been an honor to live by your side for eight years and nineteen months.»

Jordan shook his head smiling more widely and hugged him as well, but it was brief.

«See you, Nunki. Make sure I get to Earth alive.»

«Mmm... I'll think about it» he said ironically, earning a fake glare from Jordan.

And with that, the three took different paths: Yan headed to the stairs in order to go up to the Control Room, while Jordan reached Anna in front of the airlock. She had gathered her hair in a ponytail.

They exchanged looks and nodded once to show they were both ready and put on their helmets. They got out of the Rubentes Terrae when the sun was just peeking over the horizon with its spectacular blue glow. As soon as they got onboard the Atenavan, Yan's voice resounded in their helmets.

«Atenavan, Rubentes Terrae here, Yan Heng speaking. Checking ground-to-ground communication, do you copy?»

«Roger, Rubentes Terrae. Atenavan here, we're leaving now. ETA to the launchpad: twenty minutes.»

«Roger. Let me know when you arrive. Out.»

Those few minutes passed oddly fast and soon they saw the white silhouette of the ascent vehicle standing against the dark sky in the distance. It was five meters tall. They had stopped the rover about one kilometer away, hoping it was enough not to damage it and they had proceeded by foot for another ten minutes. They found themselves in front of a platform where the ascent vehicle stood vertically on its four feet. It was crossed by a vertical inscription of big blue· letters saying "ARGUS".

As they climbed on the flat platform, Jordan's gaze looked for the tip of the rocket where they were going to sit. He shivered slightly. Anna, on the contrary, looked confident.

«Yan, we just got to the launchpad. We're ready to enter the crew cabin. Do you copy?» Anna asked.

The answer arrived right away.

«I copy you loud and clear. I proceed with the opening of the hatch.»

Shortly after, a rectangular door opened slowly from a side of the rocket, while a ladder began to unravel mechanically to the ground. Anna started down towards it and Jordan didn't hesitate to follow her.

«It seems impossible that such a monster can lift from the ground» Jordan commented casually as he reached the foot of the ladder behind Anna. «Do you know how much it weighs? And what propellant it uses?»

«Oh, I promise you'll change idea during the launch» she replied with a tone that sounded almost villainous. «However, of course I know. In total it weighs eleven point five tons, of which eight point three are of propellant only, that is methane and liquid oxygen. More commonly known as methalox» the girl began to climb up the ladder and Jordan followed her. «We'll be thrust into space by a force of three hundred thousand Newtons and we'll endure a maximum acceleration of eleven point five g. But consider that this number refers to the terrestrial g, that's three times the Martian one. Three minutes after the lift-off we'll finally enter the orbit and we'll begin the docking manoeuvres with the Odysseus.»

«In your speech I find more ways to die than to make it. I mean, I gather that our percentage of survival is quite low.»

«That's it.»

«I wish I didn't know.»

«Want to know a fun fact?» the girl continued.

«Uhm, sounds better, go ahead.»

«Odysseus is the name of a mythological character, you know, one of the legends from Earth. He's also known by the name Ulysses. Ulysses had a dog, the name of the dog was Argus. Argus was very loyal to Ulysses, he would always go to him and recognize him even after many years. Did you get it? Argus and Odysseus, the ascent vehicle that lifts off and goes to the mother spaceship!»

«You just made it all up, didn't you?»

The girl let out a chuckle that sounded slightly nervous.

«No, imbecile! That's history, you should study more!»

«Well, then, I just hope Argus is still as loyal to his master as you claim.»

The ladder led them straight into the crew module, they were at a height of about four meters. Jordan looked down out of curiosity and was crossed by a chill. He was clearly about to get on the top of a freaking rocket. On one hand it felt fantastic and he couldn't wait to see how it was to be launched into space, but on the other hand he was beginning to accept the fact that it might be the end of him, matter-of-factly. Just in front of the capsule entrance, Anna turned to him.

«Listen, usually the commander sits in the centre. But I believe it's more appropriate if I sit there, since I know what to do. You'll be at my left, agree?»

«Yeah yeah, certainly, go ahead» the boy hurried to say and his friend slipped with her feet through the open hatch.

When Jordan leaned to peek over the entrance, he was taken over by confusion: at the bottom of a narrow passage he saw Anna laying on what looked more like a cradle than a chair. He tried to quickly get rid of every distress and, just as Anna did, he sat on the edge of the hatch and then slipped into the cabin, deflecting to the left not to end up on the girl. He found himself in a small, narrow space: three seats/cradles were placed in front of three illuminated screens that showcased data and graphs. Jordan didn't know much about it all, but he imagined it was the on-board telemetry. Down, in front of Anna, there was a hand control that was very similar to the one they used to drive the Atenavan. Jordan figured Anna was going to use it to manoeuvre the Argus during the docking to the Odysseus.

«Lay down like me» she instructed as soon as he was by her side and Jordan obeyed in silence.

Needless to say, he had his heart in his mouth. And so he found himself tied up to that cradle with his feet up in the air. All his hopes were in Anna who had been studying all of it for a long time, and in Yan, who was going to follow Anna's instructions on the ground. Right next to him, on the wall, there was a porthole from which he only discerned the fading colour of the sky. Perhaps, if he had leaned a little bit, he could see Mars' horizon. But for the moment he preferred remaining perfectly still, fearing that any small movement could compromise the launch.

«Where will we dock?» he asked.

«To the service module. However now I'd request you not to talk to me, please, until we're in space. I'll explain everything afterwards.»

The boy sighed and didn't reply.

«Rubentes Terrae, Argus here. We are inside the capsule, do you copy?»

«I copy you» Yan's voice replied, it sounded so distant already... «I'm now switching to the air-to-ground communication.»

«Roger.»

«Switched to air-to-ground communication, do you copy?»

«Affirmative.»

«I proceed to the closure of the hatch.»

A mechanic noise resounded behind them and slowly the dim light of the sun was obscured, leaving them to the artificial illumination of the capsule. A following metallic clack indicated the hatch had sealed.

«Can you confirm the closure of the hatch?»

«I confirm.»

«The on-board computers are in a launch configuration?»

«Affirmative. Do you remember all the steps I told you?»

«Yes. I proceed to close the cabin venting valves.»

«And all the timeframes?»

«Yes, Anna. Now let me focus.»

The girl sighed deeply as if calming down her nerves. A moment of silence followed, Jordan had began taking long, deep breaths. He felt the moment approaching.

«Time: minus fifteen minutes. Activating the inertial navigation systems» Yan's voice resumed.

This time Anna didn't reply. Long minutes of silence passed and no one of them dared to move.

«Time: minus six minutes. The automatic launch sequence is ready for ignition.»

«Wait for T minus twenty-nine seconds» Anna articulated.

«Roger. Time: minus five minutes and fifteen seconds. Activating the operational instrumentation recorder.»

«Time: minus five minutes. Activating the Auxiliary Power Unit and the on-board telemetry» Anna's voice said, after Jordan saw her moving her hands on the touch-screens in front of them.

Some more minutes of silence passed. Jordan's heartbeat continued to accelerate and any attempt to keep calm seemed useless. He heard Anna sigh deeply as they both observed the countdown in a corner of the screen. There was less than a minute left by now.

«Time: minus twenty-nine seconds. Main engine start.»

Jordan gasped. The entire structure was crossed by an unexpected quiver, a roar seemed to spread to the horizon and he felt suddenly fragile.

When Anna spoke again, her voice sounded less convinced, more resigned.

«Ignition confirmed.»

Jordan knew exactly why. All the three of those seats had to be occupied. But now one was empty. And that absence was overwhelming. They were leaving Yan behind. They were leaving everything behind. Although they were still hearing the boy's voice, he wasn't with them anymore. He was far off. He was of another world.

«Time–»

Jordan felt his right hand being squeezed by Anna's.

«–minus ten seconds. Nine, eight, seven,» Jordan tightened his grip on Anna's hand.

«Six, five, four, three–»

«Goodbye» Anna's voice whispered.

«– two, one. Lift-off.»

Jordan found himself breathlessly pressed against his seat by a sudden force. He struggled to inhale and exhale from his nose. He would never expect anything like that. His gaze was glued to a number on the screen that kept increasing, it had gone in a flash from 0.37g to 5.8g and it continued to grow. Several seconds passed during which Jordan focused on his breathing only, as it had become quite a difficult activity.

At a certain point he heard Yan's voice again.

«Successful lift-off at 6:55 WST[23] on Kanya 7th, 239, from the Huygens Crater, with an acceleration of fifty-nine point twenty-six meters per second squared.»

The pression kept increasing. Jordan continued to remain still, his gaze fixed in front of him, imagining the explosive combustion, flames and sparks, happening just few meters behind his back, pushing him straight into space. In that moment he couldn't think of anything else.

«Time: plus one hundred seconds. Minus one minute and twenty seconds to orbit insertion.»

Jordan's gaze didn't move from the indicator showing the gravitational acceleration. It kept increasing continuously and ruthlessly. It had by now reached 10g. and Jordan wasn't breathing anymore. It was all about seconds and he continued to repeat it in his mind. Few seconds only and, in a way or another, it all would finish. When the indicator touched 11g, Jordan closed his eyes. He heard Yan's voice as a distant noise.

«Acceleration: one hundred and eight point eight meters per second squared. Time: minus five, four, three, two, one... Orbit insertion! Ladies and gentlemen, welcome in space!»

As soon as the countdown finished, the acceleration ceased. All of a sudden. Jordan was stricken with dizzi-

---

[23] WST: Western Syrtic Time, fuso orario da 52.5°E a 67.5°E.

ness and motion sickness, he felt like he was suddenly precipitating, but when he opened his eyes he noticed everything was still and he was still bounded to the seat. And as if by magic, everything seemed to become suddenly more lightweight. Or rather, totally weightless. The precipitation feeling persisted and Jordan went pale, but then he slowly realized that everything was fine. He saw the Odysseus manual floating placidly in front of them before Anna caught it to move it away. Rather than magic, that was physics. He was speechless, realizing he really was still alive, and a wave of intense euphoria spread inside him.

«How are you? Over» Yan's voice spoke again and this time Jordan heard it more clearly.

«I'm fine. Over» Anna's voice said.

It's been a while since Jordan had heard her speak. He felt relieved. Although she sounded confident, the boy noticed a hint of struggle in her voice. It had been no picnic. He let out all the air he had been holding in order to speak.

«I'm still alive. Over» he said.

«Ah! So amazing to hear you guys, you're in space, Holy Olympus! Time: minus sixty-three minutes to docking with Odysseus. Tell me, how was it to bear all those g's?»

Jordan noticed with delight that the accelerometer had calmed down and he returned to breath normally.

«If your bed had broken down, last night, and you had fallen on me, I would have suffered equally» Jordan explained ironically.

«Oh, listen to you! Take care how you speak, Jordan, remember your life is in my hands and I might accidentally make you crash on the ground.»

«You wouldn't dare.»

«Are you challenging me?»

«Now stop it, you two! Even kilometres away!» Anna blared.

Jordan chuckled.

All of a sudden they heard a weird buzz, an interference in the communication.

«Hey, what – are you receiving me? Over» Yan's voice called, all chopped up.

Jordan and Anna exchanged looks. Before they could answer, the sizzle increased intently before ceasing suddenly.

«Yan?» Anna asked, hesitantly.

No answer.

«Yan? Do you copy?» Jordan tried, but also that time no one answered.

«That's odd» Anna whispered almost to herself, furrowing her eyebrows.

«Now what?» Jordan asked.

The girl let out a nervous sigh.

«Time: minus one hour to docking. With or without Yan, we go on. At this point we have no other choice.»

* * *

Huygens Crater – some minutes before.

Three rovers of the Aresland crossed together through the plain of the Huygens Crater in the dim morning light. After the sudden missing of the three kids, everyone at the Aresland had developed a rescue plan and the following sol they had started down towards the Huygens: they knew perfectly that was their destination. Regardless of whether NASA agreed or not, they were going to go after them anyway, end of the issue.

«ETA to Rubentes Terrae?» a female voice resounded in the cockpit of the three rovers.

It was Ling Yu, onboard a Hong Se De Du rover together with Tain Tseng. George Jenner's voice replied from the central rover, he was with Alexander Miles.

«Ten minutes.»

Finally, onboard the Krasnij Gorod rover, there were Viktor Taykeev and Artëm Levitsky.

«Let's just hope it's not too late» Alexander said to himself, he was sitting in the passenger seat.

He didn't receive any answer.

«What do you think, Jenner? What will happen? It still sounds crazy to me that they've fled like that, by night!» concern and frustration were evident in his voice, no matter how hard he tried to hide it.

«I wouldn't define it crazy, Miles» he replied with caution.

«Don't tell me it was to be expected!»

«Actually, it was» he pronounced slowly.

Alexander threw his hands up in a distressed gesture and George continued.

«I've already told you, Miles. They might also be Martians, but they're human beings first of all. And human beings need to understand themselves, exploring the reality around them, pushing the limits to know them. They need to understand themselves and, in order to do it, they begin from the origins.»

«Risking their lives...» Alexander added bitterly.

«Let's get this straight. Anyone who ever even thought those three kids were going to resist twenty years of their young existence inside a closed and monotonous environment such as the Aresland is an imbecile.»

A moment of silence followed, Alexander's gaze was lost on the floor. He shook his head slightly and looked at George.

«Then why does Ad Martem 12 exist? That was the goal of the mission after all, wasn't it?»

George sighed profoundly, his gaze focused on the path.

«Because we are human beings, Miles. And even we are still trying to figure out who we are. Every single choice they make, every behaviour or action is characterizing of our species.»

Suddenly they heard a rumble from the radio and shortly after, Viktor Taykeev's voice spoke.

«Stop the rovers! Look South-Westward!»

«South-West, he said?» Alexander repeated. «What the?!»

In the meanwhile George did as he was told by the commander of the Krasnij Gorod and stopped the rover after turning it to the indicated direction. Both of them, as well as Ling and Tain, leaned forward to look outside the front window, but it didn't take long for them to notice it: a dot brighter than a star or a moon, followed by a fierce trail, was crossing harmoniously the still dark sky, following a curve trajectory. It could resemble a meteorite that, burning, was precipitating to the ground like a searing ball. With the only difference that that meteorite was actually rising in the sky. And it wasn't a meteorite, it was the ascent vehicle Argus. At that sight, George let out an incredulous chuckle.

«Good heavens, that's them!»

«That's them!» Alexander repeated with a way more desperate tone. «No, no, Jenner, no! It's impossible! There was nobody with them in the Control Room! Who launched that rocket?!»

George turned to look at Alexander in the eyes for the first time and lost that half smile that curved his lips. His gaze became suddenly serious and quite worried.

«Not all the three of them have left» he concluded. «One of them is controlling the launch from the ground, it's the only way.»

Alexander passed a hand a through his hair and returned to look at the rocket that was by now leaving the rarefied Martian atmosphere. It was barely visible and eventually it disappeared from sight. There was no way back. What was done was done. And all they could do was watch.

«I bet it's the Chinese» he commented. «He's expert of computer science.»

«Very, very likely! And the girl... Anna, she studied the rockets.»

«Indeed. And... Jordan...»

«The rover» they said at unison shortly after.

«Gosh, Jenner!» Alexander sighed, «What did we create! In the face of NASA and all its employees!»

«You're perfectly right... Come on, let's go get that deranged lunatic before he decides to come up with a way to leave as well. Because, I swear, if he found it I wouldn't be surprised.»

* * *

NASA Kennedy Space Center – *ten minutes later*

It was 4:55 pm on Monday when in an office of the Kennedy Space Center, a mobile phone rang. Claire Dennis was massaging her temples, recently she had spent the most of her nights awake in order to follow the development of the events and the updates from Mars and tiredness was taking over. She hated the sound of her mobile's ringtone. Every time it rang, it didn't bring but bad news. She passed her hands in her hair to fix it, she cleared her throat and picked up her smartphone. When she read on the screen the name of her vice director, Leonard Kelley, she was already certain that bad news was coming. She answered.

«Hello? Tell me… What? I've got to see it with my own eyes?! … I'm on my way» and she hung up the call.

She flew out of her office and headed to the control centre. After several corridors and stairs, Kelley appeared at her side.

«I called you as soon as we got to know, unfortunately there's nothing we can do» he said and shortly after they entered the large room where some analysts were scrutinizing their computers and a couple of people were at the bottom, speaking among themselves. Dennis immediately recognized Reynolds and Walker.

«Finally, Claire!» Reynolds urged as he saw Dennis approaching and walked to her.

«What's the matter?»

«Look» he answered nodding his head at the main screen, «Show the images, Terry» he addressed Coleman.

And soon those images appeared, they were in sequence, satellite photographs clearly showing an ascent vehicle leaving the surface. Dennis stood paralyzed for some moments, letting that information sink in.

«That is… the Argus?» she asked, even though she already knew the answer.

«Tell me I'm wrong» she turned to Reynolds, Walker and Kelley. «Tell me it's not the way I think.»

Reynolds nodded weakly and turned to look at the repeating sequence of images.

«They're coming, Claire» he said. «They're returning to Earth. They've just started the Nostoi Mission.»

Dennis sighed and moved her gaze back to the images as well.

«It is not possible… It seems already a miracle that they've survived the launch» she commented, then addressed Walker. «How many probabilities do they have to survive a landing?»

«The gravitational acceleration will be hard to bear for them, since they're used to the Martian one. Probably they'll lose consciousness, but I don't think they're risking their lives, unless they have an accident, of course. It's what comes afterwards that worries me. They won't be able to walk, they'll struggle to breath probably, also their heart will strain more. Even the sunlight will be a problem, on Mars it is reduced by seventy percent in respect of here. They risk problems to their sight without adequate protection. We need to study a solution.»

Some moments of silence passed while everyone considered and pondered the situation. Then Reynolds broke the silence.

«Director, what shall we do?»

Dennis turned to look him in the eyes with determination and then did the same with all the others.

«If the Nostoi Mission has started, we'll carry it out. We will do everything in our power to make sure they survive and finally we'll welcome them to Earth. We are NASA, we don't flinch before twists and turns.»

FOURTEEN
~ *88 sols before* ~

Jordan Miles didn't have many certainties, but one of those was that he had never lived in a place as weird as the Odysseus spaceship before. He had been travelling to Earth for three months by now, time seemed to pass inevitably slowly and often he felt alone, lost, despite there was Anna with him.

What freaked him out more than anything was staying next to a wall of the ship and thinking *That's it, it is all about some layers of metal and then nothing. There's absolutely nothing above me or beneath me. Everything's cold, dark, far and extremely dangerous. Some layers of metal and that's it.* He had spoken about it with Anna, discovering that often she found herself thinking about it too, but finally they decided that ignoring some thoughts would be better. They had to focus on the fact that soon they were going to reach the Earth and, most of all, they had to find something to do to fill the time.

But it wasn't certainly easy in that limited space, lacking of any sort of entertainment. One hundred and forty sols had passed since the launch. During those months Jordan had been studying the whole mission project and the spaceship neatly so that he would be able to make the right moves in case of emergency.

The descent module, with the three seats, was designed to host the passengers during the landing and it was linked, on the top, to the orbital module and, on the bottom, to the service module. Jordan knew that actually there was no up or down in space, but they needed them inside the ship in order to communicate positions, therefore Anna and he decided some reference points: the orbital module, that firstly pointed towards the tip of the rocket, was the "up" or "front", while the service module, which pointed towards the boosters, was the "down" or "back".

They hardly ever went to the service module, it had the shape of a cylinder and it contained the electrical current control panel, the temperature controller, the radio telemetry, the long-distance radio, the instruments to control and orientate the vehicle and some spare components. On the back, outside the module, there was the main engine of the spaceship while all around the ship there were some small engines which served for controlling the orientation. More than that, on the outside, two large solar panels unfolded for five meters and a half. In the orbital module, cylindrical as well, there was a small room containing the hygiene facilities. Everything else was packages containing supplies of food and water and then three sleeping bags fixed to the walls.

The orbital module ended with a small window on the cosmos, the thirty-centimeters thick double glazing contained liquid water in the middle which worked as a shielding from cosmic radiations.

An inflatable module was attached all around the orbital module, it was roughly four meters wide and it reminded a sort of space donut, as the two of them called it. It rotated at a frequency of 0.21 turns per second thus creating a centrifugal force that, on the edge of the donut, made it feel like there was a gravitational pull. Clearly 0.5g was slightly more than on Mars, but they needed it to gradually get used to the terrestrial gravity of 1g and to be able to stand on their feet and not to float as they did in the rest of the ship. Generally they used that space to do physical exercise with equipment or simply to walk and run: they did it for the majority of the time. And even though at the beginning they hated that sensation of extra weight to bear, they soon got used to it, even if they tended to get tired more quickly.

Then, almost miraculously, during the second month of trip, Anna had discovered a package containing books, cards and some consoles with videogames and since then they convinced themselves that the trip was going to be a little bit more bearable. They still measured time with the Martian system, they decided to keep it until they would land as they weren't used to the terrestrial one. The sols passed very similarly to one another: the first of the two who got up in the "morning" usually woke up also the other, then they had breakfast sitting in the inflatable module, they did some physical activity, they read or played something, they had lunch and then all the same repeated till dinner and finally they fell asleep in the donut or in the sleeping bags floating in the orbital module. After they had lost signal with Yan once they had entered the orbit, they didn't hear from him anymore. Not a message, not a sign, from anyone, from any permanent base. They were completely abandoned to themselves in the darkness of cosmos. And nothing was harder than accepting that situation.

It was almost 12:30 am of the eighty-seventh sol onboard the Odysseus. Jordan was floating next to a wall of the orbital module, absorbed in reading a thick book entitled "Schrödinger's cat", where a dude named Erwin, kind of crazy according to Jordan, was convinced that closing a cat in a box, together with a radioactive substance that might activate a sensor which would spread a poison or not, the cat was going to be both dead and alive until the box was opened and one would see if the cat was effectively dead or alive. Jordan wondered how could it be possible that a living being was dead and alive at the same time. He also wondered if cats were odd creatures, capable of such paranormal activities and no one ever told him. He had never seen a cat, he wasn't even completely sure of what was it exactly, apart from a carnivore mammal belonging to the family of felids.

«Jordan?» he heard his name called by the only other person in that place.

He slipped out of his thoughts and reemerged from the book. The voice came from the descent module.

«I'm here» he answered aloud and soon Anna came out from the hatch of the module.

The girl pushed herself forward with her hands and proceeded towards Jordan, upside-down. The boy wondered if it was him being inverted or Anna. Finally, however, he decided to turn in order to face her straight-forwardly.

«There you are» she said reaching him. «Let's grab something to eat and go to the donut. We need to talk.»

Jordan nodded, he abandoned *Schrödinger's cat* in midair and reached one of containers to gather a couple of tins to heat up. He tried to imagine what the girl had to tell him. He got very curious as recently they hadn't had much to talk about. They slipped through one of the four gaps that led into the donut and, holding onto a rope, they descended more and more quickly until they touched the border with their feet, under the influence of the artificial gravity. They sat there on the ground with crossed legs, facing each other, as a habit. Jordan opened a tin of rice and beans that he had just heated up in an oven, similar to that of the Atenavan, and began to eat his insipid meal with a steel fork. Anna opened a transparent bag containing some dehydrated vegetables where she had added some warm water.

«So, what's the matter?» Jordan asked, unable to keep himself anymore.

The girl plunged the fork into her greens and sighed.

«Do you realize it is impossible that after all this time still no one has tried to contact us?» she asked, going straight to the point.

«We've already talked about it» Jordan huffed, «We won't have more probabilities to be contacted just because we discuss it.»

«No» Anna convened, «But as I already said and I repeat, it is not possible. I'm sure they tried. That's why… I believe it is us who have a problem.»

Jordan abandoned his meal temporarily to focus all his attention on Anna and found she was staring at him. Her eyes were serious and determined. He saw a spark in her gaze that he knew well by now. And he began to fear what would follow.

«What kind of problem?» he articulated.

The girl lowered her gaze and began to fiddle with her fork while searching the best words to answer.

«Well… I'm not sure, but it might be that some antennas got damaged while we were in orbit. They could have been hit by, I don't know, space debris or things of that sort. If you remember… the communication with Yan ceased all of a sudden.»

Jordan sat in silence, studying his rice and considering her words. Effectively it was a very plausible theory and he wondered how could he have not thought about it before. Then a realization struck his mind and he raised his eyes back into Anna's.

«You're not going to go out there, I hope.»
The girl pursed her lips.

«It's our only option.»
Jordan shook his head briefly.

«Do you have any idea how risky that is?» he snapped.

«Yes» she replied immediately, «I've been thinking it through for five sols, Jordan, I decided to try.»

«It's too dangerous. Can we not leave things the way they are and just go on?»

«No, we can't. Once we reach the terrestrial orbit we'll have to get in touch with Earth in order to land.»

«Then let it be me to go out, I don't want...» he stopped suddenly and dropped his gaze to the floor.

He was about to say "I don't want something bad to happen to you", but he failed.

«What?» Anna encouraged him in a low voice.
He swallowed.

«Well, you'd handle it all better than me in here, if necessary.»

Jordan took a glimpse of a disappointed twinkle in the girl's eyes, who probably expected him to conclude the sentence the way he had thought it before. But maybe it was just him, for it disappeared too quickly and her expression returned stony.

«Forget about it, Jordan. I've been studying this ship more than you and I know how to move on the outside. I need you to stay in the descent module where there are the computers and tell me if there's any signal recovery.»

Jordan stared at her in silence. He wanted to tell her he was afraid something bad would happen to her, he was afraid he could lose her and all of that was highly risky and he wouldn't be able to go on without her, but not a word left his mouth, not a sound, as if he had lost the ability to speak. He wanted to tell her all of that, but on the other hand he didn't because he feared what could happen. Therefore he did nothing but nod slightly because that was his only option.

They finished their dishes in silence and then they headed to the service module where there was a small airlock and Jordan helped Anna prepare for that space-walk. The suit was white and incredibly big. He helped her slip into it and to seal it, then he connected it to the miniature Life Support System that she carried on her shoulders like a backpack. He tied the toolbox to a belt of the suit so that she wouldn't lose it and then moved around her as Yan had done with both of them, to dou-ble-check everything. She remained still, her movements were very much limited by that spacesuit. They took some more time to run all the verifications on every sys-tem in order to make sure the suit had no pressure losses and everything worked properly.

«You're fine. Everything's okay?»

«Everything's okay» she confirmed.

Then Jordan pushed a button next to the airlock, opening it, and they entered together. There was a rope rolled up next to the external hatch, Jordan grabbed it and attached the clasp to Anna's suit, so that she wouldn't fly away in space. The two looked at each oth-er in the eyes through the suit's visor.

«Listen-» Jordan began, uncertain. «Just, you better come back, you hear me? Alive, I mean.»

The girl nodded with decision and then let out a tense chuckle at his last statement. Jordan backed away out of the airlock. He nodded once again at Anna and then pushed the button again. The airlock closed. Within few moments, Anna was going to be in the frigid vacuum of space.

Once in the descent module, Jordan slipped into the narrow compartment with the three seats and the on-board instrumentation. He sat in the center and put on a pair of headphones with a microphone.

«Anna, do you copy? Over» he called.

The answer arrived shortly after and Jordan took the first sigh of relief: it meant the antenna for the extravehicular activities communication was still intact.

«I copy you. I just got out of the airlock. It's bone-chilling.»

Jordan could perceive the deep emotion leaking out in her voice.

«I imagine, but stay focused and don't waste time.»

«Have you forgotten who you're talking to, Jordan?»

«Now's not the time.»

«So, hear me out. There are two computers. The one on the left deals with communications and telemetry, you follow me?»

«I follow you, I'm in front of it.»

«You have to try send a message to the Aresland. Everything's automatic, just find the right chat-room.»

«I proceed. Where are you?»

«At the moment I'm... moving around the service module. The antennas are on the opposite side of the airlock. Right now I could literally sit on a solar panel if I wanted.»

«Please, don't.»

Meanwhile Jordan inspected the entire computer on the left and after ending up on a section showing the telemetry until the point when all the communications had shut down, he found the way to send messages. He also found the possibility to contact Houston on Earth, but he opted for the Aresland as he was told to do.

He typed "Odysseus spaceship here, are you receiving us?" and pushed the "send" button, but a red text appeared right away on the screen, saying "No signal". Jordan read it out loud in the microphone.

«Normal» Anna commented as expecting it. «Okay, I'm on the opposite side of the service module. I see the antennas and...»

«And?»

«I need to take a closer look.»

Jordan sighed and a good minute of silence passed while the boy's eyes remained fixed on that red text on the screen while hoping with all of himself it was nothing too bad.

«Oh...» he heard Anna's voice and he straightened up on his seat.

«What? What do you see?»

«As I imagined. It's the bigger antenna, the high-gain one. The parabola. It seems impossible it's still here, I swear» a nervous giggle followed.

«What's the problem?»

«It fell off. It's hanging on a wire only. I think one of the nuts that kept it in place wasn't closed well and it ceded under an impact, followed by all the others.»

«You think you can repair it?»

«Yeah, it's nothing really. It'll take a moment.»

«Alright, hurry up.»

«Don't rush me!»

«The longer you stay out there, the riskier it gets. Just do the work and come back.»

«Be silent one moment, please» she pleaded and Jordan sighed impatiently.

Several, long moments passed before Anna spoke again.

«Now the antenna's in position. I'm about to tighten the third bolt.»

«Still no signal.»

«It's okay, it'll take some minutes.»

Jordan was about to take a sigh of relief, convinced that everything was going to be fine. But when he heard Anna's voice again, his heartbeat accelerated suddenly and he went pale.

«No no no no no!» he heard her shriek.

«What happened? Are you alright?» he jumped up, alarmed.

225

«No! Damn it!» she continued with a frustrated tone.

Jordan was horrified, the girl breathed as if to calm herself down.

«I lost the toolbox, it flew away. I accidentally hit it and now the antenna is fixed with three nuts instead of four!» she explained with glum voice, then she resumed with an almost amused hint, «Even two screwdrivers got out of it and are now floating away in different directions.»

Jordan rolled his eyes and hid his face in his hands while he realized nothing bad had happened and Anna was still fine.

«You scared me to death, you know that? Don't dare do that again!»

«This is still an awful situation! It isn't well assured and it could break again! And… For Olympus' sake, wait a second.»

«What now!?» Jordan asked once again with his hands in his hair and almost mocking a desperate tone.

«I can't believe it, that wasn't only debris! It seems we've gone through an entire swarm of meteorites» she sighed, daunted. «One of the two Star Trackers was destroyed, there are just some pieces left here.»

«But there are two, right?» Jordan pointed out.

«Yes, indeed. The backup one was activated automatically. Jordan, do you realize what trouble we're in? If we happen to meet another swarm we'll be left without communication and orientation! We'd be lost in the fuckin' nothing!»

Jordan was about to answer, when suddenly a brief notification alarm started off on the computer in front of him, capturing his gaze. He saw that the text "No signal" had disappeared and his message had been sent. Since the signal took about seven minutes to reach Mars from there, he wondered how long would it take for them to read it and answer.

«The signal's back!» he exclaimed in the microphone, «The message was sent!»

«Well, at least that.»

«Reenter, now. I'll wait for you in front of the airlock.»

«Fine, I'm coming back to the airlock. Over.»

Jordan took off the headphones and sneaked out of the descent module, heading back to the airlock. He wasn't sure if he felt better or worse than before. But at least Anna was fine and in that moment it was the only thing that mattered to him.

At least half an hour had passed since the signal had returned. Jordan was helping Anna get rid of the space-suit when suddenly a notification alarm started off from the descent module. They flew into it as soon as they finished the work and briefly exchanged looks before opening the chat-room with the Aresland. There was an answer.

[Aresland]: YOU'RE ALIVE THEN! Maybe you're not aware of it, but for three damn months the whole Martian population has feared the worst for you! Ah, I forgot, but probably you already figured it out... This is Yan talking, directly from the Hong Se De Du's main hall, Aresland station, Hellas Planitia, Mars. I'll write a quite long message because a chat with short and immediate messages is kind of far-fetched considering the distance and the time-delays. I got to tell you some things, I'll leave the questions to the end. So, the communication link had just shut down when the base was taken over by an enemy army... Alright, just kidding. Six people from the Aresland arrived with three rovers. I admit I was a little scared at the beginning, I thought they would scold me brutally, but it didn't happen. Well, of course they weren't all smiles and hugs, but when they asked why had we done it and I answered "Because it was written in the instructions for the Nostoi Mission" they didn't reply. I think I convinced them. For the entire trip back they explained to me that we weren't ready yet for that mission, speaking in terms of physical development etcetera, and so you might encounter quite serious problems on Earth. That's why they kept it hidden: they feared that what happened would actually happen. However, useless to say that once I got home I've been grounded for one month: no digital devices for twenty-eight long sols. No videogames at all, can you believe it? However I'm just fine now. Everyone here was uncertain on whether being terribly mad at us or admire us, but eventually they all passed to the second option. We've launched a kind of rocket with the two of you onboard, Holy Olympus! Then we've tried repeatedly to make a contact with you, but every attempt was in vain and so we all began to worry seriously. You have no idea of the happiness to know you're still alive! By the way, there's everyone here around me right now, literally everyone. There has been a kind of explosive party when I announced I had received a message from you. They say hi and wish you a safe trip and landing. Ah, Jordan, Hans is telling me to remind you to visit the German countryside. While, Anna, your father says on the Odysseus there's a package with many books you may enjoy. So, this is it. How are you? What happened and how did you solve it? You can't imagine how amazing it is to be able to communicate with you again.

I'm looking forward to your answer within the following twenty minutes.

I wish I were there with you, with mind and heart, I'm always there.

See you soon,

Yan.

Jordan and Anna read that message together, silently, smiling occasionally. The girl was on the verge of new tears, but she tried hard to hold them back. They read the message several times before deciding together what to write back.

[Odysseus]: Hello Nunki, you have no idea how heavy your absence is! We miss you so much, sincerely. To answer your question: we're fine, we're alive and everything's alright... or almost. We're really sorry for your grounding and, look, we'd almost feel compassion for you if it weren't for the fact that we're in way worse conditions. Not to mention that there's nothing to do up here apart from reading, playing some quite boring video-games and do gym and time seems to never pass! Anyways, after we reached the orbit, we collided with a swarm of meteorites and we haven't come out unharmed: the high-gain antenna fell off and one of the two Star Trackers was completely destroyed. Just tosol Anna got out to readjust the antenna, but she accidentally lost the toolbox before she could tighten the fourth bolt. While for what regards the Tracker, there's nothing we can do, there's the backup one. So, briefly, here is the situation: we have three months of trip left onboard a ship with an unstable antenna and only one Star tracker. Suppose we encounter other dangerous space debris. If the antenna breaks completely, we won't be able to communicate with anyone anymore. If the Tracker breaks, we'll lose ourselves in space. On top of that, it is our understanding from your message that the landing itself will be equally dangerous for us, so... wonderful.
Whatever will happen, we've loved you. Say hi to everyone. We'll do our best to stay alive.
See you soon,
Jordan and Anna.

P.S. From Jordan: tell my father I'll say hi to mum for him.

FIFTEEN
~ *The sol before* ~

NASA Johnson Space Center – 5 days before

The cold sun of September was high in the sky of Houston, its wintery rays softly caressed the building of Johnson Space Center, occasionally hidden away by clouds. Claire Dennis was in her office, busy signing and revising some official documents. It was an incredibly beautiful day, quiet and peaceful.

Since several weeks now, Dennis had begun to persuade herself of the fact that everything was going to proceed smoothly, yet she knew by experience that that tranquility wasn't destined to last. Just when she was about to convince herself that she was going to have an unproblematic working day, someone knocked on her door.

«Come in» she called without lifting her gaze from her matters.

She heard the door opening but no step came forward.

«Claire, you're needed in the briefing room» Tom Reynolds' voice spoke.

Dennis raised her head. There was one only reason why Reynolds would come to call her at that hour.

«Tom, why am I having a bad feeling?» she asked casually, returning to flip through the documents on her desk.

«Come and find out.»

She sighed profoundly and nodded before joining her colleague in the corridor.

«So» she began while walking at a deliberate pace, «What else have those three Martians in-search-of-identity messed up this time?»

Reynolds hid a chuckle.

«Nothing dangerous, they've been good kids.»

Dennis' expression darkened as she wondered for what terrifying reason had she been called then.

«How bad is it?» she asked seriously.

«Oh, it isn't» Reynolds answered calmly, «For now.»

They entered the briefing room finding some representatives of the Ad Martem 12 and Nostoi teams. There was even John Torres, older and retired many years since. He insisted on being there even if he wasn't the mission's director anymore.

«It's the only solution we have, we must contact them immediately» a young man of the Nostoi team was saying with urgency.

«Contact who?» Dennis asked aloud as she entered and everyone turned to her.

«The Odysseus crew, ma'am» the man replied.

«They must slow down the ship» Agatha Quinn spoke up, she was the space manoeuvre specialist. «They're moving very rapidly, it's about thirteen point five kilometers per second. And this velocity doesn't guarantee an optimal orbital insertion.»

«It sure doesn't! At this speed they'd see the Earth in passing and bye bye forever, to infinity and beyond!» the young man interjected.

Agatha Quinn sent him a brief glare for his tone, then returned to look at Dennis with a sigh.

«In short: they slow down... or it's over.»

The hall fell in silence.

«What's the plan?» Dennis spoke.

«My team and I have first of all taken into consideration a deceleration using the retrorockets, but we've found it wouldn't be efficient enough. Therefore, given these circumstances, the most ideal and practicable solution would be a flyby of the Moon. By flying over it very very closely, its gravity would slow down the ship enough to allow a direct reentry in the atmosphere, without risks. Of course, "without" so to say.»

«At this moment they are more than four million and a half kilometers away from the Moon, about four days of trip. In order to perform a flyby the orbital trajectory must be slightly modified and it must happen at least two days before. This is why we must contact them as soon as possible. There's their life at stake» the young man concluded.

«This is a substantial reason, the manoeuvre is an immediate priority» Dennis commented with determination, sharing a look with Reynolds and Kelley, who nodded. «Proceed to contact them immediately.»

The young man and Quinn nodded and everyone rushed out of the room to head to the control room. The administrator, the vice and the associate stayed.

«How long till the landing?» Dennis asked crossing her arms and leaning against the central table.

«It's a matter of days by now» Kelley replied.

«After such a trip... Humanly speaking, I can't do but hope for the best for their health. And that they survive the reentry.»

«You're right. Also, after living for years on a planet with a lower gravity than here, they've spent six more months in a microgravity environment. We know well how much it damages muscles and bones.»

Reynolds sighed.

«Will they continue the mission, afterwards?» he asked almost to himself. «I mean, will they go back to Mars? Will they take the colonization forward?»

«This will be up to them» Dennis replied seriously, «We won't choose for them. Not again.»

They didn't speak further, the hall fell to silence. The silence was occasionally interrupted by thoughtful sighs. Just when Dennis was about to decide to get back to her office, the door burst open and the three turned to it at the same time. A pale, distressed man who had taken part at the briefing shortly before, seemed on the verge of fainting.

«Ma'am» he addressed Dennis, trying (in vain) to hide the torment that quivered within him. «The Odysseus' main antenna has been damaged. There's no way to communicate with the kids.»

* * *

Odysseus Spaceship

Jordan couldn't take his eyes off of it anymore. The truth was he had never seen anything so beautiful before. The Earth was always closer, bigger, more real. The photographs he had seen gave just a weak idea of what was in front of him. It wasn't a dream, a mystery, a word or an image. He felt like he could touch it if he had reached out. It had begun like a far blue dot that eventually grew, approached, particularized. By now they could make out the shapes and the colours of the big continents floating on that incredible amount of blue water. Every sol they observed the clouds, white and grayish masses in continuous change of shape and disposition, as if they danced harmoniously and frantically, grazing the surface. In the sunlight they observed the blue shades of the seas, clearer next to the shores, more intense in the middle of oceans. By night they witnessed the magnificence of the greenish auroras swaying towards the North Pole. Since a few weeks the two of them were spending the majority of their sols observing that breathtaking spectacle. There was nothing more beautiful.

Luckily they hadn't encountered other problems during the trip. When they had begun to see the Earth they felt a little less alone, but still it was hard. The continuous atmosphere of tension played tricks on their nerves and Jordan happened to hear Anna burst into tears a couple of times and he never knew whether to leave her alone, try to comfort her or cry with her. But in the end no, he would never cry. They decided to talk, to tell each other anything that crossed their minds because they found out that talking made them feel better. The majority of their confessions were about the fact that they were tired of being far away from any security, far away from the Aresland, from Yan. They wanted to have something solid under their feet again. They were nostalgic for their safe rooms, their warm and soft beds, the familiar faces of the members of the bases. They had taken the habit to communicate with Mars once a month, sending messages where they reported their health status and they assured a good progression of the trip. For a few weeks though they had received no message, but it didn't seem to worry them too much. They were sure they would get a new message soon. A really long time had passed and, even if they were used to it, every sol was a new struggle. But they had to resist. They knew they were almost there. For better or worse.

That sol, on Mars as well as on the Odysseus, was sol martius 12 Dhanus 240. Jordan and Anna had just finished their dinner and were sprawled in the donut, next to some empty food cans and bags. They were playing at making a ball bounce on the ceiling as it would return back to them slowly and then always quicker, under the pull of the artificial gravity. At the moment it was the most interesting activity they had found.

«Is there something of Earth you would like to see in particular?» Jordan asked at a certain point, to make conversation.

«Everything, I guess» the girl replied.

«But something in particular?»

She sighed thoughtfully.

«Maybe the sea. Because I can't even imagine how could it be to see so much water all at once right in front of me.»

«Mmm, I agree.»

«What about you?»

«Cats.»

«Cats?»

«Cats. It seems they're capable of supernatural activities.»

«Ah, really? For example?»

«Being dead and alive at the same time, but only when you're not looking at them.»

The girl burst out laughing.

«What?»

The girl continued to laugh, incapable of keeping herself.

«What, why would you laugh? Stop it.»

She almost had tears in her eyes.

«Cats have no supernatural power» Anna explained as she got a grip on herself, «Erwin Schrödinger just wanted to demonstrate that quantum mechanics applied to macroscopic physical systems provides paradoxical results. No living being can be also dead at the same time.»

«Clear» Jordan replied with a disappointed tone, «Then, I don't know. Maybe the rain... Water falling from the sky, can you believe it? These terrestrials have water everywhere and in any form while we... well, apart from the ice we have to recycle everything.»

«Some people on Earth die of thirst.»

«Good one.»

«I'm not joking, I read it.»

«Correct me if I'm wrong, but isn't Earth covered in water for the seventy percent? I mean, we basically don't have it apart from the poles but it's iced! And yet we live decently.»

«Honestly I don't know what to say. We still have a lot to learn.»

The silence was suddenly broken by a notification alarm, similar to the one that informed them about a new message, but this time it didn't stop after just a couple of trills. Jordan and Anna looked at each other.

«It must be Yan» Anna assumed before standing up, not too sure of her words. «A little more than a month has passed since the last time, isn't it?»

Jordan did the same.

«Yes, but it didn't ring like that... What if it's not Yan? What if something happened?»

The girl didn't answer, Jordan noticed a worried twinkle in her eyes. They clung onto a rope descending from one of the four gaps and, with a jump, they flew back up until they came out in the orbital module. They passed in front of the window, next to the sleeping bags and slipped into the descent module where the alarm came from. They took their usual seats and observed the screen, dominated by a flashing red symbol.

Anna went pale, immediately realizing.

A line, that Jordan imagined was representing their trajectory, curved around a circle and then continued forward.

«What does it mean?» he asked frowning, but he received no answer.

Then he moved his gaze above the flashing figure.

«And what's that count-down? What's going to happen in two hours?»

He felt his mouth going dry. Whatever it was, it was no good.

The girl passed her hands in her hair, it seemed she was holding her breath while her eyes were fixed on that flashing image, as if she was lost in deep thoughts and measurements.

Suddenly, just like that, she began to open all the drawers under the computers, frantically looking for something in that confusion of papers, instructions and manuals. Jordan was crossed by a shiver.

«Are you going to answer me?!» Jordan raised his tone and Anna stopped frozen, as if waking up from a nightmare.

She raised her gaze to look at him in the eyes, considering whether to speak, then she resumed her search.

«You don't want to know» she said simply in a low voice.

Jordan grabbed her arm before she could open another drawer and she returned to look at him.

«You tell me what's going on. Now» his tone was resolute and didn't admit replies.

Anna swallowed.

«We... we are fastly approaching Earth» Anna explained trying to keep her voice firm as much as she could. «Too fastly. We risk a flyby.»

Jordan continued to look at her in the eyes while cold sweat formed on his forehead. The girl continued to speak.

«Flyby means that we're too fast for the planet's gravity to keep us in orbit around it» she glanced briefly at the count-down, «If we go on like this, in two hours we'll be lost in deep space.»

Jordan forgot how to breathe. He hid his face in his hands and cursed silently, letting himself lean against the back of the seat.

«Maybe I can avoid it» Anna resumed, giving up her search in the drawers and moving her hair away from her face. Jordan gave her his full attention. «We need to hurry, we have to stop the rotation and get ready for the descent. There's a manoeuvre that might allow us to land, but I can't find any document with written steps and... Holy Olympus, alright... I studied it, I know it. I can do it, or rather, I have to. It's our only way to try and make it alive.»

«Keep calm» Jordan said softly seeing how his friend began to fidget her hands. Staying calm in such a situation was paradoxical, but that just wasn't the right time to panic. «So. What is it all about?»

* * *

NASA Johnson Space Center

«How much longer?» Torres asked with urgency.

«Fifteen minutes» Coleman replied from his position, «Fifteen minutes and we're ready for the transmission.»

«It's too much, too much!» Torres repeated, «In any case, it will be too late!»

«John, we have no alternatives» James Walker intervened to calm him down, «We'll use the whole power of the retrorockets and with a trajectory closer to Earth they'll also be hindered by the atmosphere.»

«It's not going to work!» Torres concluded stubbornly, bringing his hands to his head and turning back.

Given the impossibility to communicate with the ship through the long-rage antenna, NASA had come to choose the most drastic and safe solution: the huge radiotelescope of Arecibo in the island of Puerto Rico. The power of its signal was going to be sufficient to send any kind of message to the Odysseus, which would have received through the smaller short-range antennas. The problem with the radiotelescope was that it was set to receive messages though, not to send them. Computer scientists from all around the world got to work together to reprogram it, all the ongoing scientific experiments at the Arecibo were suspended and dozens of physicists studied the alignment of the radiotelescope with the ship on dangerous approach. All of that had taken about three days and a half of intense day and night work in order to reduce the timeframes to the minimum and everything was almost ready.

It was now a matter of minutes, the alignment was almost completed, the tension was palpable inside NASA's buildings as well as at the Arecibo and in the entire world. When suddenly the silence was broken by a voice.

«Stop everything!» it was almost a shout coming from Agatha Quinn, sitting in front of another computer on the opposite side of the room. «Walker, Torres, come here! Quick!»

The two didn't hesitate to rush.

«What's the matter?» Walker asked observing the computer showing a simulation of the path the ship was on.

«I've registered a slight change in the Odysseus trajectory, they've modified the orbital trajectory» she underlined.

«The rotation stopped!» another technician said aloud.

«It seems...» Quinn continued, observing the computer screen intently, «It seems they're coming straight for our atmosphere... »

All the murmurs in the hall died down as everyone's attention turned to the woman. Quinn raised her gaze on Walker and Torres, furrowing her eyebrows, demanding answers.

«My God» Torres whispered at a certain point, still focused on the screen. «They must have realized the danger they're in and... I know what they're going to do.»

In that moment Dennis entered the room.

«I can't believe they know this manoeuvre, it was used at the time of Apollo» he continued, «It's called boost-glide, but it's also known as skip entry. The descent capsule arrives at full speed into the atmosphere and uses it to slow down. It bounces on it like a flat rock on the surface of a lake before dive-bombing into it. It is... the most complicated and dangerous reentry manoeuvre in the history of spaceflight.»

«The alignment is complete, we're ready for transmission» Coleman spoke up.

«As I recall, the Odysseus wasn't projected for a boost-glide» Dennis intervened.

«No» Torres agreed, «This isn't how it was supposed to land. But the shape of the reentry capsule might allow it anyway.»

«If that's true, then it means that there's no instruction to perform it onboard. And if they miss the angle of attack it would be fatal.»

Torres pursed his lips and nodded.

«Yes» he said, then addressed Coleman. «That's why we have the biggest radiotelescope in the world! Change of plan, forget the retrorockets and send all the data to perform a boost-glide!»

241

«Can you believe it?» Kelley whispered to Reynolds, «I've never managed to make a rock bounce on the surface of a lake and those kids are about to make a damn spaceship bounce on the atmosphere!» he passed a hand on his forehead.

«Of course» Reynolds smirked. «This isn't their problem. They're Martians. Maybe they don't even know what a lake is.»

* * *

Odysseus Spaceship – few minutes before

Something was different in the air. There was that tension that precedes something important, upsetting. It was too late to back out by now, they could only go straight for their unknown destiny. The truth was they didn't have much to bring with them in the descent module. The books, the games or food served for the trip and now they didn't feel like they needed to save them. The only thing that really mattered to Jordan was the photograph with his mother. He had guarded it carefully, as if it was a piece of crystal, until that moment.

Anna and he had spent few minutes rushing from one module to another in the ship, evaluating quickly what was important to be kept and kind of saying goodbye to those areas where they had been living for one hundred and seventy-five sols. They had just finished the tour and they had stopped to observe the capsule onboard of which they were going to precipitate to the ground with no way to escape. Jordan felt his stomach twisting as he observed Anna's distressed yet determined expression, but he didn't show it. He only wanted it to happen soon and quick. The wait felt more frustrating and painful than the landing itself.

«Shall we wear the suits?» he suggested with a firm tone.

Anna moved her unquiet gaze on him. Jordan saw his feelings reflected into her eyes and could tell the girl noticed it too. She swallowed.

«Yes, we must. The longer we wait, the harder it will be to adjust the course.»

Jordan clenched his teeth and nodded rigidly.

The ship's clock struck midnight, officially starting the one hundred and seventy-sixth sol of trip. The last one. Yet time, by now, seemed to have stopped. Anna was carefully sealing Jordan's suit, just like he had done with her few moments before. Fulminous and precise movements, attentive and cautious, in silence. They were in front of the window showing planet Earth in all her majesty. The night was advancing on the surface, hiding in the murk every colour, shape, ocean, dragging the lights of the big cities that turned on one after the other, slowly.

«Too tight?» the girl asked at a certain point, with a low voice, as if she was afraid to disturb that calm.

«No, no, it's fine» Jordan replied.

He turned to completely face the Earth outside the window, his eyes scrutinizing it all for one last time. He perceived Anna moving at his side next to the window and doing the same.

«What... what risks are we running? I mean, what can go wrong?» Jordan asked cautiously, without moving his gaze away.

He heard a long sigh and psychologically prepared himself to the worst.

«Principally we're running two risks. The first: mistaking the atmospheric entry and therefore exploding. The second: failing the so called rebound and therefore being shot out of orbit and being lost forever in space.»

Jordan stood silent for several moments, letting that information sink in.

«Tell me the truth» the boy swallowed hard, «How many probabilities do we have to make it?»

The following silence did nothing but increase the tension in the air.

«Few. Very few» her voice came out weak, «Actually… the success is almost impossible.»

Jordan's stomach twisted and his mouth went dry. He perceived his eyes tingling, but he would allow not a tear to escape.

«You've always known, haven't you?» his voice broke in the end, but he tried to hide it, «Since the very beginning.»

«I was aware of the risks as were you» she replied firmly.

«And you've insisted to come nonetheless… You shouldn't have–»

«Stop it now!» she cut him off, «Get this argument out of your head, I had my own reasons!»

«I've got my mother on Earth, but you? What reason could you ever have to risk your life at this point?» Jordan raised his tone as well.

«It's… I…»

«You shouldn't have come!»

«I came because of *you*!» she snapped all of a sudden.

Only then he turned to really look at her and met her gaze, his heart pounding as he wondered if he had heard well.

«What?» it came out almost inaudible.

She had her scarlet hair gathered up with a scrunchie so that it wouldn't float wildly in microgravity, but some locks escaped anyways. She had a spray of freckles on her little nose. Her eyes were as blue as some shades of the ocean Jordan had seen next to the shores. She was the most beautiful creature he had ever met, she was as beautiful as the Earth, full of the same light, of its apparently peaceful air, but with a spirit as devastating as the Earth's hurricanes. He thought it openly. He couldn't hold that thought, that feeling back anymore. It was too strong. Anna turned again to look outside the window, as if she was unable to hold his stare.

«I just wanted to… to do something with you» she explained «Something extraordinary and… unforgettable. With you. Well, okay, it's not as simple as that, I…» she swallowed and slightly shook her head, lacking of words.

Jordan was totally captured and paralyzed. He noticed a slight blush on her cheeks.

«I don't think I'm someone worth risking your life for» he admitted in a murmur.

Anna lowered her gaze before shaking her head like forcing herself to return to reality.

«Jordan, listen, we must go or it'll be too late» she turned away from the window and met his gaze, changing topic.

The worry in her eyes dragged him back to the reality of the situation. He felt his heart pounding and his stomach twisting. He nodded once and swallowed.

«Ready to jump?» he asked trying to keep his voice steady.

Their gazes were glued to each other.

«We're here, we can't back out anymore. Even if I weren't, who would really care?» she slightly shrugged.

The boy stopped to consider her words, but the answer escaped his lips before he could decide to speak.

«I would.»

She looked taken off guard by those words as much as him, but she seemed to recover quickly and that time Jordan couldn't read her gaze, full of something new. She slowly raised a hand to stroke his cheek.

«Jordan…» she pronounced slowly, her voice soaked in tenderness, fear, trepidation.

Then everything happened fast. They found themselves closer than ever before and, while time stopped, the Earth under them ceased to rotate, the stars shone brighter and the Northern lights became more intense, they kissed. Their helmets floated forsaken behind them and not even the lumbering suits stopped them. In that moment, in a distant part of his still conscious mind, Jordan thought that in life he wouldn't need anything else. That if the end was to come, it may also come and he would have no regret. In that surreal dimension without space or time, Jordan finally felt in peace with himself. He felt as if all his questions had found an answer, as if every doubt had vanished, together with every fear. But everything that begins will end at a certain point and that happened. They both blushed and found themselves unable to look at each other in the eyes while an air of embarrassment seemed to float in microgravity around them. Jordan swallowed and grabbed his helmet in a flash, Anna did the same.

«Let's get moving» the girl ordered shyly and floated towards the descent module.

Jordan couldn't hold back a smile as he followed her.

He did it, after all.

They took the central and left seats. They put on their helmets and sealed them. They looked at each other in the eyes and Jordan nodded once, so Anna returned to focus on the control panel in front of her.

«I proceed to stop the rotation» her voice articulated, spreading in Jordan's helmet.

Her expert hands moved on the screen in front of her.

«Three, two, one» she counted.

A sudden lateral force pressed Jordan against the wall of the capsule. He tried to hold himself onto the seat with his hands, but the bulky suit impeded his movements and the belts already did the work.

«We're almost there...» Anna commented between her teeth.

Shortly after the force stopped and Jordan could take a breath.

«I modify the orbital trajectory» Anna declared and in that moment Jordan felt a force pressing him back against the seat, but it was less strong this time. «T minus fifty minutes to the contact with the atmosphere.»

Some minutes of silence passed.

«What will you do once on Earth?» Jordan asked at a certain point.

«I think I'll go to Russia first of all, I'll look for my relatives. Then I'll visit. As I already said, I'd like to see the sea. What about you?»

«I'll find my mother. Then I'll explore. After all, that's what I'm best at.»

Before Anna could answer, a sudden notification alarm resounded in the capsule, capturing the attention of the two guys on the communication computer.

«Yan hasn't chosen a good moment» Jordan commented.

«Open it!» Anna ordered.
The boy did as he was told, and...

«This isn't Yan!» Jordan exclaimed before furrowing his eyebrows and taking a better look. «It's... Earth?! There's a series of... codes and values.»

«Boost... Boost-Glide Manoeuvre!» Anna read with increasing euphoria, «Jordan! It's a NASA document, it's the instructions!»

«They saved our lives?»
The girl returned serious.

«No, they've given us a possibility» she focused on the computer. «Separation from the orbital module: in three, two, one.»

The structure trembled. Anna was following the instructions with meticulousness as she brought the descent module, separated from the rest of the ship, on the right trajectory and tilting it with the right angle of attack. They were at about two hundred and fifty kilometers from the Earth's surface and the capsule was beginning to feel the atmosphere's friction. Jordan was paralyzed.

«T minus ten seconds to atmospheric entry, two hundred and thirty kilometres from the surface, entry speed: thirteen kilometres per second» Anna's voice declared.

Jordan prepared himself.

«Atmospheric entry at one hundred and twenty kilometres from the surface, T minus five, four, three, two, one.»

The entire capsule vibrated, more and more intensely and, almost all of a sudden, a flare of light penetrated both the capsule's portholes. Jordan couldn't do anything but move his gaze towards his porthole, petrified. Real blazing flames were enraging out there and surrounded the entire capsule. They were a fireball in free fall. And everything was becoming more and more heavy. Jordan felt his head heavy, his arms heavy, his legs heavy. He realized he couldn't move. The pressure on him was increasing constantly, unrelenting, merciless. He felt he was suffocating. His lungs begged for air but he couldn't breathe enough. He felt a weight on his chest, as if all of his organs were compressing. He struggled to move his gaze on the screen on the right in front of them and, just like during the launch of some months before, he noticed the speed with which the gravity increased, weighing on them.

«Five hundred nautical miles» Anna's breathless voice murmured, «Sixty-one kilometres from the surface.»

Jordan didn't know how long he was going to be able to still resist. He returned to look at the flames wrapping the capsule.

«Velocity» he heard Anna's far voice, «Nine point seven kilometres per second. Seven hundred nautical miles, fifty-three kilometres from the surface... Pull up!»

All the force seemed to suddenly squeeze Jordan in another direction and the boy perceived an uncontrollable motion sickness. He clenched his teeth. The sensation continued harshly for some seconds, but suddenly everything seemed to cease.

«T plus one minute and fifty-six seconds. One hundred and eighty-two kilometres from the surface, velocity: eight point eight kilometres per second. We're out of the atmosphere, we proceed to the ballistic coast. Final atmospheric reentry at T plus four minutes and forty-four seconds.»

For the rest of the time there was nothing but silence. Jordan could only think of the fact that he wasn't sure if he could resist that sensation one more time. In a distant part of his consciousness though he was rejoicing: they hadn't exploded in the atmosphere. Or at least, not yet.

Time passed quickly, Anna announced the atmospheric reentry and the vibrations returned, together with the increasing gravitational pull. The clock kept ticking, the pressure increasing.

«First parachute opening» Anna's weak voice warned, followed by a powerful blow that left both of them definitely breathless.

He wondered if that was really going to be the end. He saw Anna's shaking hands moving one last time, performing the same steps she had done shortly before. This time she didn't say anything though, he simply felt the second blow as the second parachute opened. His sight got blurry. With a last, desperate attempt to get some air, he struggled to turn his head slightly towards Anna and it seemed she tried to do the same, as if she had realized.

His eyes called, hers answered.

Then everything went black.

SIXTEEN
~ The day after ~

Jordan didn't know what was happening. He had already tried a couple of times to wake up from that heavy and kind of empty sleep. But every time he returned to his senses, he perceived an odd pain in different parts of his body and if he tried to open his eyes, it seemed he couldn't see anything. He was certain that the descent capsule had crashed on the ground. All the lights seemed to be turned off, maybe there was not an ounce of current anymore. He didn't know where the girl was, he only hoped she had survived. And then he felt literally blocked, as if the safety belt had multiplied and kept him tight, bound to the seat. Sometimes he thought he heard voices, but considering his status they might also be hallucinations. Then he gave up and let himself slip down into sleep, hoping the next time would be better. As long as there was going to be a next time.

That time he felt like sinking into a longer sleep, almost more relaxing. When he woke up for the umpteenth time, he thought he was in the donut of the Odysseus, but as soon as he tried to move and he felt blocked again, the truth hit him like a meteorite and he began to panic. But if he thought about it, some of the heaviness seemed to have disappeared. Or rather, he felt like he had grown used to that sensation. Moreover, he wasn't going to resist one more second tied up there. With great fortitude, completely returning in himself, he opened his eyes. He was suddenly taken by a sense of confusion and his head began to spin. He wasn't in the descent module either. He realized he was laying on a bed, similar to the one in his room in the Red Stone, but the sheets were white, it was narrower and more raised from the floor. For a moment he wondered how could it be possible that he was again on Mars, he wondered for how long had he slept, but then he moved his gaze around himself, realizing there was no such place at the Aresland.

He was in a dark, small and cubic room, the walls were swarthy and spoiled, the bed was in the center, on his right there was a small wooden nightstand and a big closed door, while on his left there was a square window, but it was sealed as well. Slowly he became aware of a repetitive and constant sound spreading throughout the room, but at first he didn't understand what was it. He lowered his gaze on himself and, surprisingly, he found out there was no belt binding him to the bed, even though he kept feeling its pull. He wasn't wearing anything but a pair of light shorts in white fiber. He noticed he had some sort of stickers glued to his skin just above his heart, connected to some wires that ended up behind his bed where he couldn't see, but then he understood that the repetitive sound he heard was his electrocardiogram graphically reproducing the electric activity of his heart. He had seen such a device at the Aresland too. Moreover he noticed he had a needle whose tip disappeared under a bandage on his left inner forearm. It was linked to a kind of little tube coming out of a bag containing a transparent liquid, carried by a metallic structure next to his bed. He tried not to think about it.

The first clear question that sprang to his mind was where was Anna, was she safe, was she still alive? He couldn't just lay there linked to the wires any longer, he had to go look for her, he had to understand where they were, what had happened. He tried to pull himself up to sit and never would he think that such a simple movement could require so much struggle and fatigue. When he found himself sitting he felt his heart pounding quicker in his chest while the electrocardiogram accelerated accordingly. He tried to breathe deeply a couple of times, but suddenly the dark door opened, letting a ray of light in, but it closed shortly after, leaving him again in the darkness, with the difference that now there was another person. It was a young woman with a kind gaze, a round face and raven hair gathered up. She wore a long white coat and a weird thingy around her neck. She glanced briefly at him and pushed a button on the wall. A dim light was turned on, intensifying slowly so that Jordan could gradually get used to it after spending so much time in the shadow.

«Hello, Jordan. You've recovered, finally» she greeted him with a smile, walking to his bed. «How are you feeling?»

She addressed him as if they'd been knowing each other for years and yet, no matter how much he focused on her face and tried to recognize her, Jordan was sure he had never met her in his life.

«Who are you?» he asked instinctively, his voice hoarse. «And how long have I slept?»

The woman smiled at him with kindness, as if she was expecting that reaction.

«I'm doctor Aurora Wolter. I'm a physician» she replied. «And you've slept for nearly one day and two nights, it's just morning.»

«Aurora... Like the northern lights?» Jordan asked raising an extremely heavy arm to rub the numbness away from his eyes.

Doctor Wolter smiled more widely.

«Yes, that's right» she said before taking that instrument Jordan had never seen off of her neck and putting a couple of a kind of headphones in her ears. «Please, turn around.»

Jordan hesitated briefly, but then he decided he had no reason not to trust her, therefore he followed her gestures and slowly turned his back to her. He suddenly felt something metallic and ice-cold placing on his flesh and a chill crossed him. He struggled not to wince every time she placed that thing on a new point of his back.

«Breathe deeply through your nose» the woman requested and Jordan obeyed without questions.

Later she asked him to breathe through his mouth only and cough a couple of times in the end.

«Where am I?» Jordan asked finally, almost fearfully, while the woman slipped a weird tool into his right ear and looked into it, then repeating it with the left one.

«At the Capanna Margherita refuge on the Rose Mount, four thousand five hundred and fifty-four meters of altitude, it's the highest refuge in Europe.»

«And this place is... on Earth, isn't it?»

Doctor Wolter chuckled, softly amused, and answered affirmatively.

She lifted the front part of the bed so that Jordan could lean his back against it.

«Why right here?» Jordan questioned, looking around himself.

«Because the atmospheric pressure is of zero point fifty-seven atmospheres only. It isn't certainly as low as on Mars, but it's enough to let you acclimate gradually. Moreover the air is cleaner, for now we keep you away from the big cities' pollution.»

Jordan nodded.

«By the way, I'm feeling… heavy. And fatigued.»

«That's normal» the doctor reassured him, «You're carrying forty kilograms more than when you were on Mars.»

«Yeah, I know, gravity here is almost three times that of Mars. It's just that feeling it for real on yourself is completely different.»

«You'll get used to it eventually» she said and Jordan nodded again.

Then, suddenly, he remembered. And he turned to the woman with a concerned look.

«Where's Anna? Is she fine?» he asked.

Doctor Wolter sat on the edge of his bed and looked at him.

«Yes, she's fine» Jordan took a sigh of relief, «But she hasn't woken up yet.»

«Why?»

«She needs more time to recover, but we're supervising her and we're trying to help her as much as we can.»

«Can I… see her?» he dared.

«You shouldn't move too much not to tire your heart» she seemed to speak to herself, «But we can do this, just once. But then I want you to stay in bed for some more days. Your organism needs to acclimate to the new conditions.»

«Thank you so much!» Jordan smiled. «But speaking of… *days*: what day is tosol – I mean – today on Earth? You know, we've been using the Martian system till the landing.»

«Today is September 18th, 2060. Autumn is approaching and the temperature is growing colder» the woman answered smiling as well. «And, tell me, what *sol* is it on Mars?»

«Dhanus 15th, 240. Full spring and the new year has begun since more than a month.»

«What a weird name, Dhanus» the woman commented.

«Yeah, I was thinking the same about September.»

Doctor Wolter let out a brief chuckle and headed back to the door.

«I go get you some clothes, don't move from here.»

Jordan nodded his consensus and was alone again. He breathed deeply while letting everything sink in. He was on Earth. He had just spoken with a terrestrial.

He could barely stand on his feet. Detached from every wire and wearing new clothes, he was sitting in a wheelchair. He would have preferred walking and for a moment he complained, but after moving few trembling steps around the room, he decided that staying sitting on that chair and being pushed forward was going to be generally more comfortable and less tiring. Doctor Wolter pushed him out of his room and he found himself in a long corridor riddled with doors on both sides that he assumed being other rooms. He realized that place was completely built in wood thus granting a warm and cozy atmosphere he had never felt before. He noticed there was another big window at the bottom of the corridor and it was sealed as well.

«Why are you keeping all the windows closed?» he asked then.

«Due to the solar light's intensity. We're much closer to the sun here, remember? We're trying to prevent any kind of damage.»

Jordan wondered silently how could he have not realized it by himself before, but that thought slipped away like the wind as soon as a door opened in front of him and he entered a room that was identical to his. He was pushed to the side of a bed and there he stood up, holding onto the edge. Anna was laying on her back just like him, her head was tilted to one side, her red waves were sprawled on the pillow. She was only wearing a brassiere and white shorts and, like him before, some wires were attached to her. The electrocardiogram hanging on the wall behind her resounded rhythmically according to her heartbeat, indicating she was still alive. Her chest raised and lowered slightly at every breath. Jordan stood staring at her, captured. Unable to control himself, he moved a hand and took hers. Her fingers were cold. He focused as if he could mentally speak with her and, with all of himself, he asked her to wake up, to come back to him. He told her it was over, they did it, they were on Earth. But as he expected, nothing happened and Anna remained absorbed in her deep sleep. Jordan sat back in his wheelchair as he began to feel his legs weak already.

«Do you want me to bring you back?» Aurora Wolter asked in a low voice.

Jordan shook his head, continuing to look at the girl.

«I'd like to stay here a little bit more. I'll keep her company» he replied.

Of course, he had many things to do and discover now that he had arrived here, but he didn't feel like doing anything without Anna. He didn't want to discover planet Earth alone, he wanted Anna to be with him, after all that journey. They had begun together and they were going to continue together. And then, in that unknown place, that girl was the only person who imparted security, who reminded him of the reality he was used to.

«Alright. I'll be back in half an hour, okay? We'll see if you can eat something.»

Jordan nodded and he heard the door closing.

Anna woke up two days later. Jordan had spent that time in his bed, getting up only to go to the bathroom or put on new clothes. They had placed a chair even in the shower fearing he could slip and break some bones. In the meanwhile he got to know new persons, among whom another physician, the barman on the ground floor and a couple of ladies who took care of cleansing the place, but usually it was always doctor Wolter who paid him visits. As soon as he got to know about Anna, he jumped down from his bed and started to run towards her room, chased by doctor Wolter with his wheelchair, yelling at him to stop. But he ignored her and flew inside Anna's room panting uncontrollably and he almost fell at the feet of her bed, but doctor Wolter arrived in time to make him sit in the chair. Anna struggled to pull herself up on her elbows, slightly groaning. Jordan knew perfectly well the weight and pain she was feeling and no one better than him could understand her in that moment.

«How are you?» he asked, breathless, while the doctor turned on the lights.

«Tired» the girl replied after a while and blinking.

She looked around herself and finally her gaze stopped on the boy next to her bed.

«But you've been sleeping for three days straight!» Jordan teased her.

She widened her eyes and slightly winced when Jordan used the word "days" instead of "sols".

He gave her a reassuring smile.

«Welcome on Earth, by the way. We did it.»

A week passed, Jordan and Anna had become accustomed to walking around the refuge and they had returned to be more autonomous. Every day they had to undergo about one hour of physical therapy and tests where they had to run on a tapis roulant or pedal on a cyclette, with many wires attached to their skin. Their existence on Earth was getting more and more simple and livable, but the truth was that they couldn't wait to leave those warm and shadowy wooden walls in order to go out and look around themselves with their own eyes. Actually they hadn't seen Earth for real yet. They had lost consciousness during the atmospheric entry and they had woken up in that small, protective place. They were used to live in such places, small and enclosed, considering the years spent at the Aresland, but by now they had arrived that far and they wanted to go outside and explore.

They were almost on the verge of projecting a new escape when, that September 27th, 2060, doctor Wolter announced they were ready to begin a training for their sight to tolerate the sunlight. They were brought in front of a big window on the ground floor, it seemed it offered the best view, and they were provided with very dark glasses. It was 5:00 pm, the lowering sun was going to be less bright. Jordan placed his glasses on his nose and found out he could see nothing more than slight shadows.

«Ready?» Aurora Wolter asked.

Anna was next to him with his same glasses.

«I can't see absolutely anything» Jordan complained.

The woman smirked slightly and, instead of answering, she undocked the shutters of the window and opened them slowly, letting just a crack of light in, growing wider and more intense. Despite the darkness of the glasses, Jordan had to squeeze his eyes and blink repeatedly, but he soon realized that that protection prevented his eyes from tingling, therefore he opened them a little more bravely and brought into focus what was in front of him.

From his position, he found himself dominating a valley on which a blanket of apparently soft and white clouds spread to the horizon, riddled with rocky tips of high mountains covered in a candid white layer. The clouds weren't only beneath him, but also above him.

The sharp tip of a mount stood above all the others, reigning, austere. It was slightly colored of an orange shade, the same that stained a long line on the horizon: on one side it merged into pink, on another into yellow, while above it drowned into a dim azure that grew more intense. Jordan was mesmerized.

«We're so high it seems we're still in space» Anna commented.

«For a moment I thought it» Jordan convened.

«That mountain has a name?» Anna asked pointing at the higher tip.

«Yes, that's the Matterhorn. The third highest mountain in the entire chain of Alps. In this moment we're looking toward Switzerland, while there's Italy behind our back. We're right on the boundary.»

«I see no boundaries» Anna commented, losing her gaze to the horizon.

That time the woman didn't answer.

«I didn't expect everything to be white» Jordan observed to break the silence.

«Oh, but it isn't actually. At these altitudes it's normal to find a layer of snow covering everything. Most of all in winter.»

«*Snow*, you said? That is… snow?!» Jordan asked with growing enthusiasm, widening his eyes.

«Yes, it's a state of water» the woman replied calmly.

«I know» Jordan leaned a hand on the glass, «I'd only heard about it.»

«That's true, on Mars water exists as ice only, apart from inside the bases» Anna pointed out.

«Snow everywhere, blimey, can we go out? Tell me we can go out!» the boy turned to the woman and lifted his glasses to give her a pleading look.

«Keep down your glasses!» she ordered right away, forcing them back onto his nose, then frowned. «There are eighteen degrees sub-zero, you really want to go out?»

Jordan put his hands on his hips and gave her a look.

«Really? I remind you I come from a planet where the average temperature is sixty degrees sub-zero!»

The woman shook her head smiling slightly. Anna turned with a smug smirk.

«Touchè» she patted him on the arm. «And you? Agree?» she addressed the girl.

«Need to ask?» she talked back.

«Of course you agree» the woman rolled her eyes, amused. «Follow me, we'll look for some thicker clothes» and with that she headed to the stairs that led to the upper floors.

«I like these terrestrials» Jordan whispered to Anna, winking at her and earning a glare from doctor Wolter, who had heard him.

They slipped on two pairs of warm and tight trousers each, plus a third pair, wider and waterproof, two sweaters each and, finally, a jacket made of the same material of the pants. They were wrapped in a woolen scarf and, with a heavy beanie on their head, a hood pulled up and gloves on, they headed to the exit. Jordan felt a bit uneasy thinking there was no airlock and he didn't need to carry any life support system to breathe. He had never been outside a structure without that equipment. He turned to look at Anna at the door and realized she was tormented by his same thoughts. He approached her and whispered weakly because he didn't want anyone else to hear.

«No helmet nor oxygen… Can you believe it?»

«I know… shhh» she replied quickly, just when doctor Wolter had returned, accompanied by doctor Huber, with whom they usually underwent medical tests. He was quite an old man, short and stocky, with little hair on his head, rectangular glasses on his nose and an austere gaze. Both he and Wolter were ready to go out.

«Guys, listen well» Simon Huber began with a rigid tone, «I want you to stay close to the refuge. If you sense any kind of symptom you must inform us immediately. Try to breathe through your scarf as it'll heat the air up a little bit, otherwise you might sense a pain in your chest, the air is very cold out there. It'll be dark soon therefore we won't stay out for longer than half an hour. At six ten pm at most we'll reenter. Have I made myself clear?»

Jordan and Anna nodded confidently because his tone didn't seem to admit objections.

«Take care» he added. «Come on, wear your glasses.»

The two obeyed and doctor Wolter opened the big dark, wooden door. Despite the various layers of clothes, Jordan was run over by a frozen wave of air. He shuddered. He had never felt such cold before. And that made him even more curious. He walked forward courageously until he felt his feet sinking into that white, twinkling mantle and euphoria took over him. He understood immediately why doctor Huber had asked them to stay close: they were exactly on the tip of a mount and pulling away by even a few meters would have meant slipping down its steep side. He vaguely wondered how had they arrived up there and how were they going to leave it. But right then and there he found no answer and he returned to focus on what was under his feet. He turned and saw Anna moving a step towards him. He felt a sharp, frozen breeze welting against his jacket, he slightly shivered, he struggled to breathe that air that seemed to be icing his lungs. But anyway he found the strength to speak.

«It's the first step» he said in a low voice, then he raised his tone. «The Martians have occupied planet Earth!» he raised his closed fists into air in a gesture of victory, Anna gave a battle cry raising her arms as well, then they burst out laughing out of pure joy.

Doctor Wolter and doctor Huber remained on the door, observing. Jordan crouched down, as it was his tradition, and took some of the snow in his glove, observing attentively the shapes of the small crystals, each one different from one another. They wandered around the place, observing the landscape getting darker for the following twenty minutes. When by now Jordan couldn't see much anymore, he turned to the two physicians sitting in front of the door.

«Can we take off the glasses? The sun's set already!» he asked aloud.

The two exchanged looks and said something in a low voice, then they addressed him

«Go ahead» Simon Huber conceded.

As soon as Jordan took off his glasses, all the light seemed to return all of a sudden and everything became clearer, but it didn't bother him. He felt the wind welting again his flesh and took a deep breath. He had never felt anything like that. Anna and he sat in the snow right before a steep slope began. The clouds had grown more voluminous beneath them, hiding every trace of ground, apart from the Matterhorn. They dived into the darkness of the horizon, where there were no limits.

«Do you remember when that night we saw the Earth? That bright dot among many?» Jordan asked at a certain point.

«Yes...» the girl replied with a thoughtful tone.

«Could you ever imagine such immensity?»

The girl didn't reply right away, as if she was lost in her thoughts and, when she spoke, her words sounded dragged by the wind.

«I always have felt fondness for this lonely hill
and for this hedge which screens off
such a large part of the furthermost horizon.

But as I sit and gaze, in my thoughts I envisage,
beyond it, boundless space and utter silence
and deepest still, so that it almost makes
my heart take fright. And as I hear
the rustling of the wind among these plants,
I start comparing that unending silence
with this noise and I am reminded of
eternity, and seasons gone and dead and
of the season now alive and of its sounds. And so
in this immensity my thoughts sink and drown
and shipwreck feels sweet in this ocean.»

«There aren't plants, but you gave the idea. I admit I understood half of what you said, but they did sound like the right words» Jordan commented after a while. «What was it?»

«A poem written by Giacomo Leopardi, he was an Italian poet. I happened to read it in a book at the Aresland and it really touched me because I had no idea what was he talking about. I repeated and repeated it, but it made no sense to me. But now I understand. Only now» she sighed deeply, her gaze was lost to the horizon.

Jordan continued to look in front of himself, thinking of those words that actually took a tight grip in his mind. When his thoughts were suddenly interrupted by the girl again.

«Oh, look at that!» she exclaimed, pointing at something in the sky.

Jordan raised his gaze following her arm's direction and noticed two bright stars in the early darkness. As he looked up, he noticed more and more stars, their light was dim.

«Mars?» he asked hopefully.

«No… Jupiter and Saturn.»

«Ah» Jordan growled in a disappointed tone, but his gaze was still captured by those two immense planets dominating the sky.

He laid down in the snow to enjoy the view better. Anna remained sitting.

«I think Mars will come out at about three in the morning. They'll never let us out» Anna considered.

Jordan didn't answer. The cold was getting unbearable, but he wasn't feeling it anymore. In front of all of that he had no time to worry about the temperature. He could have stayed there forever, contemplating the parade of day and night, always different from one another.

«What's going to happen now?» Anna asked him, even if it sounded like she wasn't addressing only him.

He remembered he had asked her that very question when they were still on Mars, travelling towards the Rubentes Terrae.

«What do you think?» Jordan replied as she did that time.

The girl turned to look at him and smiled weakly, probably remembering that same conversation of a long time before.

She laid down next to him and turned her gaze to the stars, without saying another word.

SEVENTEEN
~ 24 days later ~

Jordan sat at one of the wooden tables in a corner of the ground floor, in front of Anna. On a yellowish paper placemat there were the steel cutlery, a glass and a white tissue. A glass bottle full of water stood in the center of the table.

A couple of weeks had passed since they had stepped foot on planet Earth for the very first time and it had already become a daily activity. They had eventually acclimated to the sunlight and finally all the windows of the refuge could remain open, letting the light filter inside. That day they were going to leave Capanna Margherita, doctor Huber had announced several days before. Actually they were going to leave the entire continent as they were traveling overseas, to the United States, to the Johnson Space Center, where the researchers and NASA administrator herself had been waiting for them for a long time.

On one hand they couldn't wait to leave behind that small, lost hole among the mountains and begin to actually see the world; on the other hand, instead, they felt a little afraid to leave again a place they had become accustomed to and where they felt fine. But in the end, afraid or not afraid, they had to do as they were told, also because they had realized that if they had found themselves in such a place on their own they would have died early, therefore disobeying or mutinying weren't an option.

Jordan observed the bar waiter approaching their table carrying two steaming plates. He could tell he was much older than them, if it wasn't for that full beard he kept relatively short. He found himself in front of a couple of clear steaks, traced by darker diagonal strips, half hidden by a bush of green salad with slices of tomato and maize kernels.

«What is it?» Jordan asked hinting to the meat.

«Grilled chicken fillet» the young man replied with a kind tone.

«Chicken?» Jordan replied raising his gaze to the waiter, thinking he misheard it.

«Yes, is it no good?»

«Oh no, it's very good, thank you» Jordan tried to smile gently and the man walked back to the kitchens.

Then he smirked and took the cutlery, studying his plate, but he blocked before incising the steak: he felt observed. He lifted his gaze. Anna was scanning him with a frown. Jordan raised an eyebrow in response, as if asking what was she looking at.

«Any problems?» she asked then, talking about his dish.

Jordan considered whether to answer with a funny remark, but then thought better of it and simply let a crooked smile appear on his lips, while his eyes twinkled.

«No, nothing, it's just...» he pointed at the steak with the tip of his knife, «It reminded me of... those damn birds!» he sighed. «They are still at the Aresland» his tone had become more thoughtful, «I wonder how they are, I mean, it's been a while and...»

«Jordan!» Anna interrupted him, almost bringing him back to the present. «You're worrying about your hens!»

«Uh – what? No!»

«Oh, you are!» the girl talked back leaning slightly forward on the table, «After all you've grown to care for your hens and now you miss them, face it!»

«Never» Jordan replied resolutely and incised his steak.

«Do as you wish, but it is so. Just accept it.»

«Yeah, well... They'll always remain my infamous birds» he forked a piece of meat, «But this doesn't mean...»

«Yes, it does! Come on, there's nothing to be ashamed of.»

Jordan was about to talk back, but he was interrupted by doctor Wolter who approached their table, therefore he simply slipped the meat into his mouth.

«So» the woman began, while the two kept glaring at each other, «You'll leave at two pm, doctor Huber and I will be with you. We should get to the Milan-Malpensa airport at three and a private plane will bring us straight to Texas, but the trip is going to be longer, I'm talking about almost thirteen hours and a half.»

«Geez, and you call it long?» Jordan joked.

«I'm sorry, you're right. Sometimes I forget that you've travelled for six months. Therefore it will be a short trip of sixteen hours.»

«The real question is» Anna began with a serious tone, «How are we going to leave this place?»

Aurora Wolter made a face.

«The same way you got here, of course. By helicopter.»

Jordan and Anna exchanged looks. First of all Jordan wondered what a helicopter was and eventually the image of a vehicle with a huge propeller took shape in his mind. He had studied that genre of transportation in some classes of engineering and technology at the Aresland. An already familiar sensation of adrenaline ran through him at the idea of flying first on a helicopter and then on an airplane.

«And precisely what's the destination?» the girl still asked.

«We'll land at the Houston airport and a private shuttle will bring us to the Johnson Space Centre, it'll take half an hour.»

They both nodded their understanding.

«So, now I'll let you finish your meal in peace. After that go to your rooms to check if you have to take anything even if I doubt it since you arrived without any baggage» she chuckled, «And at ten to three we'll meet in front of the exit to wait for the helicopter, okay?»

They both nodded again and doctor Wolter walked away. Jordan sighed and returned with his gaze on his meat. He hesitated, then looked at Anna, who was still staring at him with a face.

«I'm not missing the hens!» he screamed in a whisper.

At 1:55 pm, Jordan was in front of the exit, all wrapped up in sweaters, jumpers and jackets to get out. After lunch he had returned to his room as Aurora Wolter had suggested and, effectively, he didn't find much to take away, apart from the photograph with his mother that had travelled so far with him. Among all those recent happenings, he had almost forgotten. He sat on his bed with the picture in his hands, as he was used to do at the Aresland occasionally. He had no idea of where she was, but at least now he was certain they were both on the same planet, which was already something. He wondered what was she doing, if she was thinking about him, if maybe she was waiting for him somewhere. He didn't know if and when was he going to meet his mum again, he could not imagine the moment. He felt nothing but shivers every time he tried. The flow of his thoughts was then interrupted by a lady whose head appeared around the door to ask if she could enter to clean. He answered affirmatively right away and, with the picture hidden in his hoodie, he headed to the ground floor.

They got outside and Jordan struggled to keep his eyes open in the light of the early afternoon. He kept his gaze low until a merciful hand appeared in his line of sight with a pair of sunglasses, that he took and put on right away. He sincerely thanked doctor Huber next to him.

«How are you, guys? Are you ready?» doctor Wolter asked with a smile.

«Yep, we're always ready» Jordan replied and Anna smiled at him.

The wait wasn't long, soon they heard the rumble of an engine getting closer from above. A dark dot became eventually bigger and noisier. The propellers whirled rapidly, creating a strong air movement while it descended ten meters away from them.

When the wheels touched down on the snow, a hatch opened letting out a figure who motioned for them to approach the helicopter. He was pushed forward by an arm and he walked towards that deafening and storming vehicle together with Anna and the two physicians. He was grabbed by that dark man and literally pulled inside, followed by the other three, who underwent the same treatment. As soon as the hatch was closed, the air ceased and the roar attenuated. Without figuring out how, Jordan found himself sitting in a small seat and bounded with a safety belt. There was Anna next to him, while Wolter and Huber were in front of them. The mysterious dark man had disappeared in the cockpit.

On the right and on the left of the passengers there were two big windows offering an excellent view. Slowly the rumble of the engine intensified and they lifted from the ground, going higher and higher, before moving forward with a smooth movement. Someone squeezed his hand and he turned to see it was Anna, but her gaze was lost outside the window. He thought maybe she hadn't even realized that act. He noticed the two physicians observing them with knowingly smiles and Jordan suddenly wished he could disappear inside the seat. But unluckily it didn't happen, therefore he simply lost his gaze outside the window as well, in order to enjoy the expanse of white mountains running under them.

As the minutes passed, their eyes couldn't move away from what was there outside the windows. As they went forward, the mountains became always less pronounced until they totally disappeared, leaving room to small settlements that seemed to converge in a big cluster of houses and buildings, always denser and always taller. Almost suddenly everything became grey and flat, in the distance he thought he saw the silhouette of airplanes parked next to a huge building and therefore he realized they had to be close.

«We're almost there» Aurora Wolter announced simultaneously with his thoughts.

The helicopter lowered as they approached the main structure and finally touched the asphalt gently before turning off the engines.

«Anna, Jordan» doctor Huber recalled their attention, he had taken out of a pocket what looked like two white bands. «Here, wear these in front of your mouth and cover your nose too.»

They grabbed those masks and followed the order silently.

«Why do we have to keep these?» Jordan asked.

«The air's not as clean as in mountain here, not to mention in this airport. A little precaution» the physician replied quickly while they jumped off the helicopter.

A kind of rover, that was actually called shuttle bus, carried them to an isolated airplane, slightly smaller than the others. Jordan noticed NASA's logo on the white tail. They got onboard through a flight of stairs that would pull away before the lift-off procedures and Jordan and Anna took their seats next to two portholes, meanwhile they took off the masks, since they didn't need them anymore. Jordan felt his heart pounding in his chest. The entire airplane was vibrating, showing that the engines were already on. A warning light turned on inviting them to buckle their seatbelts and Jordan did it immediately. Anna was sitting behind him, while doctor Wolter and doctor Huber were on the other side.

«Everything good back there?» Jordan asked addressing Anna.

«Never been better» the girl's voice answered.

«Ready to launch?»

The girl giggled.

«Affirmative, commander.»

Right then the airplane began to move and went on the runway track. The engines roared louder. Jordan was taken by a sense of excitement and nervousness, until suddenly he was pressed against his seat, once again, and the airplane started at full speed. His head felt suddenly heavier when the airplane pulled away from the track and hovered in the air. Observing the ground becoming far he almost laughed at himself for having been nervous. That was nothing compared to a launch onboard Argus.

After about three hours that Jordan saw nothing but water or clouds, he fell asleep and slept for the rest of the trip. He was awakened by doctor Wolter right before the landing in Houston, during which Jordan was only half awake, recovering from those six hours of intense sleep. He completely reawakened again as soon as he felt warm air caressing his face. His gaze searched for Anna and he noticed a tired look on her face as well. The darkness of the night was illuminated by the lights of the airport.

«What time is it?» Jordan asked with a husky voice.

«Ten thirty» Anna Wolter replied. «You alright?»

The two simply nodded and soon they were loaded on a small shuttle bus with few seats. Jordan leaned his head against the window and sat like that for the following half an hour, with his gaze lost outside, where he saw nothing but a confusion of near and far lights in the darkness. He wasn't sleepy anymore, but still he had to admit he felt tired after that trip. Without realizing it, he dozed off again, but that time he felt like he was woken up right away. He noticed Anna had fallen asleep again, her head resting on his shoulder.

«Guys, wake up, we're almost there» it was Wolter's kind voice.

Jordan sat straighter and Anna did the same, passing her hands on her face. She had her hair all messed up.

«Five minutes till we get there» she continued, «I know you're tired, but... Maybe try to make yourself presentable. You may happen to meet NASA's administrator or other personalities who've been following your mission – I mean, your life – since the very beginning.»

Jordan nodded and frantically shook his hands in his hair in order to mess it up even more, now all the strands were shot in every direction. He turned to Aurora Wolter.

«Is that better?» he asked with a still sleepy look, raising his eyebrows expectantly.

Anna burst out laughing briefly and Aurora Wolter rolled her eyes.

«But is he always like that?» she asked Anna.

«Always» she replied laughing, «He will never change.»

They found themselves in front of a colossal structure displaying, on a wall, a huge emblem of NASA and, on another one, a big American flag. A white light illuminated the building from top to bottom, giving it a nearly spectral look.

«Come on, they'll be waiting for us!» doctor Wolter exclaimed to encourage them.

The two began to follow her, keeping their gaze fixed on the building. They reached a glass door and, as soon as they crossed it they were met by a middle-aged man who was incredibly tall and wore an elegant suit that gave him an air of importance. He had a wide smile on his lips and he was accompanied by a young woman carrying a notepad, she looked friendly. The man addressed the doctors first.

«Doctor Wolter, doctor Huber, finally!» he shook their hands.

«Reynolds, hello. We've made it through the trip, the kids are fine, but they're very tired and stressed» Simon Huber replied practically.

Only then the man turned his full attention to Jordan and Anna. He looked at them so intently that Jordan wondered if he wanted to eat them with his eyes.

«I'm Tom Reynolds, associate administrator» he said to introduce himself and shook hands first with Jordan and then with Anna. «It's a pleasure to meet you.»

«The pleasure's ours» Jordan replied, unsure, still reflecting on the meaning of "associate administrator".

«Well, I suppose you want to rest» he said joining his hands in front of him, «I invite you to follow Grace, she'll show you your private chambers.»

The woman at his side smiled and nodded.

«This way» she said turning by three quarters and motioning for the two to follow her.

They started down the corridors of the JSC and went to the upper floors. They stopped in front of two doors, one next to the other, that Grace opened with two keys and turned on the lights.

«Here we are, these are your rooms. You have a bathroom and if you're hungry you'll find some sandwiches in the pantry. Have a good night.»

The two thanked her and then slipped into their respective rooms. After closing the door, Jordan sat on the blue sheets of his bed and, sighing, looked around himself. It was a very cozy environment. In front of the bed there was a big wardrobe and Jordan imagined it contained some new clothes. Under a window that was hidden behind white curtains, there was a desk with a laptop and next to it there was what had to be the pantry. The laptop captured his attention. He wondered if he could contact the Aresland from there. It'd been a very long time since he last heard from them. So he grabbed the computer and definitely laid down on his bed. He was greeted by a very peculiar screen wallpaper: Mars. The icons of several programs lingered in the black of space around it. After various unsuccessful computer explorations he heard a knock on his door.

«Come in» he called aloud.

The door disclosed a little bit and Jordan saw half Anna appearing.

«Can I?» she asked shyly.

«Sure, take a seat» he said patting on the bed next to him.

«I didn't feel like staying alone. And then, I wouldn't be able to sleep right now» the girl explained sitting next to Jordan. «What are you doing?»

«I'm trying to figure out if it's possible to contact Yan from here.»

«Mmm, let's see» she meditated observing the icons attentively, «Did you try on Satellite? Look, there's the icon of an antenna.»

He answered by clicking on it.

«Receivers...» Jordan read scrolling through a list. «Aresland!» he exclaimed, «But how is it that you always know everything?»

«It didn't take much to guess, honestly.»

«Yeah, shut up» he tried to shake her away with a hand, making her laugh.

After several moments of deep thinking on the best words to use, they wrote a message.

[NASA JSC 0938]: Aresland, are you receiving us? It's Jordan and Anna writing. You can't really imagine... we landed! That's right, we got on Earth with an emergency manoeuvre that was maybe a little risky, but we survived and we're fine. The rehabilitation period has been quite long and only today we've arrived at a NASA centre, this is why we can finally contact you. The truth? We miss you. We haven't had the opportunity to properly visit Earth yet, but what we've happened to see so far is gorgeous. Yan, we wish you were with us. Now's very late here and we're very tired. Surely we'll have the opportunity to text you more often and tell you every detail of the landing in the next days.

A total hug.

Yours,

Jordan and Anna.

Jordan closed the laptop and reached out to place it back on the desk. They laid for a while staring at the ceiling until Anna yawned.

«Can I stay?» she asked.

Jordan turned to look at her.

«You know, recently at night I happen to have nightmares» she continued, «Only now, if I think about it, I

277

realize what risk we've run. We could have died, Jordan. For real.»

The boy smiled and widened his arms to let the girl rest her head on his shoulder and cuddle up against him. He hugged her tightly.

«Of course you can stay» he whispered, «It's alright. It's gone, we're here and we're alive.»

«I've been afraid» she confessed, «As never in my life.»

«Me too. But... Deep down I knew it couldn't end just like that.»

«How did you know?»
Some moments of silence passed.

«Well» he reflected, «Everything had only just begun.»

Anna pulled up to look at him in the eyes, illuminated by a serene twinkle. Then, without many compliments, she grabbed the boy's face and kissed him, for the first time since they were on Earth. Jordan was crossed by a new vibrant rush while his thoughts halted. And he turned off the light.

The following morning Anna managed to sneak into her room just before they brought them a tray with breakfast. Jordan didn't really know if they were allowed to sleep together therefore they simply decided to make sure nobody would know. They had been told to wait in their rooms until someone would come to call them and so, after breakfast and a shower, Jordan was crouching comfortably on a blue leather armchair, absorbed in reading a book on black holes written by Stephen Hawking. The breakfast tray laid abandoned on the desk, riddled with crumbs of toast. He was reading an interesting paragraph regarding time and light when his room door opened and doctor Wolter's head came round it. He lifted his gaze from the book.

«Good morning» she greeted cheerfully.

«Hello, Aurora» he stood up and abandoned the book on the armchair.

«If you'll follow me, in a few moments you're going to meet some people who cannot wait to shake hands with you.»

And Jordan followed her, wondering if he was finally going to meet NASA's director. They called Anna and headed to the building main hall. The corridors, that just the night before were empty, were now crossed by many more people who often stopped to introduce themselves and congratulate with them. Few moments before they reached the hall, Aurora Wolter stopped.

«Oh, how careless of me, I've forgotten your medical records» she turned to the boy, «Jordan, would you do me a big favour? They are on my office table, straight ahead and down to the right, you turn in the first corridor.»

«Sure, I'll go right away. See you in the hall.»

«Good, dear boy, thank you!»

Something in her gaze or a slight variation in her tone of voice destabilized him. It seemed like she was suddenly behaving oddly. What if she had found out Anna had spent the night with him and now she wanted to talk with her in private? He tried to ignore that thought and started down the corridor. There was nothing bad in asking to go take some medical records. He kept walking till the office at the bottom of the corridor on the right. He pushed the door open and entered. He noticed a woman sitting on an armchair in a corner, but he didn't pay her much attention, while his gaze looked for the medical records on the desk. When suddenly…

«Jordan…» he heard his name whispered by a voice.

He stopped frozen where he stood, his gaze fixed on the desk. Out of the corner of his eye he had seen the woman standing up shortly after he had entered. *That voice.* He perceived his heartbeat accelerating. He felt as if he was suddenly dragged backwards in time by his own memories. It wasn't possible, he had to be wrong. Slowly he moved his gaze from the desk to the only other person present in that room apart from himself. She had long, dark hair, a soft-featured face and high cheekbones. He found himself mirrored in her eyes. His same green eyes. He suddenly forgot how to speak, how to move, how to breathe. He didn't need to check the photograph hidden in his hoodie to be sure. And it was inevitable. He had tried to be strong for too long.

A solitary tear made its way down his cheek.
Then another
and another…

EPILOGUE

Jordan was completely still. The last thing he had seen from the porthole, before focusing his gaze on the screen in front of himself, was the Odysseus II spaceship pulling away in the black of space. The entire structure vibrated threateningly while they were always more attracted by the Martian force of gravity.

«Argus II, here. Starting the landing procedures» Anna's voice articulated next to him.

Jordan sighed as he prepared for the second landing of his life, but knowing that it was going to be the last one. Yet his mind couldn't do other but travel backwards, bringing to light all the emotions and fears he had felt on that day so important. Two good years had passed since then. Well, almost three considering the trip back to the red planet. But still it felt like an entire life to him.

For the two previous years he had lived with his mother and his grandparents in Sanford, a peaceful coastal metropolis at about fifty miles from Cape Canaveral. He stabilized there after visiting a great part of the terrestrial world with his mother, discovering exotic beaches, tropical and high mountains forests, canyons and deserts, from the ruins of ancient civilizations to the famous Egyptian pyramids. With NASA's agreement, Jordan began to attend University like every boy of his

281

same age and thus he had the opportunity to learn what it meant to be a terrestrial teenager, making many new friends at the Massachusetts Institute of Technology. For nearly two years he didn't get to see Anna in person. Not that he had forgotten about her, he never could. Despite the amazing adventures he went through on a daily basis as he discovered himself and the world around him, every night, before sleeping, he spent more than an hour in video-chat with her. They told each other about their terrestrial days, their discoveries. Jordan felt like no one better than her, a Martian girl, could understand him. He thought again and again to that stolen and sincere kiss that trampled them both in a moment of total impotence and fear in front of an unknown and potentially dangerous destiny. Nothing, more than that moment, gave him the will to keep fighting, to resist, to reach the end; because finally he realized he had found something or, rather, someone who was worth it.

He wondered in which part of the world she was, if she had met her distant relatives in Russia. Every time he thought about her or Yan, something weird within him happened. Despite he believed his new life in Sanford was beautiful, he felt a sort of melancholy, a lack. An almost frustrating remoteness. Every night he spent hours on his house terrace stargazing and when he noticed a star emitting a more intense light characterized by a reddish glow, he couldn't move his eyes away. While nostalgia made his eyes twinkle, he wondered what was his real place in the universe. What was his purpose.

The answer came just one of those evenings he spent studying the sky.

«What's my task in this life?» he had asked his mother, sitting next to him.

«You know it» Laurie Williams had answered calmly, after a moment of silence.

Jordan turned to gave her a look.

«No, I don't know it. I've come this far looking for an answer.»

«It wasn't necessary.»

He frowned in confusion.

«I'm not saying I'm not happy you're here, on the contrary» she smiled, «But you already own an answer. You've always had it. And the journey itself you went on proves it.»

Jordan thought. He lost his gaze in space before returning to grasp that vermillion twinkle hundreds of millions of kilometers away. And then he understood.

«The purpose of my life is... having a life with a purpose» he whispered to himself. «Of course!» he exclaimed jumping in his chair and turning to Laurie, who observed him smiling. «This is what being human means, then! It means having a goal and once you achieve it, having another. What would we be if we had nothing to strive for? Everything's clear, now. What made me escape from the Aresland that night? What made me get on that rocket? My being a human. My need to have a purpose. To have a destination.»

He almost panted and pulled himself back together on his chair, losing his gaze once again in the sky.

«Mum, I... I have to go back to Mars. That is my place.»

Jordan was suddenly crossed by a tremble that resounded in the entire Argus II as if it had just been hit by a meteorite at full speed and only then he returned to his senses, reemerging violently from his thoughts. He was taken by a familiar sensation of heaviness and therefore he understood he had landed on the surface of Mars, exactly three miles away from the Aresland, in the Hellas Planitia. He breathed deeply to calm down his heartbeat and turned to look at the girl next to him.

«You okay?» he asked.

«I've been better, but at least I'm still conscious» she smiled knowingly and Jordan smiled back.

«They'll be here in moments.»

The girl nodded. And that was right: in a matter of few minutes the hatch next to Anna was opened revealing a figure wearing the typical biosuit of the Aresland. There were no words to describe the joy Jordan felt in simply seeing that familiar suit again. The boy narrowed his eyes to make out the face of the person behind the visor, but it didn't take much for him to recognize him.

«Dad!» he exclaimed.

«My my, look who's back» Alexander's sarcastic and amused voice resounded in his helmet, he reached out «Ladies first» and grabbed Anna to help her get out.

Soon the hatch next to Jordan opened too and he recognized Viktor Taykeev right away who, helped by Alexander, made the boy get out.

«*Privyet, milaya. Ti koroshò?*[24]» he heard Viktor say addressing Anna, who was by now on the Martian surface.

«*Privyet, papa. Da, ya skuchala po vam*[25].»

«Good to see you again» Jordan said as Alexander helped him stand on the surface.

They were sustained by the two men until they reached the rover parked at a distance of two meters. Jordan got onboard and sat next to Anna; in front of them, Alexander and Viktor occupied the driving seats. They had promised they weren't going to say anything until they would reach the base and they would be all together, therefore they spent those ten minutes of the

---

[24] Privyet … koroshò: from Russian, "Hello, my dear. You OK?"

[25] Privyet … vam: from Russian, "Hello, dad. Yes, I've missed you"

trip observing the familiar, desolate landscape that had been what they had always known for years. Jordan couldn't explain how, but as he looked at that sand and those coppery rocks and that sky of a weak sepia colour, he felt good, complete. That was his element, it was right for him. Right like the warm bed that awaits you when you're tired, right like a steaming plate prepared by your mother when you're hungry. That was his place.

When the second hatch of the airlock opened, Jordan was overwhelmed by a wave of joyful screams and claps. He took off his helmet and, without thinking, his gaze scanned urgently the small crowd in front of him until he found what he was looking for: a couple of dark, almond-shaped eyes.

Without realizing it, he dropped his helmet and found himself walking in his direction, always faster, followed by Anna.

«Nunki!» he shrieked in happiness, throwing his arms around his neck.

It was like finding a brother again after a long time. All three of them stood hugging for several minutes while an applause started all around them.

«Hey hey» he heard Yan say at a certain point and he pulled away, keeping him at arm-length. «I know it isn't your fault if there are no showers in space, pal. But you smell terrible!»

Anna burst out laughing and Jordan rolled his eyes.

«Blimey, Nunki» Jordan sighed, «You have no idea how much I've missed you!»

«I'm afraid I must admit the same» he spoke in a dramatically serious tone, «Commander Miles. But... a shower!»

Everyone burst out laughing again and Jordan shook his head, hiding his face in his hands.

After taking off the suits and having a shower for Yan's joy, Jordan and Anna told them all their terrestrial adventure in a couple of hours. They had all reunited around the long table in the hall of the Hong Se De Du. Again those smiling and friendly faces, again those cozy and circular rooms of the Aresland's bases. Jordan was happy.

«I'd like to say something» Jordan declared at the end of the tales, just before everyone decided to go to sleep. He gained the attention of all those present who were suddenly eating out of his hand. «On Earth not only did I visit spectacular places and did I get to know nature in its every form. Not only did I meet my mother after a long time, did I learn to live as a terrestrial, did I meet other guys of my age, no, not only this. I left with many questions and I'm… happy to be able to say that I've found my answers» he paused and raised his gaze on all the listeners. «Eventually I learned something: when you are in your mother's womb, you have no certainties. You don't know who your parents are, you don't know where they are, you don't know how you will be born and where you will live. At first you don't even know if you are male or female. You know nothing about yourself and the world around you. You are sure of one only thing: when you are born, wherever and whoever you are with, you will call that place home, you will call those people mum and dad. You don't care where you are, be it a city, an igloo, the jungle, a ship or even another *planet*. For you it will be perfectly normal. My stay on Earth has been wonderful, I must admit. But… I've always felt the lack of something, something that that place could not give me. What I'm trying to say is that… maybe Mars is not as fascinating as the

Earth, but it's *home*. And nothing or no one is ever going to change that.»

THE END

ACKNOWLEDGEMENTS

I'm happy to be able to say that this story is actually the result of a proper international collaboration, just the one you would need to get to Mars! There are people to whom I would like to dedicate pages and pages of gratitude, but I don't want this section to become more extended than the narration itself, therefore I'll try to be short and concise.

Thanks, first of all, to Goran Nikolašević (Croatia) who, during the regional phase of the Odysseus Space Contest, where I presented my project of a Martian base, has asked me about the birth of children on the red planet. And thus the idea started to make its way into my mind. Thank you for having encouraged me and having believed in me since the very beginning.

Thanks to professor Giancarlo Genta for writing the perfect preface to this book, preparing the reader to instantly dive into a Martian world. Thank you for your support and for believing in this story.

Thanks to Roberto Johnson (Texas) and Bruno Bassani (my father), who have performed a huge work recreating in 3D the environments that I designed and where the story is set, in order to give me a more complete and exhaustive view on what I was creating and in order to improve the future presentations of this book.

Thanks to Artëm Feofanov (Russia), Francesco Maio (Italy) and Dean Little (Australia) for having provided me with precious guidance in the field of aerospace engineering and having explained and taught me scientific topics that I haven't had the opportunity to study yet. I owe you a lot for having solved many of my doubts and having cleared my mind on specific topics of aerospace that one day I myself will go through at University.

Thanks to Thomas Gangale (Tonga) for the kind concession to use your Darian Calendar in my story.

Thanks to Martina D'Ademo (Italy) for having translated some dialogues from Italian to Chinese, language that I myself am planning to learn.

Thanks to my Maths and Physics professor, Tommaso Marino, who periodically provides me with scientific material to work on; and to my Italian professor, Grazia Gamba, who has the patience to read everything I write since years already.

Thanks to visual artist Eashan Misra (a.k.a. *Mr Kalopsia*) for creating the best cover picture I could ever dream of. Thank you for your patience and your enthusiasm while following my instructions, you were able to take my ideas and transform them into art.

Thanks to Pamela Ward, professional translator, for kindly reading my translation to English of this book and giving me precious tips to improve it.

Last but not least, I would like to thank my mother Daniela who, despite all my ideas and activities out of this world, still tolerates me.

Thank you to everyone for contributing to the achievement of a dream!

GIULIA CARLA BASSANI

Born in Turin (Italy) on January 1st, 1999, Giulia C. Bassani studies aerospace engineering at the Polytechnic of Turin. As a space programs great enthusiast, she has already achieved important success, despite her young age. After winning the international phase of the Odysseus Space Contest with the project of an autonomous space base on Mars, she went on studying and analyzing the problems of living on another planet, until she decided to extend her project and set a story in that very base, in order to "test" the effective functioning of its parts. Keen on foreign languages, she speaks English fluently, she is studying Russian and has recently begun to learn Chinese. *Ad Martem 12* is her first novel she published, a science fiction with solid scientific groundwork.

INDEX

"Sempre caro mi fu quest'ermo colle,
e questa siepe, che da tanta parte
dell'ultimo orizzonte il guardo esclude.
Ma sedendo e mirando, interminati
spazi di là da quella, e sovrumani
silenzi, e profondissima quiete
io nel pensier mi fingo; ove per poco
il cor non si spaura. E come il vento
odo stormir tra queste piante, io quello
infinito silenzio a questa voce
vo comparando: e mi sovvien l'eterno,
e le morte stagioni, e la presente
e viva, e il suon di lei. Così tra questa
immensità s'annega il pensier mio:
e il naufragar m'è dolce in questo mare."

G. Leopardi – L'infinito

Published by Giulia Carla Bassani © 2018
Printed by KDP

Printed in Great Britain
by Amazon